THE IMAGICATORS

THE IMAGICATORS

Brad Marshland

iUniverse, Inc.
New York Lincoln Shanghai

The Imagicators

Copyright © 2006 by Brad Marshland

iUniverse books may be ordered through booksellers or by contacting:

iUniverse
2021 Pine Lake Road, Suite 100
Lincoln, NE 68512
www.iuniverse.com
1-800-Authors (1-800-288-4677)

This is a work of fiction. All of the characters, names, incidents, organizations and dialogue in this novel are either the products of the author's imagination or are used fictitiously.

ISBN-13: 978-0-595-40471-1 (pbk)
ISBN-13: 978-0-595-84841-6 (ebk)
ISBN-10: 0-595-40471-5 (pbk)
ISBN-10: 0-595-84841-9 (ebk)

Printed in the United States of America

To all who helped imagicate this book into being.

You know who you are.

CHAPTER 1

▼

DIVING INTO A
DIFFERENT WORLD WITH
NOTHING BUT A ROCK
AND A FURRY CHOCOLATE

Spenser Toshiro Santiago McNillstein took a deep breath. Beneath his feet, his Aeroboard hung poised on the peak of the garage roof. He had modified the skateboard himself, mounting hand-carved wings to the sides for maximum lift. In the pre-dawn light, the lawn stretched before him like a vast ocean. He could almost hear the rough green surf crashing against the razor-sharp rocks of the gravel drive.

Spenser stretched out his arms—rocked forward on his board—and rolled. His long, black coat billowed out behind him, revealing the rainbow lining he'd hand-stitched underneath. Faster than he had expected, Spenser hurtled down the slope, hopped the garage gutter, and flew out over the sea of grass, miles below. His stomach leapt to his throat. He saw the jagged rocks racing up to meet him, glinting like monstrous, foaming fangs. Spenser focused his mind and swallowed his fear. Time expanded. He adjusted the slant of his board, catching the updraft. One tilt of his outstretched fingertip and he banked—soaring like a falcon. Spurred by his success, Spenser tucked his elbows, streamlined his body, and sped into a dive. Faster, faster—nothing could stop him. He raced forward, downward now without fear, without thought—just the raw feeling of speed and power. He dove past treetops and cliffs. He rushed toward the rocky shoreline at seventy, eighty miles an hour. Mere feet before impact, he spread his arms at the bottom of the dive and caught the warm, rising air....

Spenser crash-landed in a bush at the edge of the gravel drive. He rolled over, unhurt except for something jabbing his leg. He knew what it was—a rock he had found last week at Windy Hill. He reached into his pocket.

Piercing shrieks tore the air. Spenser leapt up, pulling his hand free. At first, he thought his parents were fighting again, but the shrieks were too musical for that. They weren't even human shrieks—more like...what? All he could think of was a dozen two-year olds playing out-of-tune violins.

He listened. The sound faded. Only Spenser's heartbeat pounded through the silence.

Spenser was tall for his fourteen years, tall enough for varsity basketball, which he didn't play. He was plenty athletic, but he could never be bothered with all the regulations and boundaries of organized sports. Likewise, he didn't follow the unwritten rules of teen fashion. He didn't care what his peers thought. He had sewn the rainbow lining into his coat because it meant something to *him*, with its intense colors rippling beneath the black surface.

Spenser went into his house, quietly setting his board just inside the front door. He crept past the high-backed living room chairs and checked the clock: quarter of six in the morning. Even his parents usually took a break from quarreling between four and seven in the morning, which was why he chose those hours to test his inventions. He hated to think what they would throw at him if they discovered he'd been wearing a track in the garage roof and crashing into the bushes. Funny, he thought wryly, it had been his parents who had taught him the prime duty of the inventor: to push the limits of the possible. Lately though, it was all "Knock it off." and "Cut it out!" and "Can't we get a little quiet here?!"

Another shriek spun Spenser toward the kitchen window. He gazed out across suburban yards, across a field of dead weeds, out toward the ruins of the Windy Hill Sanatorium.

Back in his grandparents' time, sick people had come from all over the state to drink from the spring and breathe the fresh air of Windy Hill. Back then, it was the only building for miles around, a full hour's ride from the nearest train station. Now, houses that looked just like Spenser's surrounded it on all sides. On the Windy Hill property itself, no one had built anything for eighty years, and the old dormitories and clinics had long since collapsed into rubble.

Spenser put his hand in the pocket that held his rock. His fingertips just made contact—and he heard another piercing note.

Spenser yanked his hand out into the air. No, it must have been a coincidence. And yet, there was something unusual about this rock. The moment he'd found it had been the very moment the image of the Aeroboard had appeared in his mind like a flash photo, fully formed.

Slowly, Spenser put his hand in his pocket once more. His fingers tingled as they neared the stone. Then, with a quick jab, he dug his hand all the way in and grabbed it.

Only silence.

Spenser studied the rock, which fit so easily in his palm: a perfect wedge, its surface flecked with crystals, polished smooth by countless storms. The image of the sanatorium ruins appeared in his mind.

Spenser was halfway back across the living room to the front door when—

"Boy?"

Spenser turned. His father had been asleep on the sofa, hidden by the sofa's back when Spenser had first come through.

"I have a name," Spenser sighed.

The older man propped himself up, revealing a weather-beaten face scarred by years of crushed hopes. Once, Spenser's parents had both thought they were destined to be famous inventors. *Yeah, right...*thought Spenser. It seemed like anything they tried, someone else had already done. Worse, they had given up. A wave of disgust washed through Spenser. *Given up.* Now, his parents did nothing but argue half the night and sleep half the day.

"Hmm?" said his father, just starting to focus.

"It's Spenser."

"I know it's Spenser," his father insisted. "Who do you think named you anyway?"

"About ten people, from the sound of it."

"That was your mother," his father countered. "If she could ever just agree on one single thing—"

"She used to," Spenser snapped. "You used to agree on everything."

"Keep it down," groaned his mother from the armchair. "Can't you see I'm sleeping?"

Spenser's mother looked twice as haggard as his father. Spenser rolled his eyes.
"Sorry, mom."

"Oh, Spenser, honey. I thought it was your—" She spotted his father. "Do you know what time it is?!"

"Ten of six," breathed Spenser, dreading the coming fight.

"Darn right it's—It's ten of six??"

She rubbed her eyes, rising from the armchair.

"You probably fell asleep arguing again," said Spenser.

"We were not arguing," said his mother.

"We were, too," said his father.

"We were *not*," insisted his mother.

"Stop it…*Please*," said Spenser, his throat tightening.

"No," his mother plowed on. "We were *discussing*. Discussing the fact that it's high time your father gets off his lazy—"

"Me?" his father roared. "What about you?!"

"—Gets up and *tries* something again, *does* something—for *your* sake, Spenser."

"Leave me out of it."

"Yeah, leave him out of it!" said his father, then turned to Spenser himself. "You see, Spenser? *That's* an argument. I tell you I know an argument when I'm having one! It was an argument!"

"It was a discussion!" said his mother.

"It was an argument!" said his father.

"*Please*," said Spenser.

He eyed the door. He didn't want to be here at all. Why couldn't he ever get them to *stop*?

"A discussion! A—a *disagreement!*"

"Argument, argument, argument!!"

Both his parents were standing now. Worse, they were blocking his escape. He started edging around them, hoping they wouldn't notice, hoping to get out before it got even worse.

"Spenser, wait!"

His mother had spotted him. He couldn't wait. He couldn't stand hearing any more of the petty bickering.

"Stay!" she said. Maybe she meant it kindly, but it sounded like she was talking to a dog.

Spenser feinted one way, then the other, inducing his parents to split apart just enough for him to dart between them.

"'Later," he managed to choke out. He grabbed the knob with one hand, his board with the other, and was gone.

He shuddered as he sped away. He shook out his arms and hands, trying to shed the vile feeling he got whenever his parents clashed.

Spenser made it two blocks before his front wheels started wobbling. It was almost a relief to have something else to worry about, something he could fix.

Spenser stepped off his board and sat on the curb. The whole front truck—the metal that held the wheels to the board—was loose, wrenched apart by the force of his earlier crash landing.

Parents, Spenser couldn't help thinking. Maybe one day, he'd just hop on his board and be gone for good.

Spenser jammed a wooden wedge between the board and the truck. That should hold it, at least for the morning.

Spenser took a deep breath and let it out. More than he wanted to leave, he simply longed for the time when his parents had worked *together.* For now, there was nothing he could do but head for the open space of the ruined sanatorium, his private refuge, and find the source of that shrieking tune, that fantastic fugue.

He ollied up the curb onto the sidewalk, the road itself now too crumbly for a smooth ride. *Fatter wheels,* he thought, *fatter wheels to smooth out the bumps.* Imagining it, he zipped up the overgrown entrance road to Windy Hill, a road lined with palm trees planted a hundred years ago. A hundred yards farther, Spenser came to an immense terraced slab. Once the foundation of a gatehouse, the cement had become the local skate park—until some lawyer convinced the city to put a fence around it.

The fence didn't really make a difference; Spenser's skate-buddies had quickly cut a hole in it and torn down the No Skateboarding signs. Spenser kept quite a collection of these signs under his bed. But the *idea* of the fence still gnawed at Spenser; the whole world kept screaming "*No!*"

In his mind, Spenser tracked down the lawyer and found his home in one of those uptight, gated communities with a phony name like Rancho del Monte Rio del Lago del Mar. Under the cover of darkness, Spenser slipped past the private security guard. As if the wall around the subdivision weren't enough; this lawyer had to have his own personal fence, complete with motion-detecting security alarms. That didn't faze Spenser. He knew how to move slowly enough not to trip the sensors until he got past them. He hopped yet another fence into the pool area. He found the pool controls and flipped the switch to drain it. Fifty thousand gallons, gone in *minutes.* Spenser stepped onto his board and plunged into the cement basin. His buddies from the skate park flocked in to join him. The lawyer woke. He reached for the phone to call the cops. But it didn't matter; it was too late—and there were too many of them, swooping up and down the pool walls, getting huge air, busting flips, grabs—

A bump in the sidewalk pulled Spenser from his reverie. The gray fence still surrounded the sometime skate park. Spenser sighed, doubting the power of imagination. The rocky shoreline had been a gravel driveway. His parents were still pathetic failures.

Past the crumbling gate, the grounds of Windy Hill grew wild. Grass and weeds pushed their way through cracked slabs of cement, the foundations of out-buildings where staff had lived. The once-manicured bushes and hedges sprawled into wild thickets. Even the main building barely looked as if it had ever been a building at all. A labyrinth of red brick ridges now only two or three feet high marked the old corridors, the examining rooms, the offices, and the bedchambers where countless invalids spent years in isolation, praying for a cure.

Spenser had to carry his board here, the formerly grand walkways having eroded to deer trails. He slowed his pace. The sun would be up any minute now, but still there was something spooky about a ruined sanatorium. Who knows how many patients had found their cure—and who knows how many more had died here in the cold, white-tiled rooms, miles from anyone who might have truly cared?

A voice.

Spenser froze. He listened.

Spenser knew every inch of the grounds, having escaped his bickering parents and hidden among these ruins countless times over the years. No one else from the subdivision ever seemed to venture in this far. Occasionally, some other teen-agers would party by the spring late at night, trashing the place with cans and bottles, only to be chased off by the local police. Spenser didn't think much of that sort of behavior. There was nothing creative or clever about making a mess. If they kept it up, the city would probably put a fence around that refuge, too.

Spenser continued again, quietly. Maybe he'd imagined the voice. Maybe he'd imagined the shrieking music, even. He stashed his skateboard in a thicket and noticed something else deep within. Someone—or something—had tunneled into the bushes. As Spenser peered deeper, he caught a glimpse of colored cloth. Spenser crept closer, careful not to step on a single twig that might snap and give him away. Someone had been camping here. And now he heard the voice—a girl's voice.

"She's *still* not there? Well, what if someone needs to *reach* her—like her *daughter?*…Yeah, Gaston, school's fine. Thanks for asking…Of *course* I've been studying. I'm in the library right now. Right. So I can't talk. I'm disturbing *every-body*."

Spenser looked around to see who she was talking about, then backed out of the thicket, stashed his board in another bush, and skirted around the greenery, hoping to avoid running into—

"Oh!" he said.

The girl. Popping out of a hedge just where he'd thought she wouldn't.

"Well, she knows how to reach me," she said to her cell phone. "If she *cares* to…Yeah, *au revoir.*"

Spenser stared at her, taking in her sparkling green eyes, confident pose, and the tinge of sassy smile around the corners of her mouth. She wore a too-big denim jacket with a faded sunflower embroidered on it. Her designer jeans were a little frayed at the knees, but then, so were Spenser's. She pocketed her phone and stared back.

"*You're* not supposed to be here," she said.

"I could say the same about you."

"Well, why don't you, then?"

"What?"

"You say you *could* say something. Why don't you just come out and *say* it? That's the trouble with people. They just talk and talk and don't actually *say* anything."

Spenser almost had to laugh.

"Except maybe you," she went on. "You look like you hardly talk at *all*. And what's with the rainbow coat? Do you do party tricks or something?"

Spenser thought about explaining how the colors of the world were always getting smothered by the forces of darkness, but he didn't think she'd get it. He started to turn.

"Oh…No, wait," continued the girl. "I'll bet you're a *thinker*. You look like a thinker. It still doesn't explain the get-up, I suppose, but tell me. What are you thinking now? *Right* now. Tell me. What?"

Spenser considered her. "No, you don't want to hear it."

"I *do*."

"All right, then…I'm thinking you almost had me laughing a minute ago. But you're also clearly a liar and maybe a bit of a brat. You were lying and bratty on the phone. So I'm thinking, why do I even want to stand here talking to you?"

That momentarily stumped the girl. Spenser shrugged and walked away.

"Hey!" she called. "Hey, wait just a minute!"

The girl caught up, came around him on the path, walking backward to face him as he walked forward.

"Have a chocolate? They're Fourrés. The most expensive chocolate in the world. *La crème de la crème chocolat.* Go on. Try one. I've got loads. Loads more back in my room. My father owns the company. Pierre Fourré. Unfortunate name, really. Fourré means furry. But oh well, it's our name, and we're proud of it. I'm Elaine. Elaine Fourré. You don't believe me. That's okay. But it's true. And really, they *are* the best. Just taste one. Then you'll *know* it's true."

Spenser stopped walking. He looked at the three gold-wrapped chocolates left in the shiny blue box. He took one. He pocketed the foil next to his rock, and bit into the chocolate.

"Best in the world, no?" said Elaine.

Warm flavors bathed Spenser's tongue. He held the chocolate there and let the melted syrup drip slowly down his throat. He couldn't help nodding as Elaine popped the next-to-last candy into her mouth.

"So *now* you know it's true. *Now* you believe me."

"Well," admitted Spenser, "the chocolate *is* pretty good."

"Best in the world," she smiled. "Have the last one."

Spenser hesitated, not ready to be friends.

"Go on," she said.

He allowed himself a smile, "Thanks," and pocketed the chocolate for later.

"*Anyway*," Elaine went on, "I don't really like the word *lying*. I mean, a lie is something intentionally...cruel. Besides, Gaston is my mom's *personal secretary*. That means he keeps her secrets. So why shouldn't I keep mine? That way, there isn't any battle."

"There's always a battle," said Spenser. "Even when you try not to say a word."

Elaine tried to read Spenser. She thought of herself as pretty perceptive, but he had her beat.

"So, tell me," she said, "Did you hear anything *odd* a little while ago?"

"No," said Spenser, a little too coolly. "Did you?"

"Me?"

"Yeah."

"Why do you ask?" smiled Elaine. "Maybe because you *did* hear something odd?"

"I said I didn't hear anything."

"Yeah, that's what you *said.*"

Spenser stopped. She was grinning at him.

"Did you or didn't you?" he asked.

"No," she gave a coy little shrug. "Not a thing."

"Fine," said Spenser.

He started walking again and shoved his hands in his pockets. His right fingers touched the stone, and instantly the shrieking tune began once more. He and Elaine stared at each other.

Elaine asked, "Is that what you didn't hear?"

"Yeah," Spenser admitted. "And you?"

Elaine nodded, "It's coming from the corner."

They turned and hustled together back toward the ruins. They scrambled over crumbled walls, heading for the source.

"You know," said Elaine, "Most people would be running *away* from a sound like this. But not us."

Spenser glanced sidelong at her, still not sure how he felt about being part of "us."

He stepped into the ruins of the corner room. The sound was coming from somewhere in the rubble.

"This is weird," said Elaine. "And I should know. I have seen weird the world over. You might even call me a weird *expert*. One time—I am *not* making this up—one time, I was just strolling by a private lake, and this huge, six-foot tall cockroach came up and asked me to dance. It's true! Of course," she added with a twinkling eye, "I *was* at a masquerade ball...."

"Shh!" said Spenser, trying to concentrate, cocking his head at different angles.

"Here," he said. "Definitely here."

He touched a low wall of crumbling bricks. He moved his head over the wall, listening. He scrambled all the way over the wall, then back again into what had once been someone's room.

"It's coming from inside the wall."

Elaine squatted down next to him, running her fingers over the bricks. "Right. This one's loose."

Spenser scooted closer. He reached out his hand to help, but something in his gut held him back, something that told him to leave it alone and *walk away*.

"Well, help me get it *out*," said Elaine.

Spenser ignored the sense of foreboding and dug his fingernails into the edges of the brick. He and Elaine wiggled it back and forth, but could not pry it free.

"Hold on," he said.

He took the stone from his pocket and jammed it like a wedge into the crack next to the loose brick. He clawed around in the weeds for the right piece of rubble to use as a hammer. In a puddle at the base of the wall, he found what he was looking for: a chunk of concrete the size of his fist. Again he hesitated.

"What are you *waiting* for?" Elaine asked.

"Nothing," he lied, and hammered the concrete against his own stone, driving the wedge. SMACK! SMACK! SMACK! On the third hit, the loose brick popped out.

Immediately, the shrieking grew a hundred times louder, a throbbing, piercing jackhammer pounding against their ears. Spenser and Elaine winced as they looked around. If they didn't stop the sound soon, people would be coming from miles around. Spenser put his rock in his pocket and jammed the brick back in place. He leaned against it with his back, trying to use his whole body as a muffler.

"It's no good!" yelled Elaine.

"What?!"

"I said it's no good!"

She pushed him aside and pulled out the brick once more. Behind it was a small nook. Boldly, Elaine reached in and groped around. She pulled out a piece of parchment. The sight of it made a pit open up in Spenser's stomach, urging him to shove the paper and brick back. Still, he felt sure the summons was for him. He had been drawn here from his own house, and the parchment was sealed with an ornate, yellow S.

"Let me see!" shouted Spenser over the shrieks.

Elaine held the parchment so Spenser could see it. He snatched it, broke the seal, unfolded the parchment, and read, shouting:

"Make solid what is cloudy,
Restore what has been split.
Curtail the cries that plague us all,
Obey what has been writ:
Through vortex deep shed all your fear
And bring the Stone to Windemere.
Dissolve these words to face your fate:
Imagicate ex mobilate."

If the cries had been deafening before, they were nothing compared to how they sounded after Spenser read the message. It was like being hit over the head with an ax. Spenser and Elaine screamed in pain and clamped their hands over their ears. In the process, Spenser dropped the parchment. They watched it flutter to the ground, as if in slow motion.

Perhaps it was because there was magic in the moment. Perhaps it was because the parchment came from another world. Or perhaps it was because time always flows slower when calamity approaches. Whatever the reason, the parchment seemed to take forever to fall all of three feet. Spenser and Elaine passed the eternity by joining their shrieks with those ringing in their heads. They stared at the scrap of paper floating down, down...

Finally, the parchment landed in the puddle at the base of the brick wall. The paper sizzled and sputtered, turning the puddle into a churning cauldron. Now it dissolved into yellow swirls, and the puddle began to spin. A sucking, swirling wind pulled leaves and dirt down into the bubbling stew. Along with litter and twigs, the wind sucked away one thing more: the unbearable screams. Like a vacuum cleaner inhaling dust, the cauldron seemed to draw in all the sound from every corner of the world.

Spenser took his hands from his ears. At first he thought he had gone deaf, the silence was so profound. Only when Elaine spoke did he realize what had truly happened.

"Dissolve these words..." she quoted.

Usually wind seems to blow *from* somewhere, pushing rather than pulling. This wind did not blow the puddle to make it spin. Instead, the spinning water pulled the wind. The wind sucked branches, newspapers, some polka-dotted underpants torn from a faraway laundry line—anything that wasn't rooted to the ground—into the deepening, whirling water. The bottom of the well dropped away into blackness, draining away all it sucked in. And still the wind increased.

"Ow!"

A rock hit Spenser in the shoulder on its way into the funnel.

"Hold on!" called Elaine. She grabbed a corner of the crumbling wall.

Spenser felt himself being dragged toward the whirlpool. Its contents blurred. Instinctively, Spenser reached for a low branch overhanging the wall. He grabbed it just as the sucking wind pulled his feet from under him.

Elaine cried out. Around her, the wind tore off loose pieces of the wall and sucked them into the abyss. Elaine felt her grip failing. The wind pulled her horizontal. Her left hand slipped.

"Ahh!!"

"Hold on!"

The wind pulled Spenser, too. First his black coat, then his whole body flew like a flag in a gale. He could do nothing to help her.

Elaine clutched a brick with her right hand alone. Suddenly, the brick crumbled to dust. Elaine shot into the whirlpool and swirled into a blur.

"Elaine!"

Spenser's grip on the branch was secure for the moment, but every instant the hurricane grew. He glanced at his hands, then again at the deepening well into which Elaine had vanished.

Spenser thought about going after her. He thought about his grip on the branch. He thought for a second that felt like an hour. What did he even care about Elaine? He didn't even know her. He looked back toward his home, thought about his father doing nothing, then again at the spiraling water. *Elaine.* Still he hesitated. His parents had given up. *Back or forward, back or forward.* He couldn't stand that his parents had given up. *Elaine*—Spenser bit his lower lip—and let go.

Instantly, the wind pulled Spenser into the swirl. He spun so fast, the outside world blurred to gray. Above him, above where the water spun to blue and white, were sky and air. But the whirlpool sucked Spenser the other way: down, down into darkness.

CHAPTER 2

▼

THE WIND SERF OF ALEILI BAY

The swirling storm thrashed Elaine like an old rag in a high-speed washing machine. Not that Elaine had ever actually used a washing machine herself—there were other people for that—but she was sure she'd *heard* of one once, and she prided herself in her imagination. Nonetheless, the storm whipped her with twigs, leaves, and ratty underwear.

The whirlpool sucked her down, underwater, perhaps underground, for she soon lost sight of the sky, of Windy Hill, of everything but darkness. The spin cycle ended, and she floated in black silence, not knowing up from down.

Elaine felt the urge to breathe but didn't dare. She could feel water pressing against her chest. Surely she had been pulled deep beneath the surface, maybe to the bottom of some subterranean lake. Her need for air grew. She twisted around, weightless, looking in every direction. She let out a bubble but couldn't see it, an inch from her face. She twisted again. To her left and a bit down—or was it up?—she thought she could see a patch that was not quite as black as the rest. She clawed through the dark water toward it.

Her heart pounded. Her ribs ached. She could make out strange shapes circling her. Elaine thrashed up, up—It was definitely up, she decided, and definitely blue...sky blue...*air* blue. The circling shapes became clearer: dozens of giant creatures swimming and forming—oh no—not another whirlpool! The pounding in Elaine's heart reached her throat. She grew dizzy. Her whole head throbbed. She needed air.

Ten more feet...eight...seven...She could not wait any longer. Six...Five...Four...

Elaine opened her mouth. Water rushed in. One of the creatures bumped into her from below and nudged her up. Elaine's head broke the surface. She spat out the water—and breathed.

Elaine floated on her back, gasping. The water was marvelously buoyant. Sunlight played on her cheeks. She *breathed*. Around her, the creatures continued to circle, perfectly spaced, making scarcely a ripple. They seemed a cross between dolphins and flexible, living sailboats. Their dorsal fins—towering eight feet out of the water—functioned as sails, flipping from side to side as they turned and caught the wind. The sight transfixed her, calmed her.

A splash erupted next to her. It was Spenser, gasping for breath.

"Where...What...Where are we?" he asked.

"I don't know," Elaine marveled. "But it's fan*tas*tic! I mean, some people have never learned to appreciate beauty; they've never had the chance. But someone as perceptive as you—well, even if you've never had the chance, you can probably appreciate it at least a *little*."

Spenser looked around, spotting the shore a mile away, then at the creatures surrounding them and keeping the water in motion. The moment Spenser locked his eyes on the shore, he had to twist himself around to keep it in view. Wherever he turned, all the colors of the world seemed brighter.

"This is too weird," he said. "I must have hit my head."

"Oh, it's not *that* weird," said Elaine. "One time—I am *not* making this up—one time, I *walked* on water. Right over the *top*. And I did not get one bit wet! Weird but true...Of course, it *was* a frozen Swiss lake..."

"Will you *stop?*" insisted Spenser. "Are you *seeing* those dolphins? I mean, they *aren't* dolphins. They're—I don't know whats."

"Sure," Elaine smiled. "One of them helped me up. And did you taste the water?"

"Of course! I must have swallowed buckets full! Oh..."

It dawned on him. He had swallowed buckets full and had not gagged from the salt. He took another mouthful just to be sure. The taste was not salt, but sugar.

Spenser shook his head, still not quite believing.

"It's not *that* weird, really," Elaine mused. "I mean, why should oceans always be salty?"

"Well, there *is* a reason," said Spenser. "Oceans dissolve the minerals in the surrounding…"

He trailed off. Something about the water was changing. The sea creatures had stopped circling. The water stopped spinning. The enormous beasts shifted their dorsal fins to catch the wind and sailed nearer in an intricate, weaving pattern.

"You know," said Elaine, "Most people would be swimming *away* from a situation like this."

As a final flourish, the creatures leapt from the water in unison, then plunged down right in front of Spenser and Elaine, who shrieked involuntarily. The creature closest to Elaine cocked his head to get a good look at her. His eyes showed the wrinkles of age and weather, but also of laughter—years and years of laughter. He spoke with a voice like a low flute.

"On behalf of my pod—nay, on behalf of all the Sailphins of Windemere—I welcome these young thinfins as our guests."

The other Sailphins hummed their approval.

The old one spoke again: "Eee, throw them a fish."

In one quick motion, the young Sailphin named Eee ducked his head underwater and came up with a fish in his mouth.

"Flying fish!" he laughed as he flicked his head and tossed it to Spenser.

Spenser caught the wriggling fish in both hands and struggled to keep it from squirming away.

"Uh, thanks…"

Elaine whispered, "Go on, eat it."

"Um…" Spenser looked around. All eyes were on him. "I'm really quite full…"

The Sailphins let out a high-pitched laugh.

The old Sailphin who had spoken first swam closer, and said in a hushed voice, "It's just for the ceremony. You don't have to eat it."

"Thanks," said Spenser.

"But if you're really done with it—" piped up Eee, the one who had tossed the fish.

Spenser gladly tossed the fish back to him. Eee ate it, while the first Sailphin looked on disapprovingly.

"These are serious times, Eee," said the older Sailphin.

"All the more reason to keep my strength up," said the younger, gulping down the fish.

"Speaking of strength—" said Elaine, eyeing the distance to shore.

"Of course," broke in the elder. "You thinfins swim about as well as crabs. Climb onto my back. Mind the sail, now—especially when the wind shifts. And you," he said to Spenser, "Climb onto Eee there."

"Thank you," said Elaine. "I'm Elaine, by the way."

"Welcome, Elaine. I'm—" He let out a long, high-pitched squeal that seemed to go on for minutes. "Leeeeieieiiiieiieieiaiiieiaieieieeeee…"

Elaine tried to reproduce it. "Leeiei-eye-eye-eye…"

The Sailphin chuckled, "Maybe you'd better just call me Leeee. Mind the sail!"

The wind shifted, and with it, Leeee's sail swung from one side of his body to the other. Elaine ducked just in time.

Spenser, riding atop Eee, was not having such a smooth ride. The young Sailphin swerved this way and that, going after whatever fish he saw. Spenser planted his feet skateboard-style and rose to the challenge. He'd ridden steep slaloms with ease and had twice tried wakeboarding, but not even the Z-Game course in San Diego compared to this. Always before, his own feet had controlled the board, not the other way around. Now, when Eee made a sudden jibe, Spenser had to hold the mast-like part of the fin with both hands and fly his feet out like a flag to keep from launching off. Spenser grinned into the wind, nodding in growing confidence as he learned the rhythm of his living board.

Suddenly, Eee dove down after a whole school of fish, dunking Spenser in the process. Spenser grabbed the mast and closed his mouth as quick as he could, but he still accidentally choked down a minnow.

"What's your record?" Eee asked as they came up. "Mine's nineteen."

Spenser coughed and gurgled. Something with fins wriggled deep inside him. "Nineteen what?" he managed, trying to be polite.

"Nineteen fish in one gulp."

"Oh. I don't—Aaah!!"

Eee took another dive. He came back up seconds later with Spenser sputtering.

"Twenty!" Eee squealed. "I got twenty!"

Nearby, Leeee shook his head at the younger Sailphin.

"These youngsters…I cannot imagine what Chloe would say."

"Who's Chloe?" Elaine asked.

Leeee turned his head in disbelief. "You do not know about Chloe?"

"No."

"But you—you are of Chloe's world! Surely you—I had hoped—But no, I suppose you are too young. It has been too long…"

"I don't understand," said Elaine. "What's been too long? Who's Chloe?"

"Chloe was the first Imagicator. Out of her mind, all of Windemere was poured."

"I don't get it. How? What's an Imagicator?"

"You do not even know about imagication?"

"No."

Leeee made a gargling sound, which Elaine took for clearing his throat, then spoke reverently, as if imparting the secret of the universe. "If you can imagine something wholly, completely, down to the last grain of sand, then it will *become*. That is the magic of imagication."

Elaine struggled to wrap her mind around this idea. Was he saying you could just imagine something really well, and—poof? This really *was* weird.

Leeee cocked his head to study Elaine. "Truly, you know nothing of this?"

"No," said Elaine.

"And the boy?"

"No. At least, I don't *think* so. I mean, maybe he does; we just met. I had—Well, I had kind of snuck away from boarding school—it's more like *boring* school really, so sometimes I leave and—It's like no one even *cares*. But we were just—here was this whirlpool—We got sucked in. I know it sounds crazy, but here we are."

Leeee glided thoughtfully, letting the wind fill his sail.

"Ah, child," he sighed. "There is so much that needs putting back together…I only hope you are up to whatever tasks await you."

"What tasks? What do we have to do?"

"I wish I knew. I know only this: You are a child of Chloe's world, and I daresay there is something of her about you. No one else could have entered Windemere through Aleili Bay. And that bodes well for Windemere. For this, the Sailphins give you welcome."

They neared the shore.

"I know not who summoned you, nor why. Since I know nothing, I must not delay you from that which awaits you. I can tell you only this: The power to imagicate came to Windemere from your world. There is power in the matter you bring. You must bring it to the Royal Wisps, the young ones wrapped in clouds. Above all, do not let the matter fall into the wrong fins. Imagicate well."

With that, Leeee let himself slowly sink, forcing Elaine to let go. She treaded water for a moment, then noticed she could stand. Leeee had let her off near the beach, but now he was nowhere to be seen.

Eee came zigzagging toward the shore, with Spenser clutching him for dear life but trying to maintain his composure in the process. Ten feet from Elaine, Eee jumped into the air. With a flick of his tail, he launched Spenser from his back.

"Imagicate well!" called Eee before disappearing back beneath the waves.

Spenser soared over Elaine's head and, seconds later, splashed down in shallow water among a jumble of rotting yellow driftwood twisted in almost human shapes. Elaine looked back. The Sailphins were gone.

Spenser stood and cocked his shoulders like he'd *meant* to land in such a heap, a gesture Elaine found somehow endearing.

"Come on," said Spenser. "It smells like something died here."

Elaine nodded, and the two scrambled over the rotting logs to shore. Around them curved a narrow strip of sand, bordered by a low bluff, nearly enclosing Aleili Bay. Small birds ran up and down the sand, just at the water line, playing tag with the waves. Whenever a wave touched a bird's feet, the whole flock would break into raucous giggles.

One of the birds spotted Spenser and Elaine. Elaine could have sworn it pointed at her with its wing, then let out a chortle. The laughter was contagious, and Spenser and Elaine had to join in.

Two other birds flew at Elaine and tried to land on the sunflower on her coat.

"Get off!" she laughed.

Of course, there was no real flower on which to land, and the birds giggled at the joke before flying away. As the laughter faded in the distance, Spenser and Elaine found themselves alone, staring at the wondrous scenery, then at each other.

For one powerful moment, Spenser thought he caught a glint in Elaine's eye—a look of warmth, of caring. Spenser wanted to drink in that look and keep it with him forever. He tried to think of something to say, something witty. No, it didn't even have to be witty, just *anything*.

They were both soaked from head to toe, and the water, which had seemed so delightfully warm when they were in it, now felt like bitter icicles against their skin. Instinctively, Elaine pulled her wet coat tight. Spenser shivered and looked away. Elaine looked away, too, and the moment was lost.

"There," she said, scanning the bluff. "There's someone up there."

Spenser's eyes followed hers. A rough trail cut from the beach to the top of the bluff. Near where the path disappeared from sight, a small, wiry figure with billowing cheeks darted from bush to bush, trying to stay out of sight but not doing a very good job of it.

"Let's go," said Elaine.

"How do you know he's friendly?" asked Spenser.

"I don't. But he's more scared of us than we are of him."

Spenser looked at her, then back to the bluff. The stranger above darted farther away, and Spenser had to agree. Elaine led the way through the yellow driftwood and up toward the little man. Spenser followed close behind.

"The matter..." puzzled Elaine. "What's the matter?"

"Are you kidding? I was thrashed about, dunked under—I'm *freezing.*"

"No, I mean—The Sailphin Leeee, he said something about the matter, to bring the matter to the Royal Wisps. Whatever that means."

Spenser shrugged. "The one I was on just went on about fish."

They made it to the top of the low cliff and found themselves on a wide, nearly barren plain. Two hundred yards away, a rough shack leaned against the stiff ocean wind. If the wind were to stop suddenly, the shack would collapse into the sea.

"Bring the matter..." Elaine mused. "There is power in the matter you bring...What did we bring that has power?"

Spenser felt in his pocket. "The stone," he said without meaning to.

"Right. *Bring the Stone to Windemere.* Then what? Something about plagues and fear—or was that before? Let me see the stone."

Spenser held back.

"Come on, just let me *see* it."

"No! Shh!"

Spenser had spotted the stranger crouching in a bush, watching them. The figure looked around furtively, then beckoned them closer. Spenser and Elaine exchanged looks. Coming near, they saw that the stranger was not crouching at all, but merely short. He looked skinny enough to blow away in a stiff breeze. His cheeks flopped to his shoulders like a basset hound's. And he wore a gauzy outfit that might have been made of thistledown.

"Getting down!" the stranger cried. "Out of the wind! Out of the smelling! You may not be worrying about your lives, but I am about mine!"

Spenser and Elaine hunkered down next to him.

"That's being better," he said. "Being safe."

He stuck his lips out of the bush, and they elongated like a slide trombone. He sucked in a great mouthful of air, filling his cheeks like a balloon. Then he curled his lips in, so the opening of his mouth aimed straight up toward his nostrils. He breathed out through his mouth and in through his nose at the same time.

"Smelling that?" he asked. "Foulishness, that's what it's being."

He could see from their expressions that Spenser and Elaine had not the foggiest idea what he was talking about.

"Here," he said, "Smelling it yourselves."

He took another tromboneful of air from outside the bush and blew it in quick puffs straight up each of their noses. They couldn't smell whatever he smelled, but the jet of air shooting up his nose made Spenser wince and shake his head. Elaine started sneezing.

"Begging your pardon!" said the stranger, moving his lips closer to her nose again. "Here, let me be sucking that back out!"

"No thank you!" sniffed Elaine.

"Begging your pardon! Begging your pardon!"

The stranger bent over double until his nose scraped the ground.

"Ooooch! Begging my own pardon, now."

He straightened up a little.

"Ah, er, allow me a beginning again." He cleared his throat. "Allow me to be presenting myself. Being Zephyr the Lesser, wind serf. Being at your service."

He bent low again and nearly scraped his nose once more. Pleased he avoided it this time, he let out a self-satisfied chuckle.

"Nice to meet you," said Elaine warily.

"But how shall I be calling you?" asked Zephyr. "Chloe? Your Chloeness? Your Chloesty?"

"Chloe? You mean *the* Chloe?" asked Elaine.

"*The* Chloe, then," Zephyr agreed.

"What makes you think I'm Chloe?" asked Elaine.

"Aren't you being?" asked Zephyr.

"*That* is not the question," said Elaine, sensing her own power. "The question is what makes you *think* so."

"Seeing you arriving! Funneling in! You and your friend. Who but Chloe could be funneling in?! And being escorted by Sailphins, Chloe's first creatures! *Your* first creatures, your Chloeness, *the* Chloe, as you were saying."

"Then it must be so," said Elaine. "Who but Chloe could funnel in…"

"Ah," Zephyr scraped low again. "*The* Chloe…It has been so long…Not since my grandfather's time…"

Zephyr glanced up at Spenser in his soggy, black coat.

"And this is…?"

"*This*," said Elaine, realizing she'd yet to learn Spenser's name. "Is the Count of California."

"Spenser," said Spenser. "Just Spenser."

"Ah, my dear Just Spenser," said Zephyr, bowing low, "Your countenance."

"Uh, right…," said Spenser. "Can we get out of this bush?"

"Ah," said Zephyr, and he sniffed the air again. "Smelling is good, yes. We can be going. Being after you."

Spenser emerged from the bush, followed by Elaine and Zephyr. Zephyr paused to collect a rope strung with thick glass bottles.

"What are those?" asked Spenser.

"For my wind serfing. Supposing Chloe told you all about wind serfs."

"Actually, *Chloe* hasn't told me a darn thing."

"Ah, well, that's what they're being."

Zephyr kept pulling out the rope, a different-sized bottle knotted onto it every six inches.

"You wind surf with those?" asked Spenser.

"That's right," said Zephyr, pulling some out of the bush. "Harvesting, bottling, selling the wind. Not much profiting these days. More and more giving wind to the government, and selling less and less…Some are even bottling their *own* wind!"

Zephyr laughed as if he just made the greatest joke. No one else was laughing.

"Bottling their own wind," he repeated. "From their backsides! And selling it as fresh! Ah!"

Zephyr stopped suddenly. He turned to face the wind. He bobbed his head about, tuning in to the finest changes in the breeze, the same breeze that was making Spenser shiver.

"Listen," said Spenser, "We—"

"Ah! Feeling the juiciest spots…Ah!"

He opened his mouth wide, and let the wind fill his billowing cheeks. When his cheeks had inflated to twice the size of his head, he closed his mouth, unscrewed one of his bottles, blew the contents of his cheeks into it, and quickly secured the lid.

"There!" he said with a satisfied smile. "A fair easterly, that!"

"But what do you do with it?" asked Spenser.

"What do you *do* with it?? My dear Just Spenser! Count of Cauliflower or not, if you weren't traveling with Chloe, I'd be thinking you had fuzz for brains!"

Zephyr saw Spenser's expression darken and quickly humbled himself, bowing again so his nose tangled in some weeds at his feet.

"Begging your pardon! Begging your pardon!" he said. "Forgetting my manners again!"

Zephyr straightened up and sneezed some weeds from his nose, which he then tried to plant back in the ground.

"Letting me be explaining," he said, gathering his rope of bottles around his shoulders. "Wind serfs are farming the wind. Wind is being power. It is powering the drafters, powering the nets, powering the shields—"

"What are you talking about?" asked Spenser.

"Aren't you ever hearing of wind shields?"

"Yes, but—"

"But nothing! Not knowing about your world, but here, everything is running on wind. It is even helping make the clouds at Cloud Palace—not that the palace is being much used these days. But suspecting that's why you're being here."

"We don't know—" started Spenser, but Elaine cut him off, not wanting to reveal their ignorance.

"We don't know much of what's been happening," said Elaine. "Not since your grandfather's time. Tell us what you know. Tell us about Cloud Palace."

Zephyr eyed them warily, then looked around to make sure they were still alone.

"If you're commanding it," he said. "Cloud Palace has been dissolving. No one is knowing why. Some are saying it's being the Sulfane, but he is never coming near it."

"Who's the—?" Spenser started to ask, but Elaine's elbow in his side made him stop.

"I see," said Elaine, starting to shiver. "I don't suppose you have a towel?"

"A towel??" Zephyr let out a laugh.

"Yes. We're a bit wet."

"Then be imagicating yourself a towel!" Zephyr exclaimed.

For just a moment, even Elaine was at a loss for words. But the moment was long enough. Zephyr could see that the two youngsters before him knew nothing about imagication.

"You're not really being Chloe, are you?" Zephyr said slowly.

"No?" Elaine asked. "What makes you—?"

"Chloe would be imagicating herself a towel...No, a fur coat, a warming sun if she's being cold!"

He sniffed the air again.

"Oh, the foulishness! I cannot be being smelled with you."

He quickly ran his hands along his bottle collection, searching for the right one. He pulled one from the rope labeled "Jet Stream." He tucked it under one arm, and opened the valve with the opposite hand. Immediately, a jet of air shot out, and propelled Zephyr across the bluff and in through the window of his shack.

Spenser stared after him in shock. A moment later, the serf's hand beckoned them closer.

"I guess he just didn't want to be seen with us," said Elaine. She shrugged and walked toward the hut.

"*Smelled* with us," said Spenser. "But what was all that about Chloe? Who's Chloe?"

"Leeee said Chloe was a girl from our world. She created this whole place."

"That's ridiculous."

"Oh, *is* it? Is it any more ridiculous than sailphins, a wind serf and a muddy puddle that spun us clear into a different world? How do you explain *that* one, Mr. Thinker? Hmm?"

Spenser shot her a look, not sure how he felt about her teasing. Still, he couldn't come up with an answer that made sense even to him.

"Right, then," said Elaine. "It's all a matter of perspective, my dear Just Spenser. From here in Windemere, the Chloe idea doesn't seem so ridiculous after all, does it?"

Spenser shook his head, trying to puzzle out how they had gotten here—and what his rock had to do with it all.

As they neared the hut, Zephyr opened the door. The wind serf looked furtively around, then closed the door behind them.

Zephyr's shack consisted of a single room piled all about with wind bottles and odd contraptions Spenser and Elaine could not identify.

Zephyr rummaged through his bottle collection, muttering to himself.

"Shouldn't being smelled with them…Shouldn't being smelled with them…"

"Then just give us a towel and we'll go," said Spenser.

"Oh! Begging your pardon!" exclaimed Zephyr. "You may not be being *the* Chloe and the Count of Cauliflower, but surely you are being here for doing good. The Sailphins were welcoming you. The Sailphins were being Chloe's first creatures, and they'll be the last to be giving in."

"Giving in to what?" asked Elaine.

Again, Zephyr sniffed furtively around. When he spoke, it was barely a whisper.

"To the Sulfane," he said. "To *destructing*. Surely, you were seeing the bodies!"

"What bodies?"

"The bodies! Washing up on the shore—like driftwood. Yellowing, rotting…"

Elaine and Spenser exchanged disturbed looks; they'd even scrambled over some of the "driftwood" and had only noticed the stench.

"It's being so horrible…The Sulfane…and his army…they're withering the life out of everything. My own cousins and friends…Bodies washing up everywhere…"

Elaine shivered. Spenser felt like he was going to be sick.

Suddenly, Zephyr found the bottle he'd been searching for.

"Here you are," he said. "Khamsin, 1997. As dry as dry gets."

He opened the bottle for them, and a perfectly warm, dry wind blew over them.

"It's the desert!" exclaimed Elaine.

Zephyr nodded. "Blowing from the southern city of Khamsin. Blowing from across The Dunes."

Spenser felt his whole body warming, his clothes drying in moments. Amazed, he inspected the bottle.

"Wind shouldn't work like this," he said. "You can't bottle it. I mean, think about the physics."

Zephyr laughed. "Well, I'm not knowing anything about fizzies, but I am knowing about wind."

"*Physics*," said Spenser. "The laws of how things work. This doesn't make sense…"

"Maybe not in your world. Maybe whoever was imagicating your world was imagicating different laws from the ones Chloe was imagicating for here…But then how are your serfs bottling the wind?"

"They don't. Serfs in our world used to farm the land."

"Not the wind?? Why—farming the wind is being the noblest profession in Windemere! Oh, there's not being any money in it, sure. And we serfs are always getting the flew—flying north one day and south the next. And it's being hard work, too. Just you try catching a hurricane in *your* mouth, seeing how *you* like it! But it *is* being noble…"

"Says who?" asked Spenser.

"Saying my father. Zephyr the Greater. He was being the noblest wind serf of all. Until he was being blown out to sea and never heard from again, may his breeze be resting."

Spenser and Elaine didn't know whether to laugh or to feel sorry for their host.

"I'll be telling you the truth, though," he said confidentially, "I'm planning to be making a fresh start myself. Getting out of the trade. I'm having a few ideas, inventions like."

Zephyr rummaged through his pile of creations and pulled out a piece of cloth that looked like a pillowcase.

"Looking at this!"

He opened a valve at one end. A roar of wind filled the cloth.

"It's being a wind pillow!" he shouted. "Feeling like you're sleeping on a cloud!"

"It's a little loud for sleeping," shouted Elaine.

"What?" shouted Zephyr.

"I said it's a little loud for sleeping!"

Zephyr closed the valve and the pillow deflated.

"Sorry, I couldn't be hearing you. It's being a little loud for sleeping...But looking at this!"

He pulled out another invention, which looked something like a vacuum cleaner, and opened a valve. A strong wind erupted from the nozzle and blew all of Zephyr's belongings from one side of the room to the other.

"It's being a wind cleaner. No more dusting! No more sweeping!"

"But what about *this* side of the room?" asked Elaine.

"Easy!" said Zephyr.

He aimed the nozzle again, and blew all of his belongings back to the side of the room where they had started.

"There," said Zephyr. "Now we are just cleaning *this* side..." He aimed the wind back at the first side of the room, blowing anything that wasn't nailed down to the second side once more. In the process, the wind cleaner blew a couple of bottles right out the window.

"Oops," said Zephyr, shutting it off.

"If you want to invent something useful," suggested Spenser, "You could try putting some glass panes in your window."

Zephyr burst into laughter.

"Glass panes?? Why, then the wind couldn't be getting in at all! You could hardly be calling it a wind-door!"

Just then, he spotted something out the wind-door.

"Oh, now *this* is being a treat! Coming along, coming along!"

Elaine and Spenser, now warm and dry, followed Zephyr outside, and followed his gaze up to the sky.

"Not seeing many of these anymore," said Zephyr.

There, floating above them like a black and white blimp, was a cow.

Zephyr carefully opened a bottle labeled "Caution: Cyclone" and aimed it at the cow. Immediately, the beast began flipping and spinning—not to mention mooing loudly.

"What are you doing?" asked Elaine.

"Making a milkshake, of course! Now, a bit of downdraft…"

Zephyr closed the cyclone bottle and opened a downdraft. With it, he brought the cow gently down to the ground. He approached it, ready to begin milking, then paused.

"This is being odd…" he said.

"You can say that again," said Spenser.

"Wind serfs are always reading the signs," said Zephyr. "We are smelling them on the breeze."

"You mean like omens?" asked Elaine.

Zephyr nodded.

"You funneling in among the Sailphins, that is definitely being a good sign. But then there was being foulishness in the air, a bad sign. Then a floating cow, a rare good sign if there ever was being one. Such creatures were being the height of the First Imagication. But now this…"

"What?" asked Elaine.

"Looking at its udder."

"Oh," said Elaine.

Spenser stared too, rubbed his eyes and stared some more. Half of the cow's udder seemed to be dissolving into the air. He could see through it like he was watching some kind of weird, bovine ghost movie.

Zephyr squatted down to milk what he could into an empty wind bottle.

"I wouldn't drink from that," said Spenser. "It's probably full of pesticides."

"Well," said Zephyr, "I'm not knowing about pesky sides. But it's being true, most things are having good sides and bad sides. My father was always saying that Windemere is being a battleground between the creators of beauty and the destroyers of beauty. In his time, there was being a balance. Nowadays, the beautiful things all are seeming to be crumbling around the edges."

He sampled some milkshake from the bottle.

"Mmm," he said. "But what we are having left is still being quite good. Tasting some."

Elaine put the bottle to her lips.

"Oh, fan*tas*tic. Spenser, you have *got* to try it."

"No thanks."

Zephyr leaned close to Elaine.

"I'm thinking the Count of Cauliflower is crumbling a bit himself."

"Listen," said Spenser, "You talk about the world falling apart, bodies washing up on the shore—How come you're just sitting around drinking milkshakes?"

The wind serf looked at him with surprise. "Because you're being here. You're funneling in to be saving all of Windemere."

"How could we?"

"Well, I'm not knowing *that*. If you're truly not coming here on your own powers, then only the Imagius is having the power to bring you. It's not being easy, a task like that."

"What's the Imagius?" asked Elaine.

"Not what. Who. The Imagius Rafalco—he's being the chief imagicator. Powerful good man, he's being, the powerfulest imagicator in the land. I blew over Mezmir once—that's being the See of the Imagius. I wasn't seeing him myself, of course, but still, he's being a powerful good imagicator."

"And what's imagicating, exactly?"

The serf took another swallow from the bottle, then continued.

"It's being the art of imagining something into being. But I'm hardly understanding it. They're saying everyone can be imagicating at least a little, but almost no one is being able to do it really well. And I'm having no talent for it at all. No, imagicating is being a difficult art. Only the Imagius is having the power to summon you." Here, his voice grew hushed again: "He's being the only one of the top imagicators the Sulfane isn't capturing."

"So who is this Sulfane, exactly?" asked Elaine.

"Hushing!" said Zephyr. "The Sulfane…Maybe *he's* being more of a *what* than a *who*. They're saying he was being born like a scalemander from the hot coals of Samovar Mountain. He is ruling Windemere ever since the King and Queen were splitting apart, leaving Cloud Palace. The Sulfane is not allowing imagication. The Sulfane is not allowing beauty. Wherever he is breathing, all is dissolving in a foulish wind."

Spenser found his own breath tightening in his throat. Somehow, hearing about the Sulfane rekindled that unsettling doubt he'd had before dislodging the brick at Windy Hill. "That still doesn't answer, why us?"

The wind serf shook his head. "I'm not knowing."

"Could this have anything to do with it?" asked Elaine.

"Hey!" said Spenser.

In Elaine's hand was a rock. Spenser's rock. He felt his pocket. Somehow, Elaine had swiped it from him.

Zephyr let out a low whistle. He plucked the stone from Elaine's hand and studied it.

"*Pebble, rock, flint boulder stone,*" he murmured. "*From Earth to Wind, make firm the throne…*"

A chilly breeze blew over them. The cow let out a plaintive moo and spun away on the wind. Zephyr sniffed the air.

"What is it?" asked Elaine.

"Foulishness. Foulishness upon foulishness!"

More suddenly than Spenser and Elaine had ever seen in their own world, the breeze turned to a gale. The wind serf looked about frantically. He searched the sky and horizon for any sign.

"Oh, I shouldn't have been dallying! Shouldn't have been dillying!"

"What are you talking about?" asked Spenser. "What's the rock for?"

"Begging your pardon! Can't being smelled helping you! Shouldn't being seen with you!"

With that, he took the lid from his cyclone bottle once more and shot himself back through the wind-door of his shack.

"Hey!" called Spenser.

The sky filled with storm clouds, and all the warmth they had felt from the bottled Khamsin was gone.

Spenser turned Elaine, "What was that about? You just take what you want? Right out of my pocket?!"

"If it's the rock you're worried about, we can go get it back," she said, putting the lid on the leftover milkshake.

"*Back?*" he asked, then he realized Zephyr had flown off with the stone. He groaned, and steamed after the wind serf.

"Wait!" Elaine hurried to catch up, realizing the seriousness of her mistake. She hadn't meant to betray him.

"The one thing!" Spenser yelled over the storm. "The one thing that seems to have any power—the one thing we had that meant *anything*—and you didn't just *steal* it, you let it get *stolen*! What were you thinking?! Oh, wait, you don't like *thinking.*"

Spenser could see his words had stung, but he didn't care.

"I was only trying…" Elaine began feebly.

She had only been trying to solve the mystery, which seemed the right thing to do. What more did he want from her?

In the next moment, the gale turned to a hurricane. The growing wind knocked them both from their feet. Elaine rolled half a dozen feet before lodging herself against a low rock. Spenser clung to a root. Raindrops the size of marbles pelted his face. The only shelter in sight was Zephyr's shack. Spenser, his mind set on recovering his stone, began crawling upwind toward it. For every foot he crawled forward, the gale blew him back two feet, until it backed him right against Elaine. Still he struggled forward. Elaine wondered at this side of him she hadn't seen before, this side that could suddenly care so much for a world he'd only been in for an hour.

"Spenser—" she offered. "I could help—"

Spenser ignored her, and she didn't really know how to help anyway.

If he could just get to the hut, Spenser thought, he'd be safe from the storm—and he'd get his rock back. Then maybe he could help stop the destruction of this beautiful place. Already he could feel the dark clouds pressing down, down to the point of smothering everything.

"Spenser—"

Suddenly, the wind blew the hut to pieces. Boards, bottles, and all of Zephyr's contraptions flew over Spenser and Elaine's heads, out of sight. Nothing was left. Not even the wind serf himself. And certainly no rock.

Elaine shook her head. "Oh, Spenser…I am so sorry…"

CHAPTER 3

▼

THE CLOVENS

Spenser could not believe the sight. Zephyr's shack looked like it had exploded. And where was the wind serf with his rock? Spenser rose up to look around.

Immediately, the gale caught him in the chest and lifted him from his feet like a scarecrow in a tornado. He flailed his arms, fearing being blown away. Elaine grabbed him around the ankles, adding her weight to his. He tucked into a ball and crashed back down.

"Thanks," he muttered.

"It's the least I can do, after, I mean—"

Elaine shook her head.

Spenser heard her apologies, but pretended not to. He knew he was supposed to say "Oh, that's okay" or "Don't worry about it" or "Really, I don't mind that you're a thief, a pickpocket, and a liar. Some of my best friends are thieves, pickpockets, and liars." Instead, Spenser just gritted his teeth and squinted into the storm.

They had two choices: They could stay where they were and risk getting blown out to sea like Zephyr and his father before him, or they could try crawling somewhere else—and risk getting blown out to sea like Zephyr and his father before him.

As Spenser mulled over these possibilities, Elaine suddenly cried out, "Oh!"

"What?"

"My milkshake!"

Her bottle had blown a small distance away and was pinned against the base of a scraggly bush. Now it was her turn to rise up to go after it. Spenser immediately tackled her.

"Stay down!"

"But—"

The wind shifted slightly, jostling the bottle loose from the bush. Elaine watched as the storm lifted the bottle like a leaf and whirled it out of sight.

"Whoa...," said Spenser, but he wasn't watching the bottle.

"What?"

Spenser just shook his head, speechless. Then Elaine saw it too: Floating straight down out of the sky, completely unaffected by the raging storm, was a strange creature—no, not a creature, a vehicle—a cross between an old-fashioned carriage and a bloated pterodactyl. Leathery wings stretched out from the coach's sides, blotting out what light dribbled through the clouds. Elaine and Spenser huddled closer together. What seemed at first to be the pterosaur's pointed head was in fact the driver's perch stretching in front of the passenger compartment, and a whip-like tail stretched out behind.

The cloaked driver hopped down from his seat. He had to hop, since he had only one leg. He also had only one arm. As he turned, Spenser and Elaine could see the reason: the driver was only half a person, split right down the middle, with only half a head and half a body. The carriage door opened, and out hopped the other half. The two met and merged together, a gaunt coachman in a gray cloak.

"Come on!" yelled the two halves as one.

"Come in the drafter!" called the right side of the mouth.

"That storm'll kill yeh!" called the left.

Spenser and Elaine hesitated, but not for long; there was no other shelter in sight. They realized they were still holding onto each other, still hugging each other in defense against the wind, and they pulled shyly apart.

"All right," said Elaine. "Let's go."

"Right," Spenser agreed. "Keep low."

Barely ten yards separated them from the safety of the drafter, but the storm was relentless. They crawled on their bellies in the mud to keep from being blown away. Wind-driven rain lashed at them like a million cold whips, making them wince, obscuring their vision. Whenever they dared look up, the drafter seemed no closer.

"Let's make a dash for it!" yelled Elaine over the wind.

Spenser nodded. They sprang to their feet. They took a couple of running steps before the gale lifted them from the ground. The driver again split in two.

The left half caught Elaine by the elbow. The right hand snagged Spenser by a belt loop. Together, they struggled the few remaining yards to shelter.

Inside the drafter, the half-people closed the door and merged again.

"Now that's better," said the right half of the driver's mouth. "Snug out of the wind."

"Yeh coulda landed closer," said the left half in a lower, gruffer voice. "If I'd been drivin', I'da landed closer."

"No bickering, now," said the right half cheerily. "We've got passengers."

The right eye looked over at the left eye, then back at Spenser and Elaine. Even when merged, the right half moved and spoke in a more polished manner than the left.

"Right, then," said the right. "Introductions. My name is Destry. And my associate here is Sinstry. He's a constant pain in my side, but I'm stuck with him."

"Ah, yer a fine one to talk," said Sinstry, the coarser of the two. "I'd go off on my own if I could. Glad to be rid o' yeh, I would."

"Now, now, remember, no bickering," Destry chuckled, then turned his eye back on Spenser and Elaine. "Don't mind my other half. You'll be made welcome in our drafter if I *have* to do it all myself. Get it? *Half* to?"

Spenser and Elaine each gave a half laugh, which seemed the right response.

"Now then," Destry went on, "Settle in, and we'll be under way. Sinstry, your turn to drive, since you're so slick. You get us out of this storm."

Sinstry gave a little harrumph as he split off and hopped toward the door.

"Wait," said Elaine. "You don't know where we're going."

"'Course we do," growled Sinstry. "We're the drivers."

"Politeness, Sinstry, politeness," Destry turned to his guests. "You must pardon him. Lefts are always so…*gauche*. Now then. We've been sent to find you, to take you right to where you want to go."

"*Right* to where yeh want to go," echoed Sinstry bitterly. "Why not *left* to where yeh want to go, eh? It's pure prejudice, that's what it is!"

"Now, Sinstry," the right half chuckled, "We don't mean for you to feel *left* out."

"See, that's *just* what I'm talkin' about!" Sinstry groused.

"But who sent you to find us?" asked Elaine. "The Imagius?"

Sinstry let out a half laugh of his own.

"Why is that so funny?" asked Elaine.

"Don't mind Sinstry," said Destry. "Half the time, he only has half a clue— which, if you know your fractions, means, on average, he only has a quarter of a clue. If we Clovens are good at one thing, it's fractions. Go on, Sinstry, take us to where the Imagius is."

Sinstry scowled and turned for the door once more.

"Wait," said Spenser, thinking about his rock. "We were with a wind serf. He got blown away. We've got to find him."

Destry and Sinstry exchanged looks.

"Find a wind serf?" asked Destry. "In a storm?"

"No chance o' that," Sinstry agreed.

"Why not?"

"Well," began Destry, "Supposing you people are made mostly of water. Well, a wind serf is almost entirely air. And in a wind like this, he could be anywhere."

"But we've got to find him," Spenser insisted. "It's really, really important."

"No chance," Sinstry repeated.

"Besides," added Destry, "As you say, our job is to bring you to the Imagius."

Sinstry turned to Spenser. "Don't worry 'bout yer wind serf. He'll turn up when the winds change. They always do."

With that, Sinstry left the cabin for the driver's seat. Destry again gestured for Spenser and Elaine to have a seat.

"Please," he said.

Spenser and Elaine sank into a pair of comfortable seats. The cushions seemed to billow around them.

"Comfy, eh?" said Destry. "We got this drafter off another Cloven—for half price."

Destry chuckled at his own joke again, but Spenser and Elaine were too busy looking around to pay him much attention.

The drafter had risen silently. Twenty feet off the ground, they were already above the storm. Looking down, they could see that the hurricane only covered a small area right around where Zephyr's shack had been.

Up front on the driver's perch, Sinstry was busy at the controls. The half-circle steering wheel and the single pedal had clearly been built with a Cloven driver in mind. Sinstry closed the valve on a wind bottle, and the hurricane below vanished.

"Wait a minute...," said Spenser.

Destry eyed him with his single eye.

"The hurricane," Spenser went on. "*You* made it."

Destry gave him a half-smile.

"Oh, an inquisitive mind," he said. "We like an inquisitive mind. Here's something that will suit you."

From his cloak pocket, Destry pulled a small, shiny, black box. Except for the ornate hinges on the lid, the polished, wooden box looked completely plain.

"Take a look," urged the Cloven. "Look deep inside."

He pushed the box into Spenser's hands. Spenser's fingers closed around it, but he would not let Destry distract him.

"But why the hurricane?"

Destry could see the gift of the box was not enough to placate Spenser. "We had to get you away from the wind serf," he explained.

"Why?" asked Elaine. "He was trying to help us."

Destry shook his head, "No. He just wanted you to think that. You see, you can never trust a wind serf. They're as changeable as the breeze. One moment, they're friendly, trying to help you, inviting you into their shacks. The next moment, they'll rob you blind."

Spenser's heart sank. What Destry said seemed to fit. They had trusted Zephyr, and he had flown off with the one thing of theirs Spenser sensed had value.

"Look in the box," the Cloven said kindly. "Go on. Look in the box."

Spenser looked down at the black box in his hands. It was tempting to look inside. Maybe—who knows?—maybe somehow it even held his stone. But he wasn't about to look in when someone else was pushing him to do so.

Destry tapped on the glass (the drafter's windows had glass) to get Sinstry's attention.

"Use the bottled wind. We're on official business."

Sinstry turned and snarled, "*I'm* drivin'! Don't yeh think I know my work?! I'm ridin' a fair easterly!"

Indeed, the drafter was riding a strong wind from the east, gliding swiftly over the land on its broad pterodactyl wings. But Destry was not about to let the matter drop. He rose to his foot and hopped to the door, muttering to himself.

"Why, I have half a mind to—"

He hopped outside the passenger compartment and scooted along the running board to the driver's perch.

Elaine stared through the thick glass that divided the passengers from the drivers, "He has half a mind, period."

They studied the Clovens for a moment, then Elaine leaned in toward Spenser.

"Okay," she said. "Now let's figure this out. What's so special about your rock?"

"Isn't it a little late to ask?" Spenser scoffed.

"Please."

Spenser bit his lower lip, sorry he'd said anything. He hated when he sounded like his parents, turning everything into an argument.

"Spenser?"

He took a deep breath and tried again. "All right. I've been thinking. Do you really believe all that about Chloe—that she was a girl from our world, that back in Zephyr's grandfather's time she created this whole place?"

"Yes. Yes, I do."

"Well, I'm just thinking 'what if?' here. I mean, that would have been about eighty years ago, right?"

Elaine nodded.

"Well, you know that corner room at Windy Hill—with the shrieking and the whirlpool?"

"Of course. Go on."

"Well, what if that's where Chloe lived, in that corner room? What if Chloe lived at Windy Hill?"

Elaine caught on. "Right…She was sick. Sick for years and years…"

"Bored, alone…no one her own age—"

"Nothing to do but imagine this whole place—down to the last grain of sand. Spenser, you're brilliant!"

Spenser fought to hide the smile creeping onto his face.

"Well, now here's the thing," he went on. "That room at Windy Hill, well, last week, that's where I found the stone."

"*Chloe's* stone…We're supposed to bring Chloe's stone to the Royal Wisps—whatever that means."

"We *were* supposed to bring it," Spenser muttered.

"Can't you *drop* that? I *said* I was sorry."

Spenser bit his lip again. Why couldn't he just keep his mouth shut—or at least say something nice to someone who was trying to be nice to him?

Elaine rose and paced. "We have *got* to get out of here."

She tried the door. Locked. But a little thing like a lock wasn't about to slow her down.

"We'll take over this drafter," she went on. "Get the Clovens to split. Knock them overboard; they can't have too good balance on one leg. One time—I'm *not* making this up—one time, I tipped over a flamingo just like that. Of course, it *was* one of those plastic lawn ones…But still! We could knock over the Clovens, then fly this thing where *we* want to go."

"That's stupid," laughed Spenser, then immediately regretted it.

"Don't be rude."

"Sorry," he managed.

"Oh, that's okay." Elaine paused, considering him. "See, that's what you're *supposed* to say when someone apologizes. You're *supposed* to say, 'Oh, that's okay…. Oh, don't worry about it.' Of course, if you're too proud, or too *stubborn*, to accept *my* apology, that's okay, too. If you don't want it, I'll keep it for myself. That way, I'll have an extra apology for when someone forgets to apologize to *me*."

Spenser gave a little nod, "Right," but it was too little for Elaine to see, too quiet for her to hear.

"Oh, you're impossible!" she exclaimed. "As far as we know, we're the only two people from our world in all of Windemere. We've no idea how to get back, and barely an idea how to go forward. For now, we're stuck together, like—like Destry and Sinstry."

Spenser swallowed hard, then offered, "What do you want me to say?"

"Oh, forget it! Look at the view."

She didn't really *want* him to forget it. She wanted, just *once*, for someone to care about her, about what *she* felt. And Spenser certainly wasn't acting like he did.

"Look at the view," she sighed.

In the farmlands below the drafter, colored swatches of sunlight sprouted from neatly cultivated rows. One row grew red, the next orange, then yellow, then green, then blue, then purple. Nearby, another field grew the same colors in the opposite order. The two plantings arched toward each other in the sky.

"Rainbows…" Elaine realized.

Farther on, two halves of a rainbow had grown together. Just when Elaine had been wondering if there were any regular humans in Windemere, she spotted two farmer families digging at the soil where the rainbow grew from the ground. Once they had loosened the dirt enough to expose the golden roots, the rainbow drifted off, leaving behind a fine trail of gold dust, which the farmers then collected in woven baskets. Every so often, the farmers glanced up warily at the drafter—and at its Cloven drivers.

As beautiful and peaceful as the countryside looked, this thought kept itching in Elaine's mind until it had to come out: "There's just *something* about those Clovens…"

"And what's that?"

The voice belonged to Sinstry, who had just returned to the cabin. Spenser turned away, pretending to be absorbed by the black wooden box Destry had handed him.

"Eh?" prodded the gruffer Cloven.

"Oh," said Elaine. "It's just *fascinating*. We don't have Clovens in our world."

She shot a look over at Spenser, who was opening the black cube and looking inside.

"Good thing, too," said Sinstry.

"And why is that?" asked Elaine.

"Cuz we're a mistake."

"Oh, don't say *that*…"

"Why not, if it's true. Story goes, Chloe started imagicating some kind of half-man, half-beast, but then she decided she didn't like the half-beast part. So she got us, the Clovens, half man—and half man. Story goes, Chloe thought it was one of her great jokes, like flyin' cows. But what about us Clovens? All stuck with each other, we are."

"Why can't you just leave?"

Sinstry shook his head sadly.

"It's the digestion. Yeh get all gassy if yer not hooked up right. Gassy and bloated. We know one Cloven, ooh he *hated* his other half. He stayed away as long as he could. One time, he stayed split too long, got so gassy and bloated, he *popped*. Hour later, so did his other half."

"I'm sure that's just a story," said Elaine, comfortingly. She looked over at Spenser, who was staring into the black box Destry had given him.

Sinstry shook his head, "Nah. 'Twas in the Rook. We had to clean it up ourselves. Twice."

Elaine studied the Cloven, still not trusting him.

"Tell me about the drafter," said Elaine. "Is it easy to fly?"

Sinstry shot her a piercing look with his one eye and said, "With practice."

An awkward silence passed. Elaine felt she'd better not push it, better not let Sinstry suspect she was planning some kind of escape. And Spenser was being no help at all. Instead, Elaine looked out the window.

The drafter was flying faster now, with Destry at the helm. He had opened some bottled wind to supplement the natural wind. They sped over small towns and fields, leaving the barren coast behind for the lush, fertile interior of rolling hills.

Soon they approached a sparkling cloud.

"What…?" Elaine asked.

"Daystars," said Sinstry. "They're around all the time, but yeh can only see 'em in the day."

The drafter flew into the cloud of gold and silver sparkles, then out the other side.

"Here," said the Cloven to Spenser, "Whyn't yeh give yer friend a turn?"

He pulled the dark, wooden box out of Spenser's hands and closed the lid. Spenser came out of his trance.

"What *is* that?" he asked.

"A dream box," said Sinstry. "Yeh like it?"

Spenser nodded and reached to get it back.

"Nah, nah," laughed Sinstry. "Gotta let yer friend have a turn."

He handed it to Elaine. She turned it over in her hands. She glanced over at Spenser to gauge what he thought of it. Spenser was smiling blissfully, looking more relaxed than she'd ever seen him.

"Take a look inside," urged the Cloven. "It'll pass the time."

Cautiously, Elaine opened the lid. Nothing. Just an empty box. She looked in over the rim, and then—It happened. She lost her balance and fell down, down…into dizzying darkness. She pulled herself back from the edge. She regained her balance. She was still in the drafter, the box in her hands. She had been sitting there the whole time; just her *mind* had fallen in. This thought made her even more dizzy.

"Can I have it back now?" Spenser asked.

"Nah," said Sinstry to Elaine. "Yeh gotta have a *real* look. Look all the way in."

Elaine glanced at Sinstry, weighing her suspicions, then opened the lid once more. She looked in. Again she had the sensation of losing her balance, of falling through darkness. She fought the urge to pull herself back, and this time she let herself fall. Down, down, falling, spinning…

The falling turned to floating. The darkness brightened to a warm, dappled light. She found herself astride a golden horse, sunlight filtering through leaves onto her cheeks. She *knew* she was dreaming, and yet—she touched her hand to her face and felt the sun's warmth—it was more than a dream. She sensed she could wake herself at any moment, but why would she? This dream world was perfect.

From a distance, she heard a voice crying for help. Called to action, Elaine spurred her golden horse through the trees, toward the cries. She wove between trunks at a gallop until the forest thinned to an enchanted meadow with a stream running through. On an island mid-stream stood a fairy-tale castle with one small tower. A handsome prince in a long black coat leaned out of the high window.

"Ah, worthy knight!" he called. "My tormentors have locked me in this tower for a hundred years."

Elaine nodded confidently, relishing the chance to be the heroine. From this distance, the prince looked vaguely like Spenser, only far more mature. He gave Elaine a warm, entrancing look she had never seen or felt before. She trotted her horse through the stream to the base of the tower and called, "What is your name, good Prince?"

The prince shook his head and laughed wryly. "I am afraid they call me Prince Repulso."

"Hardly!" smiled Elaine, then joked, "Repulso, Repulso, let down your hair!"

The prince snatched the toupee from his head and flung it down to Elaine.

"Ugh," she muttered, tossing the mat of hair into the stream.

"Would you like my teeth, too?" asked the bald prince, pulling out his dentures.

"Oh, no, please. Don't go to any trouble."

Too late, the false teeth landed with a plop in the water by the floating raft of hair. Still determined to complete the rescue, Elaine leapt from her horse to the castle wall and began to scale it like a world-class rock-climber. She felt a rush of adrenaline and pride in her skill. Hand over hand, she practically scampered up the rock face, but—

Someone was yanking her. A dark hand was reaching into the back of her head.

"Go away!" she wanted to say, but she couldn't speak. The hand was inside her skull, in back of her eyes, pulling her sideways, out of herself.

"Stop!" she screamed. She wanted to stay on the castle wall and complete her mission. But it was too late. The sunlit meadow, the stream, the tower, the toupee and dentures, had all vanished. She was spinning back into the dizzying darkness, and then reeling into the drafter cabin.

Sinstry had plucked the dream box from her hands.

"Now, now," he was saying, "Yeh gotta learn to share. Too bad you've only got one."

Both Spenser and Elaine were reaching for the box, but Sinstry held it high, like a wicked older cousin playing keep-away.

"It's my turn," said Spenser.

"Wait!" said Elaine, "I hardly got a chance!"

"Gotta let yer friend have his turn now," laughed the Cloven, and he handed the box to Spenser.

Elaine considered grabbing it back, but even though Sinstry was only half a man, he was a big half and looked like he could be cruel if pressed. No chance of knocking him over and out the door now. She watched as Spenser opened the box and gazed inside. His eyes became unfocused. A relaxed smile grew on his face.

Spenser's mind fell comfortably through the darkness, down into a living room. He knew it to be his own living room, even though it looked nothing like his real one. It was night. A fire crackled in the fireplace. His dad was making popcorn the old-fashioned way, holding a long-handled pan directly over the flames, giving it a little shake now and then. Spenser could smell the butter sizzling. He could hear the kernels exploding and pinging on the lid.

His mom brought in some hot chocolate. Spenser himself nestled among a pile of floor cushions. A board game had been set up in the middle of the room, set for three players. Spenser wondered for a moment who the other two players were. There was no one else in the room except for his parents, and he couldn't remember the last time he had played a game with both of them.

His mother sat down next to him, then his father brought over the popcorn and sat down, too, all three of them nestled close to each other.

"Go on, son," he said. "You go first."

Spenser took a sip of the hot chocolate. Warmth filled his entire being. The moment was perfect.

Then something poked him in the side, something from outside the room, from outside the dream. Spenser knew it was Elaine, wanting the box for herself.

"Leave me alone!" Spenser shouted.

"Excuse me?" said his mother, in that accusing tone only mothers can have.

"No, not you," Spenser started, but the poking didn't stop. "Ow! Hey, I'm not done! It's not your turn yet!"

"We know that, Spenser," said his mother, trying to remain calm. "Roll the dice."

With an effort, Spenser rolled the dice. The dice fell into a hole that had opened up in the floor and disappeared.

"No!" cried Spenser.

"Well, if you don't want to play, boy—" began his father, standing up.

"No!" Spenser pleaded, "Don't leave!"

But his father was gone. Now his mother stood up too. His dream was all going wrong.

"Wait!"

"Sorry, Spenser," said his mother, and she disappeared.

The poking turned to yanking, and Spenser felt himself pulled back out of the dream, out of the box, back into the drafter cabin. Elaine held the box in her hands. She started to open the lid.

"Hey, I wasn't done!" said Spenser. He snatched the dream box from her clutches.

"You had just as long a turn as *I* had," Elaine insisted, grabbing for it herself.

"But I'd just gotten there! I was with my parents!"

"So?"

"So it was so…simple. You wouldn't understand."

"Then give me another turn!"

"You still wouldn't understand. You *couldn't* understand!"

Elaine covered her hurt with anger. "You don't know what I understand and what I don't! You don't know anything about me!"

"Right! And I don't really want to!"

Sinstry couldn't help but let out a snort. Elaine wheeled on him.

"What are you laughing at?"

Sinstry gave his devilish half-smile. "Jus' glad yeh enjoy the box so much, that's all. Passes the time, don't it?

"Humph," said Elaine.

"Well, I gotta get back up front," said the Cloven. "Knock on the glass if yeh need anythin'."

Elaine watched Sinstry leave. Then she turned back to Spenser, who already had his nose back in the box.

"Spenser—" she started, but then stewed. *Ah, let him have another turn.* She didn't need that box—or him. *No, I definitely don't need Spenser,* she told herself. But she wanted that box more than anything in the world. She wanted to be back in that enchanted meadow, rescuing a prince no matter how bald and toothless he was. She wanted that feeling of being a hero, of helping someone who needed her. She looked again at Spenser. No, he didn't need her either; he had the dream box.

She fought back her jealousy. She wanted the box, but there was something she had to work out first. Why was that Cloven so pleased with himself? Was it really because he shared their enjoyment of the dream box? No, she didn't buy that for a second.

Elaine stared out the window. She had no sense of how long they had been in the air, nor any idea of how far they had come. They had left the rainbow fields far behind and were approaching a silvery lake. Elaine had never seen a lake so calm. It reflected the trees on the other side so perfectly that if Elaine turned her head upside-down, she could easily convince herself that the reflection was the reality, and that the reality was the reflection. As the drafter skirted the shoreline, Elaine could see people working below. The people looked up warily at the drafter.

From what Elaine could see, the work at the lakeshore was divided into two parts. Carpenters assembled wooden frames, mostly rectangular, but occasionally round or oval. Once a frame was complete, the carpenters would pass it to the second team. The second team dipped an enormous ladle into the silvery lake, and poured the water into the wooden frame. The ripples calmed immediately, filling the frame with the same pure reflections as the lake.

Elaine blinked her eyes to make sure she was seeing straight. As the workers shifted the frame upright, none of the water dripped out.

*They're making mirrors...*thought Elaine.

For a brief moment, Elaine caught sight of a girl looking out the window of a drafter, reflected in a newly-made mirror. *How sad that girl looks,* she thought. *How alone. Like she's trying so hard to do the right thing, and no one knows she even exists...*Then the image tilted away, and Elaine realized the reflection had been her own.

She glanced back at Spenser and at the dream box in his hands. No matter how many marvels there might be in the world outside the window, Elaine felt pulled toward that box. *No! Think about something else.*

On their perch, the Clovens turned their head to study their passengers. Everything appeared as it should: Spenser was absorbed by the dream box. Elaine sat gazing out the window, daydreaming.

At least Elaine *tried* to daydream, to think about anything else but the dream box. She couldn't help herself. She thought about the smooth, black wood, cool beneath her fingertips. She thought of the ornate brass hinges gliding open. She thought of the rich, mossy smell of the forest she'd first sensed when she'd opened it. She imagined herself peering over the rim into the bottomless black within...

Sinstry reached across his chest and punched his opposite shoulder—Destry's shoulder.

"Hey!" Destry protested.

"Look at that!" said Sinstry. "She's not supposed to do that!"

"What—?" began Destry. Then he saw what had so alarmed his other half. Elaine had a dream box of her own in her hands. The box shimmered, not quite solid yet, but she had brought it into being nonetheless.

"Stay here!" commanded Destry as he split from Sinstry. "Full speed! All bottles! We've got to get to the Rook before she learns what she can do!"

For her part, Elaine was just as surprised as the Clovens. She hadn't been *trying* to do anything. She'd just been thinking, thinking about the box, remembering, imagining every detail. *I wonder if this is how Chloe did it.* But the instant she had this thought—and took her attention away from thinking about the box—the nearly solid object disappeared entirely.

Destry burst into the cabin. He stared at Elaine. Her hands were empty. He relaxed a bit, letting out a deep breath from his one lung. He adopted a gentle smile.

"Enjoying the ride?" he asked.

"Oh, yes," she replied sweetly.

Both acted as if everything was normal. But for Elaine, everything was different. She had begun to imagicate.

CHAPTER 4

▼

DODGING THE DARK AND STORMY KNIGHTS

Destry took a seat opposite Elaine, scrutinizing her with his one eye. She met his gaze with determination. *I can win this stare-down*, she thought. *I've got twice as many eyes.*

The Cloven shifted in his seat, not blinking. Elaine gave up looking at his eye and studied the rest of his body. He was clad in a gray leather cloak. Where his body sometimes joined with Sinstry, his own skin was equally dark and leathery. His hand rested by his waist. Now Elaine could see, strapped to his belt, a large, black knife. Even the blade was black.

For some reason, the knife didn't scare her. Instead, it was like a challenge. She'd had to get out of tough spots before, wriggling out of the grasp of countless boarding school headmistresses. True, she'd never been locked in a wind-powered pterodactyl in a strange world, guarded by a half-man and a half-man, but then, who had? If she kept her wits about her, she knew she could escape. The trick in any good escape wasn't just seizing an opportunity, it was *creating* one.

She examined the drafter. It had one door, and Destry was guarding it. It had four small windows, one on each side, but they didn't open. Even if she could break through the thick glass, Elaine couldn't possibly squeeze through. Somehow, she'd have to get by Destry, or wait until he left to trade places again with Sinstry. Then there was still the matter of the lock—and the fact that they were too high off the ground to jump. Spenser would be no help at all, his nose stuck in the dream box. She could take the box from his hands to roust him out of it, but then he'd probably be even angrier and not want to help. A sickening pit opened up in Elaine's stomach with this realization: The whole reason the Clovens had given Spenser the dream box had been to distract their passengers and to set one against the other. And it had worked.

Elaine forced herself to look out the window. She didn't want Destry to see her panic. Still, she could feel the Cloven watching her, guarding her.

Elaine took several deep breaths and focused on the landscape. They were cruising above a muddy road, deeply rutted from years of wagon wheels and heavy rains.

The most amazing horse Elaine had ever seen—its coat shimmering like rippling water in the sunlight—came toward them on the road below, pulling an equally amazing covered wagon. The cloth covering had been painted like the sky in such detail that Elaine could even see clouds and birds moving across the fabric.

Destry rapped on the front glass. "Higher!" he called to Sinstry.

Sinstry looked around and sneered. The drafter moved lower and slower, down toward the wagon.

"Half-wit," Destry cursed under his breath. He hopped out the door and sealed it tight behind him.

"Spenser! Spenser!" Elaine shook him.

He shrugged off her hand.

"Spenser, now's our chance!" she insisted.

Spenser merely let out a sleepy "Mm, fobbawobba," and grinned into the box.

Elaine snapped the lid closed, pinching his finger.

"Ow!! What are you doing?!"

"Shh!" Elaine hushed him, not wanting to attract the Clovens' attention. She glanced around at them through the front window.

"Yeh think I don't know how to fly?" said Sinstry. "Yeh try it yerself!"

Destry took the controls. The drafter slowed even more.

"Curse her!" said Destry.

He shot a look back over his shoulder at Elaine. Their eyes met. Destry turned his attention back to the controls, fighting to keep the drafter aloft.

Below them, the sky-covered wagon had stopped. Out stepped two troubadours, scarcely older than Spenser and Elaine. The girl was dressed in robes of scarlet, with a garland of roses in her hair. The boy wore ridiculous, billowing pants, with black and yellow stripes, pointy shoes, and a pointy hat with bells jangling on the tassels. He grinned up at the approaching drafter. He caught Elaine's eye, and gave her the warm, entrancing look she had only just gotten from the dream-box prince—only this one seemed real.

In the driver's perch, Destry cursed the drafter for not following his directions. Instead, it seemed to obey the troubadour's comical gestures to land right in front of the wagon.

The troubadours produced juggling objects out of thin air—the usual balls, clubs, and knives, along with assorted ducks and chickens—and back into the air they threw them until there seemed too many objects for the two jugglers to manage—and yet they did.

"Impossible," said Spenser, for just when the troubadours had mastered the balls, clubs, knives, ducks and chickens, the chickens started laying eggs mid-air, adding even *more* objects for the jugglers to juggle.

The show was so spectacular that Spenser nearly forgot about the dream box in his hands.

"What are they saying?" asked Spenser.

"I don't know," said Elaine. "But can't you just imagine the window *shattering?*"

Just then, one of the hatchets the boy was juggling flew from his hand and crashed into the drafter's window, smashing it to pieces.

The juggler looked at Elaine, impressed. "Good work," he said, and Elaine puzzled at what he meant.

"Hey!" shouted Destry.

"Oh, forgive me!" The juggler smiled graciously to the Cloven. "Let me clean that up for you."

He conjured a dozen pink feather dusters among the balls, clubs, ducks and chickens, and juggled them toward the broken glass.

"Back off!" roared the Clovens at the jugglers, drawing their knives.

"Oh, such a cold disposition," said the girl haughtily. "Allow me to warm you up."

Her juggling balls burst into flame. They didn't seem to hurt her quick hands, though the Clovens took a step back, hesitant to challenge someone juggling fire.

The boy tossed one of the ducks he'd been juggling to the girl. As it passed through the flaming circle, it lost its feathers and became a golden-brown piece of meat.

"Ta-da!" the boy shouted triumphantly. "Roast duck! Anybody hungry?"

"Can we really eat it?" asked Elaine.

Destry wheeled on her. "Don't watch them! Don't listen to them! Sinstry, keep these minstrels back from the drafter."

The troubadours juggled the roast duck between them. The boy's juggling knives sliced perfect pieces off mid-air. The steaming slices landed on plates that he had also conjured into his act. He flung these plates Frisbee-style toward Spenser and Elaine, but Destry intercepted them, batting them down with his knife. On contact, the plates shattered—then disappeared.

"Stop this frivolity, if you know what's good for you," said Destry.

"You don't like our show?" asked the boy. "Rosetta, what *shall* we do?"

"Give them their money back, Pantalone, and let us get on with it."

"But they never paid!"

"Well, then give them back what they *should have* paid."

Pantalone stuck his hands deep into his pockets. Everything he had been juggling crashed to the ground around him and disappeared. From one pocket, he pulled an enormous gold coin. From the other, he produced a ridiculously large pair of scissors.

"Half price," he said as he tried to cut the coin in half with the scissors. The scissors bent and drooped like a wilted flower.

While the troubadours continued their antics, Destry hopped back to the drafter's broken window and spoke to Spenser and Elaine in a stern voice.

"Close your ears to these minstrels. They have powers beyond the seeing, evil powers hidden by their frivolous show."

"Come on," started Elaine, "What could be so bad?"

"They're agents of the Sulfane," hissed Destry. "They've been sent to find you, to seduce you, to lull you into believing it's all fun and games. But don't be fooled. Once they had you in that wagon, you'd be trapped."

"Better than being trapped in your drafter!" said Elaine. "If you're really on our side, why have you locked the door?"

"For your own protection! There are forces at work here beyond your understanding. The future of Windemere depends upon our delivering you to the company of the Imagius!"

"And what makes you so sure they're agents of the Sulfane?"

"They've crippled our drafter," said Destry. "Only the Sulfane has the power to destroy. Now listen, Sinstry's going to distract those minstrels while we try to find the problem with the drafter. You close your ears to the troubadours. Avert your eyes, for they have the power to hypnotize. Be warned."

He turned and headed for the driver's perch. Sinstry, meanwhile, hopped over to the troubadour's horse.

Elaine said to Spenser, "I don't believe him!"

Spenser shrugged, "Why not? Hypnosis and illusion are really similar. That duck disappeared the second it hit the ground."

"Come with us, my friends," called Pantalone.

Elaine shook her head; she couldn't possibly squeeze out through the broken window.

"The door's locked," said Elaine.

"You can open it," said Pantalone.

"Don't," said Spenser.

"I can't!" insisted Elaine.

"You *can*," said Pantalone, then wheeled on Sinstry. "Hey! Leave our horse alone!"

Sinstry had grabbed the horse's head, and the horse was baring its teeth.

Rosetta winged one of her fiery juggling balls right at Sinstry's back. It singed his cloak and caught his hair on fire.

"Ha-hah!" called Pantalone triumphantly, "Get your marshmallows ready for roasting!"

Sinstry yelped and rolled on the ground to put the fire out. He gave the horse a parting kick and hopped back to Destry on the drafter.

"Get us outta here!" said Sinstry.

"Oh, now *you're* giving the orders?" snarled Destry.

"There's a storm comin'," said Sinstry.

Destry looked around. To the north, the sky darkened. A wind blew up in advance of the approaching black cloud.

"Aye," said Destry. "It's the Dark Knights."

"Can yeh get us aloft?" asked Sinstry, a hint of worry in his voice.

Destry shook his head, "They don't dare pick a fight with us."

"No?" hissed Sinstry. "What ever happened to the Northern Squadron, eh? Eh?"

Destry shook his head, a little nervous himself.

"They got too close to Boreas. The Squadron shouldn't have been that far from the Rook."

In the cabin, Elaine whispered, "Spenser—Now's our chance!"

"For what?"

"To *escape*!"

"Why? They're taking us where we want to go."

"*Are* they?" Elaine asked. "How do you *know*?"

"How do you know they're *not*?"

"I don't, but—You know why Sinstry laughed when we fought over the dream box? Because they *wanted* us to fight. They want to split us apart just like *they're* split."

"That's ridiculous."

"It's not...It's *not*. You don't know because you had your nose stuck in that box."

Spenser wasn't sure if he should be insulted or if she was right, or both. What he *did* feel was tired of arguing. And tired of everyone else squabbling around him.

"I just *know* I don't trust them," Elaine went on. "I just know we have got to get away from here!"

"And be out there when another storm hits?" Spenser smirked.

"That's no ordinary storm," said Elaine.

"Exactly why I'd rather be inside!"

"So what do you say, my friends?" called Pantalone. "Come with us?"

Elaine rattled the doorknob.

"Can you get us out?" she asked.

Rosetta and Pantalone exchanged a worried look.

"Truly, you cannot free yourselves?" asked Rosetta.

"No," said Elaine.

"These Clovens grow too strong," said Pantalone. "Our powers have never worked within five smoots of a Cloven drafter. But yours! You brought the drafter down to us—and shattered the glass!"

"*I* did?" asked Elaine.

"It was not us," said Pantalone.

"'Ware the south!" said Rosetta suddenly.

Pantalone turned to see a second cloud approaching from the south, not as dark as the northern force, but rushing toward them twice as fast in a swirling fury.

"Stormy Knights, too," he said. "Brace yourselves."

"Inside!" yelled Destry to his other half. "Inside, I say!"

The Clovens merged for faster movement, then swung down from the driver's perch and in through the cabin door. Elaine seized the opportunity. She darted from her seat and threw herself against the door before Destry could close it. Her head and shoulders pushed through to the outside. Destry closed the door on her waist. She tried to wriggle out. Pantalone ran to reach for her, hoping to give her that extra pull toward freedom. Too late. A hand clenched around Elaine's ankle, a strong, skeletal hand—Sinstry's hand.

The Clovens yanked her back inside the drafter and pulled the door closed.

"None of that!" roared Destry, and he flung Elaine against the opposite wall of the drafter.

"Pantalone," called Rosetta, "The storm!"

Pantalone gave a last, longing look at Elaine, then turned to face the storm.

As the clouds came nearer from north and south, all could see they were not clouds at all, but two opposing forces of Knights on flying horses. The Dark Knights moved like shadows, blurring the air around them with a gray-black void. The Stormy Knights swirled chaotically, sheets of rain and lightening flying from their lances. The growing wind blew Pantalone's voice in through the drafter's broken window as he began a play-by-play commentary.

"Well, we're in for an amazing match today, ladies and gentlemen—and Clovens…To the north, heralding from the shadowy city of Boreas, all the King's horses and all the King's men…the Dark Knights!"

"This is *serious*, my brother," said Rosetta.

"Oh, don't interrupt.…And from the south, based in the sand-swept town of Harmattan, the Queen's own champions, put your hands together for…the Stormy Knights!"

Rosetta turned to the south and gave a defiant look. "Both at once—this is more than chance. How did they find us so easily?"

"Well, a good army needs its spies," Pantalone went on. "And spies the Dark Knights must have had to find us here on the Cirrus Plain. It just goes to show that being a Knight isn't all chopping people's heads off and sticking daggers in the chinks of your own armor to get at those oh-so-annoying itches. But don't count the Stormy Knights out just because they overslept. The Queen's Knights have speed on their side, not to mention fear of the Queen's scathing, scolding voice: 'If you come back here without a pair of troubadours, you're grounded! And how many times must I tell you to wipe your boots before coming in the castle? You're tracking dragon dung everywhere!'"

"Are the King and Queen really fighting each other?" Spenser asked.

"Their Knights are," Destry nodded. "You'll see now what Windemere has become: a land of turbulence and chaos. These minstrels may laugh, but it's deadly serious. And you…" He focused his eye on Elaine. "You think to escape? To what? To the peril of Windemere. We bring you to the Rook to end this chaos. There is more at stake here than you and your whims. This isn't some childish game of duck duck the noose."

Elaine swallowed hard, her anger rising.

"Hold tight," said Sinstry.

A wall of wind crashed into the drafter, shoving it twenty feet (or about four smoots, as Pantalone would say) across the plain.

"And there's the wind," said Pantalone in his sports-commentary voice. "At forty kilosmoots an hour. Not quite gale force, but a respectable opening from the Stormy Knights, who have ridden all out to get here first. And now come the Dark Knights, plunging the plain into darkness. Night-night, Knights!"

Pantalone did two quick back handsprings to dodge a pair of Stormy Knights. One more back flip and he landed next to Rosetta at their caravan. The battle became a blur of wind, rain, and flying Knights. The two groups circled the wagon and the drafter like high-speed vultures eyeing their prey. Elaine and Spenser gaped at the spectacle. It may have looked like a death-defying, daredevil circus, but the onlookers knew the danger was real.

"And there's the first contact," cried Pantalone. "A Stormy Knight clips a Dark Knight's shield and—oh!—a Dark Knight lodges his lance between a Stormy Knight's legs. A foul in any other game, but here—Watch out, Rosetta!"

A Dark Knight swooped down, trying to snatch Rosetta from the ground, but the girl was too quick. She bent impossibly backwards like a contortionist and avoided his grasp.

"The score's still tied at zero-zero. If you're new to the game, you might wonder why. But the goal here isn't so much to vanquish the opposing force, but to snatch the prize before—"

He broke off as a Stormy Knight ducked under a defending Dark Knight and charged right at him. A high bar materialized in front of Pantalone. He leapt onto it and swung himself around like an Olympic athlete. The Knight's momentum carried him under the bar while Pantalone swung over the top, then came around behind the Knight and dropped to the ground again.

"—before the other team has a chance. And that prize, ladies and gentlemen, seems to be a pair of young troubadours."

A trio of Stormy Knights now flashed and flew at Rosetta. A cloud of Dark Knights cut in between, blotted out their view and headed them off.

"Excellent defense from the Dark side! Yes, the King's always been known for his defensiveness in the face of the Queen's rage. But wait! A pair of Stormy Knights has broken through the Dark line. They're swooping! They're galloping! They're diving! They're almost to Rosetta! Rosetta ducks. She feints. She imagicates her fiery juggling balls. The lights confuse the horses. The horse on the left rears. The Knight nearly falls. The Knight on the right remains in control, charging, charging—Rosetta throws—Fireball to the helmet! A direct hit! Score!"

"Go Rosetta!" cheered Elaine.

The Knight tumbled back off his horse and crashed to the ground.

Now the rings of circling Knights lost their form. The clearly-drawn battle became a mêlée. A chaotic swirl of Knights fought their way toward the troubadours. Pantalone no longer had time for his commentary. He and Rosetta had to use every acrobatic and sleight-of-body trick they knew to evade capture.

Six Dark Knights bore down on Pantalone from six sides. The first three, he dispatched swiftly with clawing chickens; they fluttered and scratched at the Knights' visors with such ferocity that the warriors had to turn aside. Pantalone spun to face the fourth—too late. The Knight's wind lance swept into Pantalone's knees. Even above the roar of the storm, Elaine could hear his bones snap. Pantalone crumpled in a heap. Immediately, the fifth and sixth Knights swooped down and swept him a hundred feet up into the sky.

"No!" cried Rosetta. A small army cut between her and her brother. Fire shot from her ten fingertips, scorching ten horses' wings. A Knight dropped a lance, protecting his eyes from the fire. Rosetta leapt, caught the lance, and used it to pole vault herself to the back of the horse that carried Pantalone. She twisted the Knight's helmet with such surprising force that he toppled and plunged a hundred feet to his death. Masterless, the winged steed spun out of control.

"Heal yourself!" cried Rosetta to her brother. "We are going down!"

Elaine watched in horror as the winged horse and troubadours fell through the air.

Pantalone turned to face the ground fifty feet below—

Thirty—

Twenty—

"Chaos," scoffed Destry. "At least now, perhaps, we can make our escape." He threw a look at Elaine. "And we don't mean you."

An immense haystack suddenly appeared outside the broken drafter window—just in time to cushion the fall of Pantalone, Rosetta, and a crippled winged horse. A new phalanx of Knights charged after them.

Destry split from Sinstry, and hurriedly put his key in the door.

"Sinstry! We need two hands! But keep one eye on our passengers!"

"One eye's all I got," said Sinstry.

He followed Destry out into the storm, heading for the driver's perch, locking the door behind him.

Pantalone did a flip over a Knight, his legs healed, and landed outside Elaine's window.

"See you soon, I hope," he winked, then disappeared in the blur of the storm.

"Did you see that?" Elaine asked Spenser in a hush.

"What, that he likes you?" chided Spenser.

"No!" exclaimed Elaine. "Under his coat!"

"I'm afraid I wasn't looking."

Spenser started to open the dream box again, but Elaine snapped it closed.

"Spenser! Come *on*! You may not have been looking at Pantalone, but I *know* you were looking at Rosetta, and she has it too!"

"Has what?"

"Clouds!" said Elaine.

"What??"

"It's the weirdest thing! Watch when they do flips. You can see wisps of clouds under their costumes!"

"I'm sorry," said Spenser, "I'm *not* gonna look under their costumes."

"There! Look!"

In the whirlwind of the battle, Pantalone and Rosetta fairly flew past the drafter, pursued by both armies. In a flash, they were gone. But the flash was just enough to reveal what Elaine was talking about.

"There!" Elaine exclaimed. "Wait—*wisps*—the Royal Wisps! Those aren't just a couple of jugglers!"

"Who knows what they are?" shrugged Spenser. "You heard the Clovens. Those minstrels are hypnotists."

"You believe the Clovens?"

"Well, the Clovens didn't steal my stone."

"You still mad about *that*?"

"No!" He bit his lip again, afraid of this turning into yet another argument. But still, he had to make his point. "I'm just saying, the Clovens didn't steal my stone. You did. Then Zephyr did. Zephyr stole it and he was running from the Clovens. If Zephyr's against me, the Clovens must be for me."

"But you believe Zephyr when he says to find the Imagius?"

"I don't believe anybody!"

Elaine stared at him. "That's true, isn't it…"

Spenser stared back. He realized it *was* true. Elaine had him pegged. He really didn't believe anybody anymore. He felt fenced in—by the Clovens, by Elaine's questions. He could feel her staring right through him, and he turned away.

"Listen, Spenser," said Elaine. "These Clovens—It's okay not to believe *them*. Everything they say is only half true. I mean, they say they're taking us to the Imagius. But even if that were *all* true, it's not where the Sailphins said to go. Take the matter to the Royal Wisps, they said."

Spenser shook his head. He didn't even belong here. This world was crumbling worse than his own. It would be so much easier just to get lost in the dream box.

Up front, the Clovens seemed to have fixed the drafter. They eased it into the air. The battle raged in a blur all around them as the Knights fought to capture the young troubadours. Elaine looked down on the landscape below. The troubadours were nowhere to be seen. A few Dark Knights poked around the rocks where the horse and wagon had been. Another group had gathered at the mouths of two caves. Knights emerged on foot from each one. The caves were empty.

Without anything to fight over, the battle ended. The Dark Knights flew off to the north, the Stormy Knights to the south.

"Ugh," moaned Elaine. "We missed our chance."

She threw a look at Spenser, who had just so recently been passionate about getting his rock back and somehow stopping all this chaos. Now he hardly seemed to care—not about her, not about anything. *Well,* thought Elaine, *I'll care enough for both of us.*

CHAPTER 5

▼

THE DANGER OF DREAMING

Merged with Sinstry, Destry jiggled the drafter's controls. He had gotten the machine off the ground, but now he couldn't move it forward or backward or up or down.

"The witch..." he hissed, forgetting his own manners.

"How can she?!" asked Sinstry.

"She can't. Yet. Curse her imagination!"

"Yeh want us ta kill her?"

"That's not for us. It's *because* of her powers the Sulfane wants her."

"Jus' knock her out, then. We could clonk her over the head."

Destry shook their head. "Undamaged. Those were our orders. Collect the stranger from Aleili Bay, undamaged."

"What then?"

"Watch her," said Destry. "And we'll use the last of our bottled wind."

They mounted two canisters on the jet racks and opened the lids. The bottled breeze pushed the drafter forward at little more than walking pace. Destry scanned the label.

"Summer Breeze," he scoffed. "Five kilosmoots an hour!"

"We could pick up some Jet Stream in Cirrus," Sinstry suggested.

Destry shook their head again.

"We don't like going so near the cities. The people there are not always sympathetic to our cause. We'll find some hamlet along the Samovar. It's nearer, too."

Inside the drafter cabin, Elaine paced as best she could in the cramped space; two steps and she had to turn.

"Ugh! I can't even *pace* in here!"

She turned, faced Spenser, who was just about to open the dream box again.

"Will you keep your nose out of there?!"

"Why? It passes the time."

"I don't want to pass the time! I want to *use* the time. You pass the time and it may pass *you*! I thought you cared so much! What happened?"

"There's nothing for us to do, Elaine. Face the facts. Fact one, even if we were supposed to bring something to the Royal Wisps, we don't have what we're supposed to bring—thanks to you, I might add. Fact two, we don't even know where they went—if that really *was* them. Fact three, the only one who can help us now is the Imagius, and that's where we're going."

"That's *not* a fact. You don't *know* that. You just say that because you've suddenly given up. You're not going to *change* anything unless you *do* something."

Spenser gritted his teeth. Why did she have to sound like his mother?

"What were you doing at Windy Hill so early, anyway?" Elaine went on, trying to shake him out of his stubbornness. "Running away?"

"Shut up."

"Running away from home on your home-made skateboard? Do you do that a lot? What then? Go back home every night to your mommy and daddy?"

"Shut *up*."

"No. I won't shut up. Because like it or not, we're in this together. If you want to be with me, you better be ready to *keep* running."

"Maybe I *don't* want to be with you. Maybe I don't want to be here at all." Spenser watched his words sting.

Elaine covered her hurt with bravado. "Tough. You're here. But okay. Choose. Somehow, *I'm* going to get free from those Clovens. What are *you* going to do?"

Spenser shook his head. Why was it always me or them, stay or go, mom or dad? He didn't want to choose. He wasn't going to choose. Except maybe to escape them all. Escape. That's what he craved—escape from everything, a quiet place where he could be by himself.

He opened the dream box and looked inside.

"Spenser!" yelled Elaine.

But it was too late.

Spenser's mind spilled over the edge, floating once again, then plunging through the darkness.

He touched down on a gently sloping hill of dried grass. He looked around at the rolling, oak-dotted hills rippling away in all directions. He was alone.

He took a deep breath, and the summer smell filled him with warmth and drowsiness. *Ah, to take a nap in the sunshine…*The idea pulled at his mind and body, sinking him down. Still, Spenser knew he was in the dream box, dreaming of this comfortable place. *How would it be to dream I'm going to sleep? And what if I dream I'm dreaming?*

Spenser fought the urge to lie down for a nap. There was something about this place that was too familiar to close his eyes on before he figured it out. He strolled over the rise and looked down the other side.

He was on Windy Hill. Spread out below him were the familiar ruins of the old sanatorium, the out-buildings, the paths…But beyond the paths, down the long drive, there were no houses, no subdivision, no home. As far as Spenser could see, there were no people and no fences anywhere—just the beautiful, golden, rolling hills dotted with oaks and willows. Being so alone in the world might have scared most people, but it gave Spenser a strong sense of balance, of peace.

Spenser listened.

Birds. A breeze rustling the grass…No parents yelling, not a single person fighting, no one saying "no."

Spenser looked down the hill to where his house should have been. *I must have dreamed that house*, he thought. *Now I am awake. Here among these golden hills.*

He wandered down the familiar path, past the spring to the ruins. It gradually dawned on him where his feet were taking him—to the bush where he'd stashed his Aeroboard.

He had chosen this bush because it was too thick to see into, even if you were right next to it. Spenser reached in and pulled out his board. The wedge was gone, the front truck showed no sign of damage, and the wheels were the fat wheels he'd imagined would smooth out the bumps.

He mounted his board and took off down the slope. He didn't have to lean. He didn't even have to pivot. He just *thought*. "Left" or "Right." The slightest intention changed his direction. Spenser felt as if his board was floating off the ground. The rolling hills formed a giant off-road skate park, complete with half-pipes in the creek beds and slalom courses around the trees, no barriers to where his mind could take him.

After riding for some time, Spenser let his momentum carry him right back to the top of the hill. He coasted to a stop. He took a deep breath of the warm summer air. Peace still flowed into him. The moment was perfect. He lay on his back and stared into the deep blue. He wondered if somewhere up there was the rim of the box. *Ah, who cares? This is where I want to be. This is where I belong.*

For now—forever—Spenser felt content here on this golden hill. He'd never go back. He closed his eyes—and slept.

Elaine screamed—and with good reason. She had been pacing again. Two steps, turn. Two steps, turn. Every time she turned back to face Spenser, his nose had sunk deeper into the dream box, his expression more glazed over.

I don't really need *him*, she thought. *What do I care if he rots in there?*

At the same time, she knew these thoughts didn't quite ring true. And she couldn't quite get over the feeling that they were bound together in this for a reason. As she paced, she tried to tease that reason out of the mystery. What had Zephyr said? Flint, boulder, stone—something about the throne...

Ah, Elaine scolded herself. *Why can't I remember the simplest rhymes?!* But the stone was obviously important. If it had something to do with the throne, it probably had something to do with Cloud Palace, which Zephyr had said was dissolving. It probably even had something to do with the King and Queen fighting. And if it had to do with the King and Queen, then it was also connected to the Dark and Stormy Knights—and to the troubadours, who just maybe were the Royal Wisps the Sailphin Leeee had told her to find.

The stone was the key, and it was her fault it was lost. No wonder Spenser didn't think much of her; how could she blame him? No wonder he'd rather keep his nose in that—

At this point, Elaine again reached the end of her two steps, turned—and screamed.

Deep inside the dream box, Spenser had just closed his eyes to sleep. What Elaine saw was Spenser's whole, real body dissolving into a cloud. She could see through him. A second later, this ghost-Spenser was sucked into the dream box like a genie in reverse. His hands were the last to go. When they did, his ghostly fingertips released the box. The black cube clattered to the floor, closed and silent.

"Spenser!" Elaine cried.

She picked up the box and tried to open it. There was no lock, not even a catch, but the box would not open. She looked around for a screwdriver, a knife—anything to pry the top free. The sparsely furnished drafter had nothing to offer. Elaine dug her fingernails between the box and lid, grimacing with the strain.

"Spenser!"

"You're not part of his dream."

Elaine turned. Destry had come into the cabin, having heard her screams. He was smiling.

Elaine fumed, "You treacherous, villainous, deceitful, two-faced—"

"Well, *that* part's true," Destry laughed. "But your friend is perfectly safe."

"How can you say that?!"

"How can you *not* say that? You've seen into the box yourself. It's perfectly safe. We're sure he's having a wonderful dream. May we?"

The Cloven plucked the box from her hand before she could react and put it to his ear.

"Yes, yes," he said. "Everything seems to be in order."

He set the box down on the small shelf above the seats, then produced an identical box from his cloak pocket.

"Would you like one of your own? We'll be sure to wake you when we get to Dreck."

"You said there was only one box," said Elaine in a low voice.

The Cloven laughed, "No, Sinstry said *you* only had one. Well, we'll leave this one here for you in case you change your mind."

He set the new box on the shelf next to Spenser's.

"Ah, we're coming to the Samovar. That's the steam you see rising off of it."

Elaine took her eyes from the Cloven long enough to see they were approaching a thick fog.

"The Samovar River comes from a gap between the Samovar Mountains and The Coals," said the Cloven, "high above Dreck. If you think it's steamy here, wait until you see it at the Cauldron."

"I won't be going that far," Elaine insisted.

"So you say," said Destry, studying her.

"I do."

Destry sighed, "Then I won't waste a perfectly good dream box on you." He picked up a box, considered it. "Perhaps it'll keep Sinstry out of my hair for a while. Now we just need to find a serf to sell us a couple bottles of jet stream."

He left the cabin once more, locking the door behind him.

Elaine watched him hop around the front to the perch. The drafter descended again, down through the mist. Through the broken window, Elaine could hear the roar of a rapid river nearby.

"Keep an eye on the girl," she heard Destry say to Sinstry. Sinstry turned around to watch her as Destry took over the controls.

Elaine didn't have much time. She wanted to wait until Destry set the drafter down somewhere, but what if Sinstry came back in the cabin before then? No, she couldn't wait. The fog was on her side. She was out of the Clovens' reach. She didn't even have to worry about Spenser. She could put him in her pocket and escape with him. If he couldn't choose, she'd choose for him. He'd thank her for it later. Yes, she'd save him. *He may not like me much now,* she smiled to herself, *but he'll be so grateful...*

So it was just a matter of the locked door. Elaine had thought hard about this. The troubadours had insisted she could open it. But how? The troubadours had said their *own* powers wouldn't work within five smoots of a Cloven drafter. It was power, magic power, that could open the door. And Pantalone had said she could do it. But that didn't make any sense. Elaine had seen the troubadours in action. Making balls of fire appear out of thin air wasn't some cheap sideshow trick. How could she have some power they didn't? She remembered Leeee's words: *If you can imagine something wholly, completely, down to the last grain of sand, then it will* become. *That is the power of imagication.* Pantalone and Rosetta had power. They used no fancy wands, no elaborate gestures, no magic spells. They simply imagined. Perfectly. Elaine remembered how she'd nearly conjured her own dream box, just by imagining every detail. She *could* do it. Somehow, she could.

Elaine checked the front window. Destry and Sinstry were busy scouting through the fog, looking for a wind serf's shack. Elaine snatched the dream box from the shelf and tucked it into her coat pocket. She turned to face the door. She put her hand on the knob. She thought as hard as she could: "Unlock."

She turned her hand—

But the knob didn't budge.

"*Unlock,*" she said through gritted teeth, and twisted her hand again.

Still locked.

Sinstry glanced back. Their eyes met. Sinstry could see Elaine was still locked in. He smiled his half-smile, then turned his attention back to the fog.

Elaine tried again to will the door open.

"Unlock, unlock, unlock!"

Struggle as she might, wishing wasn't enough. Nor was the word.

Imagine it wholly, completely...

There were no magic words, she reminded herself, no spells, no secret gestures. It wasn't the *word* unlock she had to focus on. It was the *thought*, the *image*, the *feeling* that mattered.

Elaine took a deep breath and calmed her mind. She imagined the feel of her fingers on the cool brass. She pictured the knob turning easily in her hand. She could practically hear the well-oiled gears inside moving the latch. She imagined the door swinging outward, silently on its hinges. She imagined it wholly, completely.

She put her hand on the knob once more—and effortlessly, it turned. The door swung open. Elaine could hardly believe it. Was she still imagining? She stepped silently out onto the running board. The fog had gotten so thick, she could not tell how far above the ground the drafter glided.

"Oy!" Sinstry shouted. He had spotted her.

Elaine froze. This was no dream. If anything, it was now a nightmare. Two hops and the Cloven was almost to her. No, this was worse than a nightmare; it was real. She jumped.

"Half-wit!" Elaine heard Destry cursing Sinstry. "I told you to keep an eye on her!"

Elaine fell. She imagined that the fog slowed her descent, and perhaps *because* she imagined it, it did. She tumbled onto a moist, mossy bank. She could hear the roar of the nearby river, but could not see more than a smoot in any direction.

"There!" shouted Destry's voice. "Land!"

Through the mist, Elaine saw the drafter's belly coming down almost on top of her. Then she saw a more terrifying sight: Destry, leaping from the perch before the drafter even touched down, his black blade drawn.

Elaine ran. The soft ground quieted her footsteps, but not enough. Somehow, the Clovens followed, keeping pace. The Clovens could go nearly as fast while split and hopping as they could when together and running. And as Elaine rightly feared, they could search twice as much ground.

"Head her off!" cried Destry.

Elaine sprinted through the fog, barely able to see her own feet, the mad thumping of hopping Clovens close on her flanks. She dodged tree trunks that suddenly sprang up in her path. She leapt over rocks and small streams. Her foot caught on a root. She tripped. She fell.

"Hold!" cried Destry.

All noise stopped except for the beating of Elaine's heart.

Destry's voice broke through the fog, clear and close—too close.

"Hunting, is it? Well, Sinstry, we'll just listen for our quarry, shall we?"

"Right," agreed Sinstry from just on Elaine's other side. "We'll listen."

The fog hid Elaine's body from view, but her heart beat so loudly she couldn't imagine the Clovens not hearing her. She struggled to calm her breath and heartbeat, but the quieter she tried to be, the louder her heart pounded in her chest and in her ears.

Thump. A hop on her left. *That'll be Sinstry,* thought Elaine.

Thump. A more careful hop just on her right. *Destry.*

They haven't heard me, thought Elaine. *They'll go right by me.*

After a moment, *thump*—another hop on the left, then—*thump*—one on the right. Then silence. Listening.

Go on, thought Elaine. *Pass me. Miss me.*

Thump...Thump. One more hop from either side. The Clovens had each landed just a bit farther away. Elaine breathed easier.

Thump...Thump. Even farther away. Elaine eased herself to her feet, ready to run for it. CRACK! A twig snapped under her foot as she stood.

Silence.

Oh, just kill me now and get it over with, Elaine thought. Then she thought, *no...twigs snap all the time in the woods, don't they? They don't know it was me.*

Thump...Thump. Closer this time. Then waiting. Listening.

Something flew by Elaine in the fog: a small bird. A second later, it flew back the other way with another bird following it. Elaine recognized them as the giggle birds from Aleili Bay. At first she smiled, remembering how silly they were, but then her smile was replaced by a feeling of horror. The foolish birds brought back a whole flock. They giggled raucously as they pretended to land on the sunflower on her coat.

"Shush!" said Elaine, swatting them away, but the giggle birds laughed even louder.

Thump...Thump. Thump, thump—*thump THUMP.* Closer and closer.

Elaine panicked. She had no choice. The giggle birds had given her away. She again summoned her strength and ran as fast as she could, away from the river. Why she had chosen this direction, she couldn't say—except that it was back toward where she had last seen the troubadours. After ten more exhausting, heart-pounding minutes, she realized the horrible folly of her choice. The farther she ran from the river, the less the moss dampened the sound of her footsteps, and the farther she ran from the river, the thinner the mist that kept her hidden.

The Clovens were back to their mad, thumping hopping, right on her tail. Ahead of her, the fog dissipated, but Elaine could not risk turning back for fear of running right into her pursuers. She had to find a place to hide, and quick.

"There!" shouted Sinstry.

Elaine looked over her shoulder as she ran. She had two dozen paces on the Clovens, but she was tiring—and the fog was thinning. She looked forward again as another veil blew between her and her pursuers. Ahead of her stood two caves carved into a pair of low hills. She darted inside the nearest opening. She pivoted to look back, to see if she'd been spotted going in—and slipped on the slimy floor. The inside of the cave was strangely warm and spongy, but Elaine had no time to ponder why. She raised herself up and looked out once more. Just as the Clovens came into view through the fog, a rushing wind pulled Elaine off her feet. The wind swept her back, deep into the cave. Elaine could feel herself being sucked down a long, reddish-black tunnel.

The last thing Elaine could see was the cave mouth closing, sealing her in darkness.

Sinstry arrived first at the hills. He paused as Destry merged into him.

"Did we see her?" asked Destry. "Did she climb?"

Sinstry shook their head.

"What?" Destry insisted. "What did we see?"

"These weren't cliffs," said Sinstry. "They were caves."

"And the girl?"

"We don't know. She got away."

Destry scanned the cliff.

"Oh, the Sulfane's breath!" moaned Sinstry.

"No," insisted Destry. "The Sulfane won't ever know."

"How can we say that?! He sent us to get the strangers, and we lost 'em! We'll be dissolved!"

Destry shook their head, mulling it all over. "No, the Sulfane sent us to get the *stranger*. We don't think he was expecting *two*. If we deliver just one, he won't ever even know."

"But we lost 'em both! The girl took the dream box with her."

"She took *a* dream box with her," grinned Destry, producing another box from his pocket, "But not the *right* dream box."

He handed the box to Sinstry, to the left hand. Sinstry put the box to his ear, listening. He allowed his grin to mesh with Destry's. Their face eased into balance as the two halves agreed.

"To the Rook," they said together.

They turned as one, and walked back toward their drafter.

CHAPTER 6

▼

THE ROOK

Spenser knew nothing of Elaine's escape, nor of her attempt to steal him away from the Clovens, nor even of the Clovens' treachery, which kept him captive. Spenser knew only the deepest sleep of a dream within a dream.

The Clovens, united in their mission, marched back to their drafter. In the dense steam rising off the Samovar River, they did not find their vehicle on the first try. Instead, they came first to a shack with no glass in its wind-door, a shack that slanted into the prevailing breeze, a shack that could only belong to a wind serf.

Destry knocked on the door and got no answer.

"Aw, come on!" said Sinstry, breaking down the door with his left shoulder.

"We were trying to be polite," said Destry.

"I don't care about polite. I care about gettin' to the Rook!"

"*I? I?* There is no I. Only we."

The Clovens' left eye shot a look at the right, then Sinstry gave a grunt and split off. He went straight to the serf's stash of bottles and grabbed an armload of jet stream.

"Yeh wanna be polite? Be polite. Leave the serf some coppers."

Destry sighed heavily and left some coins on the table. At the door, the Clovens rejoined.

After a time, they found their drafter, mounted a pair of jet stream canisters on the rack, and flew the drafter at a fair clip for the northwest. They rose above the Samovar River, trying to avoid the steam. After quarreling for some time, the Clovens tried a lower elevation, to the side of the river, which they found to be clear enough. They skirted the city of Windham and paralleled the river course toward Dreck.

Deep within the dream box, Spenser woke. The hills around him no longer looked golden and welcoming. The warm colors had mostly faded to dusty gray.

Spenser shuddered, startled by the change. He got to his feet and studied the sky. The dusty blue at the horizon curved upward to gray, then straight up to black. Somewhere up there was the rim. He tried to remember his body outside the box. He tried to picture himself outside, holding the box in his hands. He tried to place his mind back in that body in the drafter. He did not know he no longer had a body outside the box. He did not know he had tumbled completely within.

Destry felt the dream box quiver in his pocket when Spenser awoke inside. The Cloven dared not risk another escape, so he split from Sinstry and hopped back into the cabin. He took the dream box from his pocket and set it back on its shelf. He took the seat opposite, and watched the box, his one hand on his knife.

When Destry took the box from his pocket, the colors in the dream world around Spenser brightened a few shades. Spenser again tried to pull his mind back out of the box, but with no body on the outside, Spenser was stuck.

Oh well, he thought, *better to be stuck in this world than that other one.*

Spenser hopped on his board and cruised down to the spring. As he knelt to drink, he caught sight of a strange reflection: A black square rippled in the sky above him. Spenser looked around and up, but the square appeared only in the pool's reflection. He reached into the water, but felt only the refreshing cool of the water and the smooth stones at the bottom.

Spenser sat on the bank and gazed into the reflection as he had gazed into the dream box in the drafter. The black square solidified, and Spenser felt himself tipping down toward it. The view was as dizzying as the whirlpool that had first transported him to Windemere. *A dream pool*, Spenser thought. *I wonder where it leads?*

Spenser could almost smell the next world contained in the dream pool—a world green and forested. Whatever dream the pool contained, Spenser was sure it provided a way out of this one.

Before he tipped in all the way, something stabbed him in the side. He turned, but no one was there. Another poke, this time in the opposite side.

"Hey!" he called. "What the—"

Before he could finish his sentence—

"Ooomph."

—the flat of an invisible blade knocked him to the ground. Another sharp stab poked his stomach, then his head. With every jab, his world grew dimmer until all was black. Yet even in the darkness, the knife kept stabbing. Spenser heard Destry's voice protesting through the silence.

"It's the Sulfane's business."

A strange, crackly voice cut him off, "Sulfane's business! Sulfane's business! What do yeh think *we're* doin'?!"

One last poke in Spenser's lower back drove him straight out of the dream box, back into the drafter. Spenser felt as if he had just been squirted from a tube of toothpaste. His head, his shoulders, his hips—his whole body—were sore from squeezing out of the box. A strange Cloven, the one with the crackly voice, held the black cube in his hand. His other half had been poking it with his knife until the box looked like a woodpecker's lunch. Having spent so much time in the dream box, Spenser felt groggy, half-drugged, and the Clovens cramming around him in the drafter wavered in and out of focus.

"Ha-hah!" cackled the new Cloven, "Smuckling, is it?"

"Not smuggling at all," Destry insisted in a dignified way. "A prisoner for the Sulfane." Here, he lowered his voice, "A creature of Chloe's world. See for yourselves. See the colors."

The new Clovens eyed Spenser up and down (one eye went up, the other down), taking in the lining of Spenser's long, black coat. The new Clovens edged back in awe.

"Yes…Yes, of course…But—how did yeh get him?"

"That is not for you to ask."

"Yes, of course…Yeh can pass."

"*Thank* you," said Destry in a snide voice that showed he didn't really mean it.

The new Clovens hopped from the drafter shouting, "Make way! Make way! The Sulfane's business! Make way!"

As Spenser tried to clear the fog from his mind, two words stood out loud and clear—prisoner and Sulfane. Spenser could no longer deny it. He was Destry's prisoner, no doubt on his way to the Sulfane, and Destry guarded him with a knife.

"Where's Elaine?" Spenser asked.

"A laine?" half-smiled Destry. "What's a laine?"

"*Elaine.*"

"There is no Elaine. There never was an Elaine. And if you value your life, you'll remember that."

Spenser's stomach cramped, but his mind cleared more, and he strained to focus on the world outside the drafter. They were in a line of carts, people, livestock, and drafters barely off the ground as they approached the gates of a walled city. A sign posted on a fortified tower read: "Drafting Elevation Limit: Two Smoots. Punishable by Fine or Maggots."

A group of peasants passed close by Spenser's window, close enough that he could see their blistered skin, scalded by who-knows-what kind of torture. Hundreds of Clovens hopped and crawled over the carts, inspecting everything and everyone. Sinstry stood up on the driver's perch, a whip in his hand, thrashing peasants and peddlers out of his way and echoing the other Cloven's call.

"Make way! The Sulfane's business! Make way!"

The drafter pushed its way through the crowd at the gates. Not all the creatures clamoring to gain entry were human. Spenser could see a pair of giant, hairy spiders carrying coils of homespun rope to market. They used their eight legs to great effect, walking on some, carrying their twine with others, and still leaving two or three gangly appendages free to shove other creatures out of their way.

A pale gnome, his skin almost translucent, stood out in the mob inching toward the gates. He held a twisted musical instrument over his head, trying to protect it from the crush. The gnome was so small that Spenser kept losing sight of all but the instrument, which occasionally let out obscene noises. Finally, the gnome scrambled onto a spider's shoulders, then hopped from head to head over the crowd. Every time he landed on someone's head, his instrument let out a terrific raspberry. Peasants tried to knock him off, but the creature was quick, and soon passed out of view into the great, walled city.

A gray, scaly creature, dripping with runny mud, strolled through the mob selling steaming eels from a basket.

"Muckworms!" he croaked. "Fresh, roasted muckworms!"

Destry pulled a coin from his pocket and held it out the broken window.

"Oy! Muckraker!" he called.

The muckraker pushed past some peasants, knocking over a basket of their eggs on his way to the drafter. He took Destry's coin, and handed him two steaming muckworms. The muckworms were about a foot long, as fat around as a quarter, and coated with slimy mud. Destry sucked one down like a piece of spaghetti, without a single chew, then tucked the other in his pocket.

The drafter crossed a bridge over the steaming Samovar River. Below, more Clovens threw yellow logs into the misty river. On closer look, Spenser realized with horror that these were the bodies—dead bodies, horribly blistered—of wind serfs, a pair of Clovens, and people like him.

"Enemies of the Sulfane," Destry warned. "Do not dare to cross him."

Just before the gate, the drafter passed a small troupe of troubadours, bound together with yellow chains, guarded by two pairs of Clovens. The players looked tired and poor, their costumes dirty and torn. Spenser studied their faces, but they bore no resemblance to Pantalone and Rosetta. An older woman in the troupe noticed Spenser. She nudged the man chained next to her. He followed her gaze until he spotted Spenser as well. A look of relief crossed the man's face. He almost smiled as he looked into Spenser's eyes—and winked.

Spenser wanted to question him, but the drafter passed the minstrels too quickly, and the moment was lost.

"Make way!" cried Sinstry. "The Sulfane's business! Make way!"

The drafter reached the gate. Spenser looked up at the battlements towering above the city's entrance. From a distance, he had had no sense of the walls' immense scale. Smooth, gray stone stretched straight up for two hundred feet. The Clovens patrolling the top looked like rats.

"Impressive, eh?" said Destry proudly. "Forty smoots to the top, three smoots thick. Dreck is a city that knows the value of stability, a people willing to fight for peace."

Something about "fighting for peace" didn't quite make sense to Spenser, but he was too sick with dread to argue. This sickness, combined with the commotion throbbing outside the drafter, had kept Spenser from noticing his own feelings. Now, looking up at the stronghold waiting to swallow him, Spenser realized he was terrified.

He should have resisted the dream box. He should have listened to Elaine. More than that, he should have gone back to bed this morning and not to Windy Hill at all. He could hear Elaine's taunt echoing in his head: *What were you doing, running away? You're not going to change anything unless you* do *something.* How could he do anything now?

The drafter passed under the great arch, lined by a phalanx of Clovens.

"Pass! Pass!" called the Cloven who had escorted them through the crowd. He stepped aside and waved them on. "Straight on for the Rook!"

Destry let out a breath and half smiled. He was on the home stretch, his mission nearly complete. Sinstry guided the drafter through narrow cobblestone streets, twisting left, right, left, but always up.

After the commotion outside the gates, Spenser expected the streets of Dreck to be equally packed with the bustle of commerce. Instead, the drafter met few other people, and most of the windows along the road were shuttered closed.

"Where are all the people?" Spenser had to ask.

"Where should they be? Dreck is a city that knows the value of hard work."

"But what about kids? Surely school's out by now."

"School?" Destry smiled his half smile and repeated, "Dreck is a city that knows the value of hard work."

Soon, the road broadened to a wide boulevard. The putrid, rotten-egg smell of sulfur hit Spenser's nostrils. Without the buildings crammed so close, Spenser could now see the Rook towering ahead. Spenser tried to swallow his own fear, and practically choked. A sickly yellow haze rose from the moat and swirled into a rusty cloud, all but obscuring the tallest turrets. Everything about the cold, gray stone emanated power, oppression, and misery.

The drafter coasted over the drawbridge, over the moat. Again, Spenser gagged. Sulfuric steam rising from the yellow acid in the trench burnt his nostrils and throat until he held his breath. A pair of scaly, orange salamanders the size of overgrown crocodiles broke the surface of the moat, wrestling viciously. Spenser shrank back from the broken window at the sight.

Destry half-smiled at Spenser, who still held his breath, "Don't worry. Scale-manders only eat things that breathe."

The scalemanders sank back below the yellow surface, and Spenser let out a low whistle.

The drafter cruised through the gate to the courtyard, where hundreds more drafters filled an area the size of two football fields. An army of Clovens prepared the drafters for battle, loading them with lances, spears, and buckets of steaming yellow liquid.

Sinstry parked near the castle itself.

"On your feet," said Destry. "Move."

Spenser did as he was told. He climbed down from the drafter. Destry held him on one side, Sinstry on the other. Together, they marched toward the main entrance.

An enormous, shaggy beast lay with its horned head blocking one of two doors. Its equally spiked tail blocked the other. It breathed heavily, but did not sleep, and a yellow-green drool spattered in and out with each breath. As Spenser and the Clovens approached, it growled like a dutiful watchdog.

"Ah, the Dilemma," said Destry proudly. "This is the only castle in Windemere guarded by one. You don't want to get caught in its horns, I'll tell you that."

He tossed the Dilemma the second muckworm from his pocket. The beast slammed its horns together with a deafening clang, pinching the muckworm midair with such precise force that the worm's mucky guts spurted halfway across the courtyard. The Dilemma then stuck out its enormous dripping tongue and sucked the muckworm down. It licked its lips and let out a belch Spenser could smell from three smoots away. The Dilemma raised itself up on its front legs, allowing the Clovens to guide Spenser underneath its matted, hairy belly and through the door.

"Be warned," said Destry. "Getting out is not as easy as getting in."

Living gargoyles lined the broad entrance hall, drinking and gargling liquid sulfur, then spewing it out in arching fountains.

Spenser fought to keep from shaking. *Fine*, he forced himself to think. *If I can't get out of here the way I came in, I'll find another way... The dream box. Back to the dream Windy Hill, then out the dream pool to—not to here again—to somewhere new.*

"Could I have the dream box back, please?"

"The Sulfane is always just," said Destry. "You give him what he wants, and he'll grant you your heart's desire."

That's it then. The dream box. Who knows how many worlds might be strung together by boxes and pools?

The thought calmed him enough that he could focus on the task at hand. He was about to meet the Sulfane. If he survived that meeting, *then* he could worry about escape.

The Clovens led Spenser down corridor after corridor. At each corner, Spenser became increasingly unsettled. Soon he realized the reason. An irritating sound permeated the entire castle, but for the first few corridors, it was so subtle that Spenser hardly noticed it. Five hallways later, though, the noise was unmistakable: it was the same shrieking music he and Elaine had first heard on Windy Hill. Every now and then, like a fugue punctuated by percussion, the eerie tune blended with a blistering scream.

As Spenser drew closer to the music, closer to the Sulfane's inner chamber, he could no longer force himself to have a single hopeful thought. Now he feared he would never escape. He tried to remember what it was like to be happy. He tried to remember an innocent time, before his parents had given up everything but arguing—surely he had been happy *sometime*—but the only feelings he could summon were those of pain, dread, abandonment, sadness—and absolute despair.

The Clovens led him around a final corner. The triangular room pointed them to the doors at the tip. Spenser froze.

"Come along, now," said Destry, pulling him roughly.

Spenser dragged his feet. What had stopped him was the decoration on the doors: an ornate, yellow S—the same ornate, yellow S that had sealed the parchment they had found in the wall of Chloe's old room, not an S for Spenser, an S for Sulfane.

CHAPTER 7

▼

THE TRUTH ABOUT THE TROUBADOURS

Elaine came to rest in darkness. She had been sucked deep within the cave and could no longer see the mouth.

Weird, she thought, feeling the spongy floor. *And I've seen a lot of weird...*

She stood and bumped into an equally spongy ceiling, not damp, but not quite dry.

She listened. *Thump-ump...Thump-ump...*A pulsing sound, quite different from the terrifying thumps of the Clovens' hops, this sound was rhythmic and soothing—like a heartbeat, only much, much slower.

In the pitch black, Elaine imagined she could see. And the cave walls slowly became visible. Indeed, it looked like the inside of a sponge, with tunnels of all sizes branching in every direction. She followed the main tunnel down a gentle slope, down toward the soothing *thump-ump.*

When she reached a place where the *thump-ump* seemed loudest, she put her hand against the cave wall and felt the pulse through her fingertips. *Thump-ump...Thump-ump.*

Just then, the warm wind swept her off her feet, blowing her back out the tube through which she had come. She could see the cave mouth opening in front of her. She flew between squarish, white stalactites and stalagmites and out onto a grassy hill. She landed as softly as a dandelion fairy blown on the breeze. She looked around to take stock of where she was, out in the late afternoon of Wind-emere. The Clovens were nowhere to be seen. Elaine turned back to look at the caves and practically jumped out of her skin.

The two caves rumbled and shook the earth. The quake knocked Elaine to her knees. The cliffs around the cave mouths stretched and shrank, then turned into the heads of Pantalone and Rosetta. The hills in which the caverns had been carved shifted and shrank as well. Elaine's mouth dropped open as the entire hill-side shrugged off the dirt and transformed into the two troubadours.

"But—But—" Elaine stammered, rising back to her feet.

The minstrels dusted their clothes, then bowed elegantly to Elaine. Pantalone coughed, a cloud of dust spewing toward Rosetta.

"Sorry," he wheezed.

Rosetta waved off her brother's cough with a courtly flourish.

"Allow us to introduce ourselves properly," she said haughtily. "I am Tallia, firstborn child of Queen Quoirez by King Orrozco, Heiress to the Airs, Princess of Whales, Dauphina of Dolphins, Duchess of Boreas, Contessa of the Far Isles, Crown Princess of all Windemere."

Pantalone smiled at his sister's show of manners, then—not to be outdone—he bowed with a flourish of both hands *and* one leg, "And *I* am Tyrrel, sec-ond-born child of King Orrozco, Prince of uh, you know, and Duke of um, uh…whatever. It's all written down on a big crown back at the palace. You should really see it someday."

Tallia shot her brother a reproving glance, then studied Elaine, who was still trying to wrap her mind around seeing cliffs and caves transform into living, breathing human beings. And not just any humans—these included the prince whose gaze she recognized from the dream-box tower.

"Perhaps," said the former Rosetta, "you think this still part of our comedy."

"Oh no," said Elaine. "I understand. At least, I think I do. You're the Royal Wisps."

Tyrrel broke into an easy laugh.

"You sound like a Sailphin," he said.

"Yes," said Elaine. "They told me to bring the matter to the Royal Wisps."

"Only a Sailphin would call us that," said Tyrrel. "A bit pompous sounding, I'd say, but as the first creatures, I suppose they have the right to a bit of pompos-ity, don't you think?"

"Oh, I suppose so," said Elaine. Even in his minstrel's costume, Tyrrel's gaze flustered her more than she would ever want to admit. "But this matter I have to bring to you—Well, it's a little confusing, because the matter I had *then* isn't what I have *now*. I mean, *now* my problem is *this*. My friend Spenser is in this box."

She pulled the dream box from her pocket and held it out for them.

"So what's the problem?" asked Tyrrel.

"Well, getting him *out*, of course."

"You know not how to get him out?" asked Tallia.

"If I did, it wouldn't be a problem."

"You see?" said Tallia to her brother. "I told you we could not accomplish it."

"Maybe she just needs to rejuvenate," eased Tyrrel.

"Nonsense," said Tallia. "She is not the one. Come. Before we are found again."

Tallia started to walk away, scanning the skies. Tyrrel didn't budge.

"*Are* you Chloe?" he asked Elaine.

Tallia turned back, waiting to hear the answer.

Elaine hesitated. A lie would gain her nothing.

"No," she said, "I'm Elaine."

She watched Tyrrel's hopeful expression fall.

"You see?" said Tallia again. "Aster's plan failed. We are on our own."

Tyrrel sighed and nodded.

"What?" asked Elaine. "What made you think I was Chloe anyway?"

Tyrrel shrugged. "We tried to summon her. We failed."

"No you didn't. You got me. And Spenser. You got us both. We're from Chloe's world. Just help me get Spenser out of this box and he'll tell you too."

"We are wasting time," said Tallia. "She does not even know how to get someone out of a dream box."

"She escaped two Clovens," said Tyrrel. "That's something."

Tallia scoffed.

"Tallia. We need every ally we can get."

Meeting no further protest from his older sister, he turned to Elaine.

"Let me see your box."

Elaine held it out for the Prince. He took it gently in his hand, then held it to his ear.

"This box is empty," he said.

"No, it's not," Elaine insisted, "I saw him go in."

"Not into this one."

"He did!"

"Hmm…There is but one way to tell."

He raised his hand, ready to smash the box on a rock.

"No!" shouted Elaine.

"It's the only way," said Tyrrel gently. "Were your friend truly inside, it would hurt him no more than a bucket of cold water. If he is not in here, well, you should smash it anyway. These things are dangerous. Some people go in and never come out. They die of starvation."

"'Tis true," said Tallia. "One cannot live on dreams alone."

Tyrrel paused, awaiting Elaine's go-ahead.

"Okay?"

Elaine nodded, "Okay."

Tyrrel raised his hand again, and hurled the box onto the rocks at his feet. It smashed to splinters. Nothing came out, not even a puff of smoke.

Elaine stared. She picked up a fragment of wood, a hinge swinging off of it. She shook her head.

"The Cloven must have tricked me. I guess it was the wrong box."

"Only a fool would trust a Cloven," said Tallia.

"And only a prig would point that out," Elaine retorted.

"Hold your tongue," snapped the princess.

"That's gross," Elaine replied with dignity. "I'd get saliva on my hand."

Tyrrel held back a laugh and intervened. "Come. Darkness approaches. Let us get somewhere safe."

"But we have to go after Spenser. He's still with the Clovens!"

Tyrrel and Tallia exchanged looks.

"Like so many others…" said Tallia bitterly.

Tyrrel tried to explain, "I'm afraid we can't risk going after your friend. Not yet. By now, they must have him back at the Rook, guarded by a thousand Clovens, and the Sulfane. Tallia, what did you do with Grace?"

"I?" she said, "Not a thing. But I daresay those boulders have a certain look about them."

"Grace!" Tyrrel called. "Here, girl!"

As he spoke, the boulders turned into the troubadours' horse and cart. The horse grazed contentedly, as if turning into a boulder and back again was the most ordinary thing in the world.

"Did you do that?" Elaine asked.

"What?" asked Tyrrel.

"Turn that boulder into your horse."

"No, not me," laughed Tyrrel. "One thing imagication cannot do is control another living, thinking being."

"Then how—?"

"People are not the only creatures with imaginations."

"Are you saying *animals* can imagicate?"

"Well, not most animals. Most animals are like Clovens—or Knights—they have no imaginations at all. But the occasional horse—"

"And cat," added Tallia, coming out of her sulk.

"Yeah, but cats are so careless about it. They lie around dreaming all day. We had one cat that liked to imagicate her own private ball of sunlight. She set a silk rug on fire."

"That is nothing," said Tallia. "My friend, the Duke of Windham—"

"Her *special* friend," said Tyrrel with a wink.

Tallia blushed, but pretended to ignore her brother.

"*His* cat imagicated the ballroom was a gigantic fishbowl—right as the orchestra was tuning up for the Duchess's grand ball. All the guests were soaked."

"And you did not get your dance with your young Duke," teased Tyrrel.

Tallia stared at him.

"We need to get going," she said, abruptly turning and climbing to her seat on the wagon.

"Yes, we do," agreed Tyrrel, lingering with Elaine by the horse.

Elaine stroked Grace's coat, which shimmered like rippling water.

"It's a very special horse, you know," said Tyrrel, "A gift horse. Look, it raises its hoof to you."

Elaine reached out for the horse's offering. Balanced on top of its hoof it held a small, triangular piece of metal. Elaine took the tarnished object in her hand.

"Ach," cried Tyrrel to the horse. "You call that a proper gift? I should put you out to pasture."

Tallia defended the gift horse. "Leave Grace alone. 'Tis not her fault that Cloven looked her in the mouth."

"I told the halfling not to do that!" Tyrrel stewed. "Never do that to a gift horse…"

"But it's a fine gift," Elaine said graciously. "I'll treasure it."

"You're too kind," said Tyrrel.

"No, really," said Elaine. "It's, um…What is it?"

"An aeros. From Mirage."

Elaine shrugged, not understanding.

"You've never played Mirage?" Tyrrel asked.

"No."

"Can we please get going?" broke in Tallia.

"But of course," said Tyrrel.

He turned to Elaine.

"After you."

Elaine climbed into the seat next to Tallia. Tyrrel followed and wedged Elaine in the middle.

Tallia made a rapid clicking sound, and Grace obediently started to trot. They soon left the road and headed for the setting sun across a grassy landscape dotted with rocks and trees. Though the ground was uneven, the wagon floated along, barely disturbed by the ruts and bumps.

"But what's Mirage?" Elaine began. "And when can we get Spenser? And how did you get away from the Knights? And how did you find me in the first place, in the drafter? You *were* looking for me, weren't you? And why were you trying to conjure Chloe?"

"Easy, there," Tyrrel smiled. "We have a long way to go."

"Right," Elaine said, taking a deep breath. "It's just—It's been quite a day."

"Yours, too?" Tallia asked with a bit of a barb.

"I wasn't saying yours *wasn't*," Elaine shot back.

"Let us begin with Mirage," Tyrrel cut in.

Elaine and Tallia spoke in unison, "*Please.*"

"Mirage is the most popular game in Windemere. It's a board game, but also a game of imagication. It's the way most people practice. You play the role of a character on the board and imagicate solutions to puzzles and obstacles on the way to creating your own palace. The piece Grace gave you is called the aeros. It's the only piece that can fly. If you get the aeros in Mirage, your character can fly above the board and play in three dimensions."

On close inspection, Elaine could see how the aeros resembled a miniature paper airplane dipped in metal, practically black with tarnish. Still, Elaine could feel the energy pulsing inside it, itching to break free of its own weight and catch the wind. Elaine could imagine the corrosion crumbling away. The wings gave a little ripple, shone silver, and caught the breeze. The aeros shot from her hand.

"Better hold onto that," said Tyrrel.

Elaine looked all around, but the aeros was gone. Seconds later, it soared back past her ear.

With the agility of a professional juggler, Tallia plucked the aeros from the air. She caught it between thumb and forefinger, and held it right in front of Elaine's face.

"Imagication is not all fun and games," said Tallia.

"No," said Elaine, "I don't suppose it is."

She took the aeros back. Again it was a lifeless metal triangle, though the tarnish had disappeared. Elaine tucked it into her pocket.

"It used to be, though," mused Tyrrel.

"What used to be what?" asked Elaine.

"Imagication," said Tyrrel. "It used to be all fun and games. Back when we were young."

"Aren't you still?"

Tyrrel shrugged.

"We have aged a lot these last two years," agreed Tallia.

"She means since Cloud Palace started dissolving," said Tyrrel. "And we left."

"What do you mean, you *left*?"

"Well, Cloud Palace was no longer a very comfortable place to live. One would get up in the night to go pee, and fall through the floor to the kitchens. It was pretty embarrassing. Not to mention what might get into the food."

"But that is hardly why we left," Tallia added.

"Then why?"

"Well, our parents were fighting," said Tyrrel.

"Don't all parents do that?"

"Not with armies of Knights on flying horses," he replied.

"Oh. I guess I wouldn't really know," said Elaine.

"But the thing is this," said Tyrrel. "The Dark and Stormy Knights fight each other, but mostly they are fighting over *us*. Each army tries to capture us to bring back to the King or Queen."

"Why don't you just go? I mean, your parents *want* you."

"Only because they *need* us," said the prince bitterly. "Only because they each need an ally. You see, Cloud Palace does not hold together with only one ruler on the throne. So each wants us to side with one against the other. Yet we don't want to go with the King *or* the Queen. We want to go with both."

"Or neither," said Tallia. "Tyrrel thinks that if our parents merely got back together, everything would be fine."

"And Tallia thinks nothing will ever be fine until she personally conquers the Sulfane's army."

"And conquer it I shall," said the princess with a conviction Elaine couldn't help but believe.

"Still," said Elaine, "The battle Spenser and I saw wasn't with the Sulfane."

"No, we would not have had such an easy time with him," said Tyrrel. "Do you know how he kills? By corrosion. The Sulfane dissolves all your joy. He blisters your skin and soul alike. His enemies die screaming at what remains when all hope is gone: Pure...empty...*horror.*"

"I can imagine...," said Elaine.

"No. You cannot," said Tallia, "Not until you have seen it done."

"Even then," said her brother, "It is better not to imagine..."

"Meanwhile," Tallia went on bitterly, "Our parents are too busy fighting with each other to notice this *real* enemy: the Sulfane and his army of Clovens."

"It is true," said Tyrrel. "Every day something else beautiful gets destroyed while the King and Queen fight over us. Look there. Do you see it?"

Elaine looked where Tyrrel pointed. In the distance was a rainbow farm, much like the one she had seen from the drafter.

"Yes, but—Oh no..."

Now she saw clearly—and understood. These rainbows were black and white.

"'Tis the Sulfane growing stronger," said Tallia. "Everywhere, more is destroyed than is created anew. Soon, even imagication will be no more."

"We have tried everything," said Tyrrel. "We have tried talking to our parents. And we have tried fighting them."

"Now we have our own army—readying every day to fight the Sulfane— under my command," said Tallia. "You shall see when we get to Kayseri Caves."

"We have tried everything to avoid a battle," continued Tyrrel, "And nothing has worked. Then we heard the Sulfane was conjuring something from Chloe's world—something to tip the balance—to give him even more power. If he can get something from Chloe's world, we thought, why couldn't we get Chloe herself? So under Aster's guidance—he's our closest advisor—we tried to summon Chloe back to Windemere, hoping she could set things right. We knew not for certain where she would appear, so we set off for Aleili Bay. We sent Aster to Cloud Palace, Gnarl to the Rook itself—"

"Nothing worked," said Tallia. "All we got was you."

Elaine bristled, but held her tongue—figuratively.

By now the last light had faded from the sky. Something black flitted over-head, something like a bat or a small pterodactyl.

"Spy!" Tallia cried, and imagicated a ball of fire hurling at the winged creature. Elaine tried to catch how she did it, but quickly realized one couldn't see another's imagination at work.

The pterodactyl swerved, trying to dodge, but the fireball changed course as well. The pterodactyl did a loop, the fireball hot on its tail. The pterodactyl swerved the other way, but Tallia anticipated the move and sent another fireball to meet it. Direct hit. The pterodactyl burst into flames and plummeted to the ground.

"Good shot," said Elaine.

Tallia shrugged. "We're target enough without a passenger," she said to her brother. "Get her settled in back."

Tyrrel nodded. He climbed over the back of the seat into the covered part of the wagon. Elaine followed.

"Whose spy was that?" Elaine asked.

"The Sulfane's," said Tyrrel. "But the pterospies are nothing. We can see them. Worse are the spies we cannot see." He lowered his voice. "When we get to Kayseri Caves, be careful to whom you speak. We know not how the Knights found us. We thought only our most trusted people knew our route."

"One of them told?"

"It wouldn't be the first time. So far we have been lucky. Only half of our people have been captured or killed."

"Only *half?*"

Tyrrel nodded somberly, then cleared a space for Elaine. "The costumes make a pretty cozy nest. You should get some sleep."

"What about you?"

"I should stay up with Tallia for a bit."

He watched Elaine sit among the brightly-colored fabrics.

"Elaine?"

"Yes?"

"My sister can be a little, well...She can act a little *too* much like a princess, you know?"

"It's okay. She is one."

"Yes, she is," Tyrrel agreed.

"Tyrrel?"

"Yes?"

"You never told me how you got away from the Knights."

Tyrrel smiled, proud of his trick.

"Well, imagication is a difficult art. It's not enough just to think of a thing, or even just to picture it. You have to *imagicate* it. Completely. And *sustain* it. That is the real trick—to imagine it so fully that it remains, even after you turn your attention elsewhere."

"But the Knights—"

"We sustained enough confusion that the Knights did not see us take the form of caves. And they did not even guess. That trick is just about the hardest thing we know how to do. Because to imagicate, you have to imagine a thing completely. Yet had we imagined ourselves completely as caves, we would not have been able to turn ourselves back into ourselves."

"Because caves can't imagicate."

"Exactly. We had to keep all our organs intact, but in the shape of caves. We were just about to turn back into ourselves when we saw the Clovens chasing you."

"I must have run right into your mouth!"

"Better than up my nose," laughed Tyrrel.

"Ew, right," said Elaine. "I guess they don't call it the mouth of a cave for nothing."

"True," Tyrrel smiled. "Anyway, I saw them coming after you. I took my chance and moved. I breathed you in."

"The wind," said Elaine.

"Exactly. I did not wish to swallow you. So I breathed you in and closed my mouth."

"I must have been in your lung."

"Yes. It was a strange feeling. You were in my lung. And I felt you touch my heart."

A strange shiver ran though Elaine.

"Are you cold?" Tyrrel asked.

"No, I—" she began. If anything, she was feeling a little hot. "I'm fine. All these costumes should keep me warm."

"Good," said Tyrrel. "That is good."

He watched her settle into her nest.

"Get some sleep," he said. "We shall reach Kayseri by morning."

"Right. Thanks."

Tyrrel nodded. He turned to head back outside.

"Tyrrel?"

"Hmm?" he turned.

"Goodnight," she said, hoping to get another glimpse of his warm, entrancing look. She settled for a simple smile.

"Goodnight."

Alone among the troubadours' costumes, Elaine took a deep breath. She felt the wagon's gentle rocking. She listened to the steady clip-clop of Grace's hoofs, muffled by soft earth, the rocking, the hoofs, the rocking…It was all too much for Elaine's heavy eyelids.

Tomorrow, she thought, *tomorrow I have to find Spenser.*

CHAPTER 8

▼

THE SULFANE

Destry and Sinstry opened the doors carved with the ornate yellow S's. A thick yellow fog poured out. Spenser coughed and gagged on the stench as the Clovens dragged him inside. Spenser's eyes stung. He blinked away tears and looked through the mist.

A small orchestra of scaly, gray gnomes, dressed in formal black and white, stood by an open window. Among them, Spenser recognized the pale gnome from outside the city gates. The swirling, yellow fog revealed the flow of the wind: in the wind-door and through the orchestra's instruments, which looked mostly like organ pipes and slide-whistles. This wind orchestra whistled and screeched, playing the same shrieking tune Spenser had heard in the corridors outside—and back home on Windy Hill. Here, the music, if you could call it that, was more than deafening; it was piercing, sending needles through Spenser's eardrums into his brain. The noise crescendoed feverishly. Spenser winced as the musicians' fingers and arms blurred with the fog. Still the noise grew, drilling into Spenser's head, practically splitting him in two. With a final flourish, the musicians fell silent.

The yellow fog lifted a bit, revealing the vastness of the chamber. At the far end rested a gray stone throne, partially submerged in a gurgling bath of steaming sulfur. The fog lifted more, unveiling the throne's occupant. There, his feet soaking in the steaming pond, sat the Sulfane, a powerfully poised humanoid, clad from calf up in unusually pale leather. Only the shoulders of his jersey hinted at the material's source: Protruding from the fabric like epaulets were some unfortunate person's ears.

On top of his revulsion, Spenser found himself unsettled by the Sulfane's almost dignified appearance: His sleek, black hair was parted impeccably. His smooth gray scales glowed like polished, chiseled alabaster. His piercingly bright yellow eyes shimmered like a jaguar's. And when the Sulfane raised his hand to acknowledge the musicians, Spenser could see the webbing between his fingers, a further hint of the scalemander blood coursing through him.

The Sulfane ignored Spenser, Destry, and Sinstry, and turned his attention to a pair of Clovens closer by.

"Now, my faithful," he rasped solemnly, "You may each help yourselves to a plum."

The near Clovens bowed as if this were the greatest gift in all Windemere.

"Thank you, your lordship," they said as one.

"Let it be known," the Sulfane continued, "That the Sulfane rewards well those who serve."

"We shall, your lordship."

These faithful Clovens each took a gray plum from an equally gray bowl. They bit into the fruit. Blood-red juice trickled down their chins.

Destry and Sinstry shifted impatiently. Destry cleared his throat.

"Your lordship," he began.

"You're late!" snapped the Sulfane.

"We had to stop for wind—"

"These two didn't," said the Sulfane, referring to the blood-plum-eating Clovens.

"But your lordship, we brought you this human."

"Ah, yes. Well, as I said, you're late. I already have what I need."

Spenser swallowed hard, trying to control his rising panic. Did this mean he already had Elaine?

"Forgive us, your lordship," Destry said. "But we met this human at Aleili Bay—just as your lordship instructed."

The Sulfane dismissed them with a wave.

"I no longer require a child of Chloe's world. As you can see, the matter is already in hand. Yes, step forward. Behold. The future of Windemere is within my grasp."

Destry, Sinstry, and Spenser all stepped closer, through the yellow haze. The Sulfane held out his hand. Resting on his scaly palm was Spenser's stone.

"Boy," said the Sulfane, his breath a withering yellow. "Do you recognize this stone, boy?"

Spenser swallowed, but could not summon the life within him to answer.

"Oh…You think yourself important, do you? Too important to answer the Sulfane, the Lord Protector of the Realm? Well, think again. You were the errand boy, nothing more. It was for the stone alone that I summoned you to Windemere."

Spenser called up his last bit of defiance. "You're no Imagius," he practically cried. "It was the Imagius who summoned me."

The Sulfane nearly choked on his own laughter, "The Imagius? Oh, what a fabulous day! The stone, and a good joke, too! No, boy. It was I. *Make solid what is cloudy, Restore what has been split. Curtail the cries that plague us all; Obey what has been writ.* You obeyed, boy. You obeyed *me*. Did you not recognize the Sulfane's seal?"

Spenser had to admit to himself that he had recognized the ornate, yellow S immediately—but he would not admit any such thing before the Sulfane.

"Answer me, boy," the Sulfane hissed.

Spenser shook involuntarily, all hope draining from him.

"Answer me…"

Just then, the pale gnome accidentally let a small, obscene sound escape from his instrument. The Sulfane's head spun.

The offending gnome quivered. "Forgive me, your—"

Before the gnome could finish his apology, the Sulfane let out a breath. A toxic, yellow cloud shot out, scorching the unfortunate gnome's skin. The gnome screamed and writhed, his skin sizzling, bubbling, cracking. Sickly brown smoke rose, and curdling pus puddled on the stone floor where it steamed and evaporated. The gnome's shrieks grew as blistering as his skin. Spenser cringed and shivered. The gnome's suffering flooded the chamber, forcing Spenser to share the unfortunate creature's pain deep in his own soul as all joy evaporated in the corrosive acid of the Sulfane's power. The gnome's screams faded as its spirit dissolved—a final horrible, whimpering cry of pain, sadness, and utter loss.

The gnome toppled like so much rotten, yellow wood, one more enemy of the Sulfane for the river to wash away, slowly poisoning the Sweetwater Sea.

Spenser stared, a pit opening in his stomach like he was going to be sick.

"You may have noticed something of what Windemere lacks," said the Sulfane, as if nothing had happened, "A beautiful country, yes. But a peaceful, stable country? No. Here, one hardly knows if the cup from which you are drinking will dissolve into mist before reaching your lips…Have you heard of Cloud Palace?"

Spenser nodded hesitantly, still staring at the withered gnome.

"What stupidity! How do you expect the country to function with a royal castle that changes shape with the very breeze?!"

Spenser wanted to stand up for Cloud Palace, to say he thought it sounded beautiful, but between the sulfuric fumes and his own despair, not to mention the sight of the gnome, lifeless on the floor, Spenser could hardly gather his thoughts.

"Perhaps," the Sulfane went on, sounding genuinely concerned for Spenser, "Perhaps you know what it's like—to live in a place where people fight over the most trivial matters." He paused, assessing the effect of his words. "Yes, I can see that you do. You want to escape such a place. You want to be free of such pain. But more than that, you want to heal it. Because, after all, it's your *home* we're talking about. Is it not?"

Spenser nodded, following reluctantly along, "It is my *home*."

"Then you understand," said the Sulfane. "Windemere is *my* home. I was born right over there. Do you see that red glow out the window? Those are the Coals, the foothills of the Samovar Mountains, where I grew up. I don't want my home ruined by trivial fights. I want to bring stability to this land. Do you understand?"

Through the yellow haze, the Sulfane's words made sense. Again, Spenser had to nod.

"Good," said the Sulfane. "Then perhaps you are more than an errand boy after all."

The Sulfane gestured for his orchestra to begin again. They did, playing a slow, haunting tune that tunneled into Spenser's head, muddling him even more than the yellow haze. Spenser struggled to piece his thoughts together. The stone. The Sulfane, holding it in his hand. What did the Sulfane want? He already had the stone. What did he need Spenser for? But what if the stone held some power that even the Sulfane couldn't figure out how to use? That was it—or else, why didn't the Sulfane just use the power and be done with Spenser altogether? Instead, he was trying to get Spenser on his side, in that twisted way each of his parents was always trying to do. In his own conniving way, the Sulfane was asking for Spenser's help.

"I won't do your work," Spenser blurted out.

"Oh, but you already have," the Sulfane calmly replied. "You brought me the stone. *Make solid what is cloudy, Restore what has been split.* I meant that in all sincerity. Windemere is crumbling. The King and Queen have left Cloud Palace to the mercy of the wind. Every day, battles between the Dark and Stormy Knights rage across the land. The people cry out for peace. They cry out for order. Only we can curtail the cries that plague us all."

Spenser wanted to close his ears to the haunting wind orchestra, to the Sulfane's raspy, hypnotic voice, but the Clovens still held his arms pinned against their sides.

"I am no imagicator," the Sulfane went on. "You were right about that. I was never given that power. But the stone you brought from Chloe's world will give me that gift. Show me how to use it. Then together, we can stop all the nonsense, the bickering, the fighting that is tearing my home apart."

Spenser shook his head slowly. The Sulfane's argument was starting to sound convincing. Yet if Spenser admitted that he didn't know how to use the stone either, then the Sulfane would surely have no use for him. Then what? Would this scalemander of a man just let him walk away? Spenser didn't think so. He had to make the Sulfane think he was going to help him—at least until he could escape.

Spenser shifted his head from shaking to nodding.

"Imagication is a difficult art," he found himself saying. "I'll need a few things."

"Then imagicate them," said the Sulfane.

"No, I—" Spenser paused. He was playing a dangerous game. "I just need some rest first. Traveling between worlds isn't easy, you know. I'll need a quiet room, a dream box, the stone, and the night to myself."

The Sulfane's eyes tried to probe Spenser's mind. The Sulfane could be patient. He had waited nearly eighty years. He knew how to savor a moment. He could see only one danger in going along with Spenser's plan.

"I think I shall hold onto the stone," the Sulfane said. "Go on. Get your rest. Tomorrow, our work begins."

The Sulfane nodded to Destry and Sinstry. On either side of Spenser, they marched him out of the room. At the door, Spenser glanced back. The Sulfane was still gazing at the stone, smiling.

"Saved our hides, he did," said Sinstry.

"Yes, in fact, he did," said Destry.

The Clovens escorted Spenser up a stone staircase, treating him more gently now.

"Yes, we have something of value here," said Destry.

"Except *we* weren't given any blood plums," said Sinstry.

"What would we want with blood plums?" asked Destry.

"Isn't that just like a Right!" said Sinstry. "You know *exactly* what we'd want with blood plums!"

"You'd miss me," said Destry. "You'd come back."

"What are blood plums?" Spenser asked. The rotten-egg smell of sulfur permeated the entire castle, but Spenser had felt his head clearing the moment he left the Sulfane's chamber.

"Blood plums? The fruit of life," said Sinstry.

"The fruit of loneliness," said Destry.

"Freedom," said Sinstry.

"I don't understand," said Spenser.

"Freedom," Sinstry repeated. "Ordinarily, Clovens can't stay split for too long. We need our other halves or the plumbing's not right."

"It's more than plumbing," said Destry.

"That's what Rights always think," said Sinstry. "Cuz they wouldn't have anyone to boss around without the Lefts."

"We wouldn't be complete," Destry insisted.

"Blood plums close the loops," Sinstry continued. "After a Cloven eats a blood plum, he's single. He's free."

"Or not," said Destry. "Most stay together."

"Maybe so," said Sinstry, "But only when they *choose* to stay together."

"There's no point discussing it," said Destry irritably. "The Sulfane only gives out about two plums a year."

"They should've been ours."

"They weren't. Those other Clovens brought him the stone."

Spenser and his escorts arrived at the top of the spiral staircase. A dozen closed doors ringed the landing. Destry and Sinstry led Spenser to the door farthest around the circle. Destry fit his hand into a palm-shaped depression in the otherwise smooth surface. Spenser heard a click. The door opened.

"There you are," said Destry. "Make yourself at home."

They released his arms, and Spenser stepped inside a small tower cell, completely bare except for a low stone bench. Spenser saw at once that his fortune had yet to change completely; he was still more a prisoner than a guest. The Clovens, their job complete for the day, moved to seal Spenser inside.

"May I have the dream box, please?" Spenser asked.

Destry smirked, "Of course."

He produced Spenser's old dream box, riddled with holes. Spenser took it in his hand, hoping it would still work. He peeked inside. He recognized the bottomless black. Again, the Clovens moved to leave.

"And something to eat," said Spenser. "If I'm to help your lordship, I'd better get my strength back."

"His lordship said nothing about food," said Destry, closing the door.

"But I haven't had anything since—since I don't know when!"

"Then imagicate yerself a feast," said Sinstry.

"If you can't do that, you're of no use to our lord," smiled Destry.

"Nor to us," said Sinstry.

With that, the door closed.

Spenser tried imagicating himself a feast. It didn't work. He tried imagicating himself a loaf of bread. Nothing. He tried imagicating himself a single grape. Still nothing.

"Imagication," he scoffed. "Whoever said there was such a thing."

Spenser studied his cell. A single window looked out on the deepening night. All he would have to sleep on was the cold, stone bench.

But I won't be sleeping here, he reminded himself. *Somehow, I'm going to escape.*

Spenser continued his inspection. The window was thick glass, too thick to break without a tool. And even if he could break it, the opening was too small and too high above the sulfuric moat to do him any good. A dizzying distance below, the city of Dreck brawled and belched. Spenser could just make out a pair of troubadours in chains, being led toward the castle by four Clovens. Spenser didn't think they were the troubadours he had seen with Elaine, but he couldn't be sure.

Elaine. Where was she now? he wondered. Mentally, he kicked himself. He'd had a chance and he'd blown it. *Stupid, stupid me,* he thought. *I should have listened.*

He tried to put that thought out of his mind, along with another thought that kept gurgling up—that he and Elaine hadn't been called to Windemere to do good. Instead, they had been used for the Sulfane's own purpose, a purpose Spenser still didn't fully understand. But he understood it well enough to know he wanted no part of it. He had to get out. And he had to get back to Elaine. He recalled those few times she'd tried to make him smile—with her exaggerated tales of six-foot cockroaches and tipping flamingos. *Elaine. She* hadn't given up. Even though she'd called him a thinker, she was the one who had seen the truth through the Clovens' lies. And she *had* really liked him, hadn't she? She had wanted him to come with her. And he hadn't listened.

The cell door had neither hinges nor doorknob on his side. The surface was perfectly smooth except for one palm-shaped depression where a knob would normally go. Spenser tested his hand in the space. It did not fit. He shifted his hand around, but still the door stayed locked. He felt every stone around the doorframe, hoping to find some small chink, some little flaw he could exploit. No luck. The masonry was perfect.

That's it, then, he thought. *I'll have to go out through the dream box.*

Spenser sat on the bench, the dream box in his lap. He took a deep breath—and opened the lid.

Once again, Spenser tumbled through dizzying darkness. Once again, he landed on firm ground. This time, though, he remained in darkness. Instantly, he drew in his breath. Something wasn't right. He felt a chill skitter down his spine. He peered through the darkness, trying to get a bearing on his surroundings. The smell, he recognized—the oak and grass of Windy Hill. The familiar scent comforted him. At least he wasn't lost. He could find his way home from Windy Hill in the dark if he had to. But the chill lingering on his spine told him this wasn't the same Windy Hill, or even the same dream Windy Hill as before. This was a nightmare Windy Hill.

Spenser looked up, searching in vain for the black rim of the box in the black sky. As his eyes adjusted to the dark, he could make out light patches, like holes in the sky. They weren't stars; they were too big. Then what?

To Spenser's left, a gray figure dropped to the ground. Spenser jumped to his right, and nearly crashed into another. A third gray form dropped in front of him, blocking his way. This one was close enough to see. It was a Cloven. A nightmare Cloven, missing more than its other half. It was missing half its flesh.

Spenser spun around.

More Clovens dropped to the ground on all sides. Half heads on half bodies hopped closer, surrounding him. Spenser looked up. The Clovens kept coming, raining down through the holes in the sky—the holes the Cloven knife had carved in the dream box outside the gates of Dreck.

Spenser fought back his panic. He had to get to the spring, to the pool.

A cold hand touched his shoulder. He whipped around. The force of his turning ripped the bony Cloven hand from the Cloven's arm, but still it grasped Spenser's shoulder. Spenser screamed. He knocked the hand from his shoulder before it could get a firm grip. Another Cloven reached out his hand. Spenser ducked under it and ran.

He ran down the hill, dodging the raining Clovens, darting around a slalom forest of bony halflings, all reaching out their hands.

He collided into a gray fence. He turned and crashed into another.

If only he could make it to the spring—

Another Cloven hand tore at his back.

Skip the spring. The bush hiding his skateboard was closer. If he could just get to his board, he could outpace them. He could outdistance the whole nightmare.

The bony hand on his back was still there. He thought he had shaken it off, but he could feel the skeletal fingers crawling up between his shoulder blades. He could see the bush where his board lay, silhouetted on the next hill. Another fence rose up in front of him. The hand on his back inched still higher. It was almost to his neck. Spenser would never make it to the spring. He would never even make it to the bush. He had to get out *now*.

With a supreme force of will, Spenser pulled himself from the dream box. Back though the dizzying dark, he found himself back in the cell, slamming the box shut, gasping for breath. He set the box on the bench and stepped well away from it. He stared at it, not convinced something wouldn't follow him out of it into the cell.

He stared for a long time. Gradually, his pounding heart slowed. He took a deep breath. Then another.

And then—

Spenser felt it—five cold fingers creeping up his neck.

Spenser let out a yell and slammed his back against a wall.

The bony hand dropped from his neck and skittered into the corner. Spenser moved to chase after it, and it skittered the other way. Spenser dove for it, and crashed to the floor, inches short. He grabbed, missed. He dove again—and missed again. He tried faking one way, then going the other, but the hand was too quick.

Spenser paced around the room. The hand kept to the opposite side. Spenser found himself back at the bench, back at the dream box. He picked it up. He tested its weight in his hand. Suddenly, he hurled the dream box at the hand as hard as he could. The hand dodged. The dream box missed and smashed to splinters on the cold, gray stone. The hand's momentum carried it a few feet farther, then it rolled over on its back, lifeless.

Spenser stepped closer. He suspected the hand was just playing dead. Any moment, it would spring back to life. Spenser took another step, then he gave a quick, fake start, trying to get the hand to react. He reached out his foot and prodded the hand with his toe. His shoe met with a cold, stiff lump of thin flesh and bone. The Cloven hand was definitely dead.

Spenser stepped back, not taking his eyes off it, until he stumbled against the bench. He sat. He let out a breath. His dream box was smashed. He was locked in the Sulfane's Rook with a dead Cloven hand, with no hope of escape.

CHAPTER 9

▼

JUGGLING ELEPHANTS IN KAYSERI CAVES

Elaine dreamt she was as small as a gnat, minding her own business, sipping nectar from a flower. Suddenly, a giant nose came down to sniff the scent. Elaine saw it coming—too late. She tried to hold on, but was sucked right up the nose. She found herself stuck in gooey mucus. She wriggled and twisted, trying to set herself free. All her squirming tickled the inside of the nose. It sneezed.

Elaine shot back out into the air, but not for long. Immediately she was wadded up in a tissue and practically smothered.

Elaine woke in a sweat—or did she wake? She was still stuck, wadded up in fabrics of all colors. Panicking, she thrashed herself free. She was in the back of the troubadours' wagon, surrounded by the rumpled costumes she had thrown off.

She poked her head out of the covered part of the wagon. For a moment, she thought her dream had been true after all. The wagon was inside a large cave. But then she saw sunlight streaming in through an opening and remembered Tyrrel saying they would be at their hideout by morning.

Elaine climbed out of the caravan. She was alone. She walked toward the cave mouth and looked out. As far as she could see were sandstone valleys and cliffs, all dotted with tent-rocks carved into pinnacles by wind and rain and riddled with caves. She took a deep breath of refreshing morning air. The sky was clear. The early morning sun bathed the cliff walls in orange warmth.

"Fancy some breakfast?"

Elaine turned. Tyrrel stood behind her.

"Oh," said Elaine. "Where did you come from?"

"Ah, it's a tricky cave," said Tyrrel. "You can only see one chamber at a time. Follow me."

The young prince turned and walked straight toward the back wall. Elaine caught up so they were side by side. Two more steps and Elaine felt sure she would smack her nose on solid rock. But the smack never came. It wasn't even that they walked through a wall. It was more as if they walked through a doorway, except—just as Tyrrel had said—she could only see one chamber at a time.

Elaine gasped at the sight of the second chamber—an immense cavern with a vaulted ceiling. Sunlight streamed in through natural skylights. The floor billowed as if made of cloud. Elaine stepped onto it and felt her gait change to a floating stride.

A hundred people sat around a long banquet table. Many of them had wispy clouds trailing from their shoulders like epaulettes, symbols of the royal court. As Tyrrel and Elaine made their entrance, the lively laughter and conversation died to a hush.

"My friends," said Tyrrel. "This is Elaine. Of Chloe's world."

Elaine was certainly the youngest person in the room. Some grizzled warriors and advisors kept their white beards tossed back over their shoulders so they wouldn't get them in the food. Still, Elaine could feel a wave of awe and respect pass through the crowd at the mention of "Chloe's world." Only for a moment did she remember Tyrrel telling her that one among these hundred seemingly dedicated followers was the traitor responsible for the capture or death of just as many.

"Welcome," said one grizzled warrior.

"Yes, welcome," echoed some others.

"Um, thanks," said Elaine somewhat awkwardly.

"Come," said Tyrrel, guiding her to the head of the table.

A man with star-shaped spectacles stood to make room for Elaine. "Here," he smiled warmly, "Draw up a chair."

"Oh, thanks," said Elaine, taking his.

"Not at all," said the star-spectacled man. "I'll just draw up another."

A paintbrush appeared in his hand. With a few quick strokes, he painted a chair in the air, which soon became solid enough for him to use. Elaine marveled at the artistry—and the artist. The jovial painter was as old as her parents, but at least as young as herself in spirit. His scraggly blond hair fell to his shoulders, and his premature bowling ball of a belly jiggled with the slightest smile.

Tyrrel took the seat at the head of the table, saying, "Elaine, this is Aster. He is my tutor in breath and art."

"*Was* his tutor," Aster corrected.

"But shall be again, my friend," said Tyrrel. "Though now I call on Aster more often regarding matters of political strategy. He is just back from Cloud Palace."

"Still dissolving, though the thrones looked intact. They're just waiting for a pair of strong-willed rulers to sit in them."

Elaine nodded, and looked down the long table of courtiers, all of whom pretended not to be staring at her.

Tallia sat at the opposite end, engaged in a confidential conversation with a young nobleman only a few years older than herself. Tallia's eyes met Elaine's, and Tallia gave a little nod. When the nobleman turned his head to gaze at Elaine, Tallia touched his arm and brought his attention back to her.

"Some hibiscus soufflé?" Tyrrel asked.

"Oh, absolutely," said Elaine hungrily.

She took the dish the prince offered her, and served herself a huge, steaming portion of the fluffy, purple concoction. She dug into it, not having eaten anything since the milkshake the morning before. Bits of spongy food flew from her fork as she forgot all the manners of her upbringing. The platter was half empty before she looked up and noticed Tyrrel and Aster both staring at her. She stopped eating. She held her fork above her plate, frozen like someone who just let out a whopper of a belch right when a bride and groom were about to kiss.

"Oh. I'm terribly sorry," she said, putting down her fork.

"Not at all," said Tyrrel graciously. "It is I who must apologize. The flavor is fine, but it is not nearly filling enough."

"Oh, no, it's not that at all," Elaine said. "I was just a bit hungry."

"You're too polite," said the Prince. "I have wanted to say something to the cook for months. But he is with us at his own risk."

"And devotion, your majesty," put in Aster.

"And devotion, I grant you that. I have nothing but deepest appreciation for everyone in this hall. I mean that most sincerely. Still, I wish you could have dined with us at Cloud Palace. Our chef there—well, she was the Imagius of chefs. Some days we ate nothing but desserts for breakfast, lunch and dinner—

desserts that were actually good for you. She was a true follower of Chloe, in that way."

"How so?" asked Elaine, eager to hear more about this girl from her own world.

"Oh," Tyrrel smiled, "There's a popular legend about Chloe—that Windemere was the *second* world she created. The first world was Sugarmore, made entirely of candies, chocolate, and creamy desserts—no people, no plants, no creatures—all for Chloe's personal enjoyment. Well, she couldn't possibly eat it all, and the rest melted into a massive, sticky, gooey mess on the first hot day, and went bad by week's end. From this, the moral goes, Chloe learned the importance of moderation and balance."

"What happened to Sugarmore?"

"Who knows?" shrugged Tyrrel. "Some say it's still floating out in space somewhere."

"Attracting a nasty host of interstellar flies," Aster added with a wink.

"So anyway," Tyrrel continued, "the best cooks still follow Chloe's lead. Though they do try to add a modicum of nutrition for balance. And our cook here in hiding, well, how can I blame him? He was only an apprentice imagicator at the start of the troubles. And he does have a fine nose for it."

"Yes," Aster agreed, "He has a good sense of scents—if I can put in my two cents."

Tyrrel laughed along with his former teacher. "And who else among us could imagicate food at all? It's not as easy as it might seem. You might get something that looks like food and smells like food—even tastes like food—but one bite and your eyes spring out of your head. Do you remember Svinnagale?"

"Aye, who could forget?" Aster groaned.

"Svinnagale was our cook before Olema. No imagination at all. He picked fruit right off the trees and dug potatoes straight from the ground!"

"Shocking," agreed Aster.

"Still, he kept us fed until Olema found us," said Tyrrel.

Behind him, Tallia cleared her throat. She and the young nobleman had worked their way to Tyrrel's end of the table.

"I trust you have been discussing battle plans?" she said.

Tyrrel and Aster exchanged looks.

"Not exactly discussing plans," Aster winked, "But planning to discuss—"

"Please, Aster," said Tallia. "I need you. As I need everyone. Every day, the Sulfane grows stronger. We've all seen the rainbows, the daystars falling like dead leaves. We must strike before he grows stronger still. Our call to summon Chloe has failed—"

She shot a glance at Elaine, who bristled.

"—And we are as strong as we will ever be. We must delay and discuss no longer. We must act: create a diversion to draw the Sulfane's forces from the Rook and strike him in his own lair."

Aster's face lost all its joviality. "I beg your pardon, my Princess," he said, "But I believe this to be a foolish plan."

The young nobleman, full of bravado, stepped right up to Aster, who remained in his seat.

"It is not for you to criticize the wisdom of our plan."

"I am merely suggesting," said Aster coolly, "that we wait until we gather more imagicators to our cause."

"The imagicators are routed!" the young nobleman insisted. "Even simple conjurers, troubadours, minstrels—everyone with any imagination at all—captured by the Sulfane's Clovens. What happened to the all-powerful Imagius? Intercepted on his way to meet us, caught—and locked up in the Sulfane's Rook. And *how* caught? Who here knew his plans, the path he would take? Tell me, Aster, who?"

Aster waved the accusation away with a paternal smile.

"Ah, my young Duke...You say the imagicators are routed. But all of us here are imagicators—even you, to some extent."

"You are out of line, sir," said the young nobleman through clenched teeth. "You sit there *mocking*, laughing, twiddling your thumbs—"

"Elaine," Tyrrel cut in, "May I introduce you to Meertis, the Duke of Windham."

The young Duke glared at the Prince for interrupting him, but, being outranked, he held his tongue.

"Nice to meet you," said Elaine. "Are you the Duke with the cat?"

As she said this, she pictured him standing waist-deep in a flooded ballroom. The young Duke let out a sudden whimper. His pants had somehow become soaked.

Tyrrel and Aster burst into laughter. A goldfish hopped from the Duke's pocket, causing Tyrrel and Aster to laugh even harder. Tallia looked aghast at Elaine.

"How dare you!"

"I didn't mean to—" Elaine began.

The Duke looked down, looked around at the courtiers joining the laughter, and scurried from the room.

"I tell you, Elaine's a natural," Tyrrel laughed to his sister, "She is merely untrained."

"Then train her," said Tallia, and she stormed out after the Duke.

"You mustn't mind the Duke," said Tyrrel, leading Elaine through a series of passages. "Last year, the Sulfane dissolved his father in a duel. The young Duke watched it happen."

"Or so he says," said Aster. "You might have noticed the young Duke tends to overstate matters."

"At any rate," Tyrrel went on, "the Sulfane left with the old Duke's sword. And the young Duke left without a father."

"Every day," said Aster, "the young Duke wakes, looks in a mirror, and rehearses saying—"

Aster and Tyrrel stopped walking, struck an overly dramatic pose and declaimed in unison, "'Sulfane, I have come for my father's sword.'"

They held the ridiculous pose for as long as they could without laughing. Finally, the giggles started squealing out like air from two balloons. They slapped each other on the backs, best friends despite the difference in age.

The corridor ended at a slit in the rock, barely wide enough for one person to squeeze through, all but invisible from the outside. Elaine found herself on a flat slab of rock ten smoots across, ringed by a low sandstone wall. Elaine squinted at the bright morning light pouring down from a cloudless sky.

"Welcome to the Sun Stage," said Tyrrel. "In olden times, light nymphs and sun fairies held their Solstice dances here. Now we use it for private training. Have a seat."

A sturdy-looking wooden chair appeared next to her. She touched it.

"Impressive," she said.

Tyrrel shrugged, "A prince gets the best teachers—sometimes even the Imagius Rafalco himself."

"More often, Tyrrel was stuck with me," said Aster.

"Stuck is right!" joked Tyrrel. "Aster would give me the most impossible exercises! 'Imagicate something that is bright black!' 'Imagicate hot ice cream.' 'Imagicate something that can't be imagicated!'"

Aster laughed, "Your ice cream tasted quite good, as I recall—even if did turn my tongue *bright black*."

The spectacled tutor turned to Elaine. "I trust *you* are a model student?"

Elaine hesitated, "Uh…"

"No matter," said Aster. "If I could manage a rascally prince, I'm sure we'll get along just fine. Now then. Quite simply, imagication is the intentional application of acute imagination. Anyone can do it. And anyone can improve with proper training and practice. Of course, like every talent, some people are naturally better at it than others. It's the same with music. Most children can play a few songs, but only a few become great composers. The rest stop trying long before they are grown-ups. Only true naturals grow up to be imagicators, and they are as rare as one in a thousand."

"And you think I'm a natural?" Elaine asked Tyrrel. She would never have called herself a model student, but she did pride herself in her imagination.

"Without a doubt," said the prince admiringly, and Elaine felt a flush go to her cheeks.

"You are of Chloe's world," said Aster. "That may, perhaps, give you some power beyond that of any of us here, a power we desperately need."

He paused. Excitement surged through Elaine, but the weight in her teachers' voices kept her focused. They were counting on her. She would be their secret weapon. And maybe *she* would rescue Spenser.

"How do I start?" she asked.

"With control," said Aster. "Most begin by exercising their imaginations, but I daresay you already have plenty of that. Too much, perhaps."

"What's wrong with too much imagination?" Elaine asked.

"It's hard to control."

Tyrrel added, "You become the cat who sets her own bed on fire."

"Right," said Aster. "Now listen."

He imagicated himself a chair like hers and sat facing her, very close.

"There are four types of imagination: intentional, daydream, dream, and nightmare. As I said, imagication is *intentional* imagination. Of course, we shall focus on that, but we must also work to control the other types."

Here, he stood again.

"What happened back there with the Duke was funny to some of us, but not to all. Do you know how it happened?"

"I suppose I just remembered Tyrrel's story about the flooded ballroom."

"And you pictured it clearly?"

"I suppose so."

"Even the goldfish?"

"It just happened," said Elaine.

"Amazing," Aster laughed, shaking his head. "You certainly have the talent. But now listen."

He took a seat again.

"You must be careful. What you had was an actualized daydream. It was not intentional, but still, you imagined it fully enough for it to *become*. Now, tell me. What would happen if your sleeping mind created images as vividly as an act of imagication?"

Elaine thought about her dreams. Had she created that castle in the meadow somewhere in some other world?

"I don't know," she said. "Would they...*become?*"

Aster nodded, "They might. Now, think of your nightmares. If you learn to imagicate fully, but you do not learn to control the other types of imagination, then who knows what horrors you might unleash? They say that in the far north, north of Boreas, beyond the Nightmare Mountains, is the land of Terridor, a land populated only by nightmares, a land from whence no Windemeran has ever returned."

"Is that where my nightmares would go if—if I actualized them?"

Aster shook his head. "Not necessarily. More likely, they would haunt whatever place you dreamed. And nightmares do not just come from bad dreams. Article Four of the Windham Convention on the Moral Uses of Imagication states that no imagicator may create creatures or situations that may get out of his or her control. The inevitable consequence of such an imagication is a nightmare."

Elaine was hardly paying attention. Who cared about some convention on the moral uses of imagication? She was too busy worrying about all the nightmares she'd had over the years. How often had she dreamed about showing up in class unprepared for a big test—and then shown up in class unprepared for a big test? How many times had she dreamed about her parents sending her off to boarding school just to be rid of her? And isn't that just what had happened? Then, an even more horrifying thought: How many stabbings, murders, bombs—how many wars had she brought into her world without even knowing it?

Aster could sense her mind processing all this. He gave her time to form her question.

"Could I have, well...Could I have made my own world as rotten as it is?"

"Oh, no. No, Elaine, you could not."

She thought about her mother, and her father whom she hardly knew, leaving her with strangers for months at a time. Had she dreamed that into being, too? Aster watched her face fall.

"You could not," Aster repeated. "You have not learned sustenance."

"What's that?"

"To sustain. To keep something in existence after you've imagicated it. That is, it's one thing to imagicate a chair—Go on, try it."

Elaine half-heartedly tried to imagicate another chair like the ones Tyrrel and Aster had created. Nothing happened.

"No, truly try," said Aster.

Elaine took a deep breath, calming herself. After a minute, the ghostly outline of a chair appeared next to Tyrrel. She filled it in, imagining it solid.

"Excellent," said Tyrrel.

At the sound of his voice, Elaine's attention broke from the chair, and the chair disappeared.

"You see?" said Aster. "Imagicating is one thing. Sustaining is another. The moment you turn your thoughts to something else, it's gone. I'd wager even the Duke's pants turned bone dry once he left the dining hall. So even if you have had actualized nightmares, which I doubt, they wouldn't have been sustained."

Elaine nodded, "I see." But already she felt exhausted by the effort and fearful she might unwittingly bring more nightmares into the world.

She stood up restlessly, turning to Tyrrel.

"Can we do something else? I'm not sure I'm ready for all this."

"No and yes," said Tyrrel. "No, we cannot do anything else. This is why we are here. The young Duke of Windham may be pompous, but he is also correct. Every day the Sulfane *is* growing stronger, and we must act soon. And yes, you are ready for it. Right now. Stand up."

Even if Tyrrel had not been Crown Prince of Windemere, Elaine would have had a hard time resisting the command in his voice. She stood up without even realizing it. Only after she was standing did she think, he'll make a good king— gentle, yet firm at the same time.

"Now," said Aster. "Imagicate a ball of light in your right hand, like so."

He demonstrated.

Immediately, instinctively, Elaine did the same. It came so easily, Aster was amazed. But he hid his smile, not wanting to break the flow of the lesson with too much praise.

"Toss it to your left hand," he said.

He tossed his; she followed suit.

"Now. Add another to your right hand."

They each held two balls of light, one in each hand.

"And now," said Aster, "You shall learn why nearly all imagicators are jugglers. Juggling is the best possible lesson in sustenance. And you've already discovered something about it. You just put your attention into the second ball to imagicate it, yet your first ball remained."

Elaine nodded. She understood the difficulty of what she had so easily accomplished and did not want to break the spell by speaking. She held both balls firmly in her mind, as well as in her hands.

"Throw the first ball back from your left hand to your right, in an arc that passes in front of your eyes. When that ball is at the peak of its arc, toss the second ball from your right hand to your left. Like so."

Aster demonstrated, but Elaine dared not take her attention from her own balls to look.

"Your turn," said Aster. "Throw."

Elaine threw the first ball from her left hand toward her right. When it was at its peak, she tossed the second ball from right to left. She caught the second ball flawlessly. She smiled, pleased with herself. Only when she heard Tyrrel's laugh did she realize she only held one ball.

"Ah, I am so glad," said Tyrrel. "You are not perfect. I was afraid we'd have nothing to teach you."

"What happened?"

"When you threw the second ball, you completely forgot about the first. You did not sustain it. Try again."

Elaine imagicated a new ball for her left hand and tried again to hold both in her mind. She threw the first ball. She threw the second ball. She caught both.

Tyrrel tried to hide his pleasure. Aster took a step back and let Tyrrel take over the lesson.

"Three balls," said the prince.

Elaine, who had never juggled even one ball before in her life, imagicated herself a third ball. Juggling three was really the same as juggling two. When one ball reached the peak of its arc, she threw the next—then the next, then the next. The key, she realized, was not focusing on any one ball. Instead, she imagicated a sense of knowing that the balls would continue to exist even when she wasn't paying them strict, undivided attention.

"Four balls," said Tyrrel.

She swallowed, but added a fourth ball without breaking the flow. Her rhythm changed, but the game was the same.

"Five balls," said Tyrrel. "Six."

Elaine kept adding balls, and her transitions were seamless.

"Seven balls…Eight."

No number of balls could throw her off. Her imagication was sustained.

Aster started to laugh. Never before had he seen someone learn so fast.

"Here," he said. "Have a bowling ball."

He tossed one to her.

She tried to catch it, but it crashed to the ground. All her balls of light suddenly disappeared.

"What happened?" Aster asked.

"It was too heavy."

"What do you mean? I threw you a light one."

"What?"

"What made you think it was heavy? It was made of the same stuff as the others—imagination."

"I thought it was heavy."

"You *imagined* it was heavy," Aster corrected. "And so it was."

Aster and Tyrrel worked with Elaine all morning, then into the afternoon without stopping for lunch. By mid-afternoon, Elaine had mastered any number of balls, heavy or light, as well as plates, knives, ducks, and egg-laying chickens. She could sustain every object she imagicated as long as she wanted, while still adding more. Soon, the Sun Stage was filled with so many balls and farm animals one could hardly take a step.

Elaine had just imagicated an elephant when a ball of fire nearly took off her head. She ducked. The fireball missed. Elaine whirled around to Aster.

"What the—" she started to say.

"Duck!" shouted Tyrrel.

A flaming duck flew straight at her. She ducked.

"Chicken!" shouted Aster.

"Am not!" she shouted back, standing up.

"No, *chicken*!"

Elaine looked up, just in time to see a chicken laying a fiery egg right over her. She sidestepped as it fell—right onto a plate at her feet.

"Well, I've had them scrambled and poached, but never—"

A new fireball zoomed straight at her head. She tried to imagine it wasn't there, but it kept coming. At the last second, she dodged it. The fireball whizzed past and smacked the elephant in the rump. The elephant trumpeted and rose up on its hind legs. Elaine backed up, afraid of getting trampled by the beast she had created herself. She stumbled over a bowling ball and toppled backwards just as another fireball whizzed by, just missing her nose as she fell.

This time, she saw where the fireball had come from: Princess Tallia sat on the sandstone wall, flames in her hand. She threw the new fireball at Elaine with deadly precision. Elaine rolled. The fireball missed. But now it curved back toward her again.

"Imagicate, Elaine, imagicate!"

The voice was Tyrrel's.

She didn't have time. The ball was nearly to her, and a second one was homing in, too.

Elaine tried to will them away. She tried to remember the Sun Stage as empty as it was when she first saw it. Nothing worked. The two fireballs shot toward her. She dodged both.

Then Tallia launched a third.

Why is she doing this?! Elaine wondered. *Could Tallia herself be the traitor?*

Three fiery balls pursued her. Four. Then the agitated elephant started rampaging around the ring.

"Imagicate! Imagicate!" called Tyrrel.

How?! she wanted to scream, but had no time.

She darted between the elephant's feet. Five fireballs chased her. And an angry elephant.

She tried making it all go away, but it wouldn't.

Brainstorm, Elaine told herself, *brainstorm*.

A fireball caught her on the leg. Her jeans burst into flame.

Then she had it.

Not brainstorm, rain*storm*.

Elaine imagicated a bucket of water dousing her pants, then a cloudburst drenching the whole Sun Stage.

Rain poured down—cool, refreshing rain. The fireballs sizzled to steam. The elephant flapped his ears and took a calm drink from a puddle. The ducks quacked happily.

Elaine looked around for Tallia, hoping to make a thundercloud shoot a bolt of lightning at her. But Tallia was gone.

As quickly as the storm had come, it disappeared. Elaine hadn't tried to sustain it. The late afternoon sun came back out.

Elaine sank into the chair Tyrrel had first imagicated for her. She looked around at the shattered dishes and the other two chairs, trampled by the elephant.

Someone was clapping.

Elaine looked up. Tyrrel and Aster sat on the sandstone wall opposite where Tallia had been, applauding a crazy performance.

Elaine stared at them, shaking her head.

"It didn't work," she said. "I tried to make it all go away, but it didn't work."

Aster smiled.

"You have learned in a day what most imagicators fail to learn in a year. Imagication is a *creative* art. Only the Sulfane has the power to destroy. You succeeded by *adding* something to the world, not by taking away."

Tyrrel hopped down from the wall and reached out his hand.

"Come. The mess will all go away. None of it was *permanently* sustained. Yes, there are levels of sustenance, too—something like how you can hold an image either in short-or long-term memory. Let us go down to dinner."

She took his hand and followed him back into the hidden passage.

When Elaine stepped into the dining hall moments later, the courtiers already sitting around the great table stood and applauded. Those who could imagicate produced umbrellas and opened them up.

Elaine turned to Tyrrel with a questioning look.

"They have heard of your exploits. They will look to you with the respect they show for a High Imagicator."

"But what's with the umbrellas?"

"You have found your element. Yours is water, just as Tallia's is fire. Perhaps that is why you two seem to clash so often."

"I don't see her here."

"No. She is probably out with Grace."

"I need to find her."

Elaine turned without a further word.

Elaine followed hoofprints up a dusty trail and soon had Tallia and Grace, the Gift Horse, in sight. Elaine watched as Tallia and Grace arrived at a natural rock arch. They paused there, scanning the endless cliffs and valleys.

Probably waiting for a secret meeting, thought Elaine.

Elaine paused, too. If Tallia was really dangerous, Elaine should have brought Tyrrel with her. But no, Tyrrel would never believe his own sister was the traitor. Elaine had to confront Tallia herself.

Elaine looked around for another path up to the rock arch, but in this landscape of cliffs and tent-rocks, no other way was passable. Elaine walked as quietly as she could, but when she was still ten smoots away, Tallia turned.

Elaine hesitated.

"Come closer," said Tallia.

Elaine did.

"You did very well today," said the Princess.

"Thanks," said Elaine, a bit warily.

"You'll need every bit of that skill."

"Especially with traitors around," said Elaine.

"Yes, isn't that true," Tallia mused, gazing into the distance.

Elaine couldn't stand even a moment of silence.

"How could you!" she blurted out. "Is siding with the Sulfane the only way you see of getting power now that your palace is gone?"

Tallia turned to stare at Elaine, then she burst into laughter.

"Why, you're an even bigger fool than I had imagined!"

"You think so? Well, who else could have known it was you and Tyrrel pretending to be troubadours—and called in the Knights? Who else could have told the path the Imagius was taking to meet you so he too could be caught? And why else would you be throwing fireballs at someone who's come here to try to set things right?!"

Tallia had stopped laughing. Her tone became piercing, commanding, yet just as fair and even as her brother's.

"I threw those fireballs to test you, to train you. Tyrrel is an amazing juggler, but he is no warrior. We need more warriors. And as I said, you did very well."

"But what about the Knights, the Imagius—" *And Spenser captured, too,* she thought. "Who told your enemies?"

"I wish I knew," said Tallia, and her wistfulness hardened to determination. "The traitor, when I catch him, will suffer far more than a few flaming juggling balls."

Elaine nodded. She understood. If Tallia had truly intended to harm her, then harm would have been done.

"I'm sorry," was all she could think of to say.

Tallia shrugged.

"I wish we still had time for fun and games. A year ago, you and I might have been friends. Instead, we are merely comrades. The battle has already begun. Listen. Do you hear the wind? Dark Knights, Stormy Knights, but that's not all. There is the sound of a thousand drafters. The Sulfane's entire army is on the move. And if the Sulfane has the boy who came here with you—along with the Imagius—well, we need all the comrades we can get."

CHAPTER 10

▼

THE IMAGIUS RAFALCO

Spenser must have slept, for in the early morning, he woke to the growling of his empty stomach—and to the shrieking of the distant wind orchestra playing a nightmarish rendition of reveille.

Spenser looked out the window. He could just glimpse a corner of the courtyard, and the corner he saw was alive with activity. A thousand Cloven troops marched in formation. Hundreds more carried steaming cauldrons of yellow liquid from the moat to the drafters. Still others loaded on bottles of wind.

Spenser looked about his cell. The Cloven hand rested lifeless in the corner. The door remained closed. He pushed on it. Still locked. He ran his finger over the palm-lock, trying to figure out the mechanism. *It doesn't make sense,* he thought desperately. *I can't—No! Don't give up. Don't give up.*

He couldn't give up; he'd already wasted far too much time in the dream box, then even more time feeling sorry for himself.

And then it hit him. He had frittered away the whole night while the key sat right there in the room. In its own perverse way, the dream box *had* worked; it had given him what he needed—an escape from the cell. He had torn the Cloven hand from his own nightmare and conquered it. For hours, it had lain in the corner, dead, yet beckoning with upturned fingers.

Spenser grabbed the lifeless hand and fitted it into the lock.

The door opened.

Cautiously, Spenser peered out. The circular landing was deserted. Spenser stepped from the cell, taking the Cloven hand with him. He crept quietly to the top of the spiral stair and had just started down when—

Voices echoed up from below.

"Big days ahead…"

"Blood plums for all, they say…"

Spenser hesitated. The spiral staircase was the only way down. And the voices were coming closer, their footsteps rising on the stairs.

"…Bring the boy to the Sulfane again, and claim our reward."

Spenser whipped around and scurried back up. He closed the door of his own cell from outside. *Let them think I imagicaled my way out,* he thought quickly. *Then they won't come looking.*

The footsteps on the stairs kept coming. Spenser darted across the landing to a door on the opposite side. He put the Cloven hand into the palm-lock. It clicked. He pulled the door open just enough to squeeze inside.

A Cloven appeared on the stair, its half-head looking the other way. Spenser fought against a wave of dread that he might have to face the Sulfane again. He sealed himself into the new cell, trying to control his panic. A new voice turned him around.

"Ah, welcome, welcome."

A bedraggled, white-bearded old man spoke to him from the stone bench. His body looked weak from hunger and neglect, but his eyes shone brightly on either side of his falcon nose.

"May I offer you some tea?"

Spenser shook his head and whispered, "There are Clovens at the door!"

"Clovens!" the old man exclaimed in mock surprise. "You don't say…Clovens!" He called as if to a pet, "Here, Clovens! Here, Clovens Clovens! Clovens want some tea?"

"Shh!" said Spenser.

The old man shrugged. "No Clovens. Nothing to worry about."

Spenser held his ear to the door. A pair of shrieks erupted from the other side. The Clovens had discovered his disappearance.

"Well, let me just finish my mending," the old man went on, "Then we'll have a nice hot cup together. These stone floors can be so hard on one's stockings, don't you agree? Oh, sure, I've thought about redecorating. A nice carpet—paisley, perhaps—but that would ruin the overall prison cell motif, don't you think?"

Spenser looked at the old man, who was pantomiming darning a sock. The old man finished his work and set the imaginary sock aside.

"Now then. Hibiscus or Mellow Mint?"

"Neither!" snapped Spenser, "I'm trying to listen!"

"Oh, come now. Surely you can listen and have a cup of tea with old Rafalco at the same time."

Spenser turned back to him. "Rafalco? The Imagius Rafalco?"

"The Imagius? Oh, no, maybe once. But now it's all I can do to make a cup of tea. Here."

Rafalco held out his hand to Spenser as if it held a teacup. Spenser looked at the empty hand. Rafalco followed Spenser's dismissive gaze to his own hand.

"It's not working, is it?"

If Spenser had been in one of his crueler moods, he would have scoffed out loud. But the former Imagius looked so distraught that Spenser just shook his head.

Rafalco sank back onto the stone bench.

"For a moment, I thought I was getting my power back. For a moment, I thought—no, it's too absurd."

"What is?"

"I thought I'd conjured you."

"Maybe you did," said Spenser, still hoping he'd been brought to Windemere to do something good, not just as the Sulfane's errand boy.

"No," said Rafalco wearily. "I wish I could have."

"Why?" asked Spenser, moving away from the door. "Do you even know who I am?"

"Well, not exactly…I know you are of Chloe's world by your colors. But it's true; I don't even know your name."

"Spenser. Spenser McNillstein."

"A pleasure to meet you, Spenser McNillstein," said Rafalco, bowing his head. "Sit down, and I'll tell you a story."

"I can't sit. I've got to go!"

"Not until you hear me out."

Rafalco had not raised his voice, but the words froze Spenser in place. The Imagius may have lost his ability to imagicate, but he retained an awesome, authoritative presence that he could summon at will.

"Windemere cannot afford to have you running loose until we determine what powers you have and what of it the Sulfane might want."

"But his Clovens are looking for me," Spenser pleaded

"Then don't go out through the door," said Rafalco, almost laughing. "Blast a hole in the tower!"

"And then what? Soar away on a flying carpet?"

"A flying carpet? What a wonderful idea! How does it work?"

Spenser almost blurted out, "It doesn't!" but instead, he clenched his teeth and went back to listening at the door. Rafalco gave a dismissive wave of the hand and poured himself some imaginary tea.

"Once upon a time," began Rafalco, "A girl named Chloe imagicated the whole of Windemere."

Spenser tried to focus his attention on the sounds outside the door. He thought he heard Cloven feet going back down the spiral stairs.

"While her mind came back to Windemere many times over the years, her ultimate gift of magic was to imagicate that Windemere would be here always, even when she wasn't thinking about it. Sustenance, we call it. One of the most difficult tricks of imagication."

Yeah, yeah, yeah, thought Spenser. *None of this is helping me escape. I've still got to get past the Dilemma, the moat, an army of Clovens—to Elaine. Elaine.*

"After she imagined the whole world, Chloe was bored. She got tired of imagining new blades of grass. She even got tired of flying cows that could make milkshakes. They were alive now and could grow on their own. Her world was perfect. Windemere was perfect. But a perfect world is boring. The people in it just lazed around all day admiring the flowers, and that was no fun for the girl who had thought it all up in the first place. So she created the Sulfane."

"Wait, Chloe created the Sulfane?"

"Who else could have had the power? She gave all of us quite a challenge when she did, and many people missed the boring world. But it's kept us on our toes, kept us vigilant against destruction."

"But how do I come into this?"

"When Chloe imagicated the Sulfane, she built a protection into the system— that no matter how much he destroyed, there would always be imagicators to create anew. In a sense, we needed him, or the world would overflow with creation."

"Overflow? I don't get it."

"Well, think of the world as a forest—always growing, always creating. If it weren't for rot and decay, we'd all drown in fallen leaves.

"For eighty years, Windemere has been in balance, the creators versus the destroyers. Yet the Sulfane has never been satisfied with that balance. He's had a bit of luck with the King and Queen splitting up; that has shifted the balance in his favor. Still, he's chained by the power of your world, limited by the talents Chloe gave him, and he knows it. He knows he can never win. Unless, of course, he can tip the balance *all the way.*"

"How could he?" Spenser asked, fearing the answer.

"The power of your world is always stronger than the power here, for out of a mind in your world, ours was created. So the Sulfane has always wanted something from your world to give him the edge. Matter. Some matter. Matter is the key. We must make sure he doesn't get it."

"Well, he didn't get a key. He just got a rock."

"A rock? From your world? Are you *sure*?"

Spenser nodded. The Imagius rose to his feet, dropping his imaginary tea set. Spenser wasn't sure, but he almost thought he heard the tinkle of fine china shattering on stone.

"*Pebble, rock, flint boulder throne,*" Rafalco quoted. "*From Earth to Wind, turn cloud to stone...*"

"What does that mean?"

"It means, we haven't a moment to lose! You must imagicate our escape!"

"Imagicate?" scoffed Spenser. "You're the Imagius. You do it."

Rafalco shook his head, "My powers faded with my capture. There are only two things that can destroy imagication: the rotten smell of sulfur and the utter lack of wind. The Sulfane has yet to control the wind—though you'll notice it's stiflingly still in here—but everything in his presence is suffused with his putrid fumes."

"Then what makes you think I can imagicate?"

"Look to your clothes," said Rafalco. "All that is bright fades to gray—or yellows—when in the Sulfane's Rook. But look to your clothes. They have colors."

It was true. Everything Spenser had seen since crossing the moat was gray or faded yellow. Yet his old jeans and the rainbow lining of his long, black coat had refused to give in.

"Your clothes are not of this world. Your clothes do not fall under the Sulfane's power," Rafalco said.

"Then let my clothes imagicate their way out!" said Spenser.

"No, you. *You* are not of this world. If a simple stone from your world has power here, think what *you* can do."

Spenser tried to imagine a hole in the tower wall and a magic carpet waiting in the air outside, but part of his mind kept saying, *This is ridiculous.* The wall remained solid.

"Come on, then," said Spenser.

He put the Cloven hand to the palm lock, and the cell door opened.

"Ah, wonderful," said the Imagius as they stepped out onto the empty landing. He held out his hand for the Cloven hand. "May I?"

Spenser shrugged, gave the old man the lifeless hand, then crept to the top of the stairs to listen.

Rafalco started around the circle of cells, opening every door, saying, "Hoo-hoo! An enemy of the Sulfane is a friend of ours. Oh, hello, Renard! Hello, Oso!"

A young man with a face like a fox came out of the first cell, followed by a great, golden bear. When they saw the Imagius, Renard bowed his head, "Your Imajesty," and Oso the bear gave Rafalco a wet lick on the cheek.

"None of that," Rafalco chuckled as he continued unlocking doors. "Now I'm just an old fool."

"Not for long, I warrant," grinned Renard.

Soon the landing was filled with the happy voices of two dozen long-lost friends reunited—imagicators, troubadours, and assorted magical creatures.

"Imagius! You've got your strength back!"

"Not yet, not yet."

"Ho, there! Is that Gnarl beneath that hood?"

"Rockbane! My dear friend…I haven't seen you since the Battle of Boreas."

"Yes, that's so. But why so glum? We're free!"

"What, is the Sulfane dead?"

"Not yet, not yet."

"Did you see the courtyard?"

"My cell looks the other way."

"Every Cloven in Windemere is assembling—preparing for a mighty battle."

"Why, if it isn't Guffaw! They got you, too, eh?"

Guffaw, who looked as much like a bowl of jelly as a man, gave an embarrassed chortle. "I'm afraid my laughter gave me away."

He giggled, then snorted outrageously, trying to stifle it. No use—his laughter escalated. Those immediately next to him took up laughing, too. This made Guffaw laugh even harder.

"The judge gave me twenty years," Guffaw guffawed. "I said, 'Thanks. My doctor only gave me ten!'" His chortles and guffaws grew until they spanned the octaves. Even those who didn't get his joke had to laugh, and waves of contagious laughter spread throughout the tower.

"Shh!" cried Spenser.

All eyes noticed him. All voices quieted.

"May I introduce," said the Imagius, "Spenser. Of Chloe's world."

Murmurs went through the crowd.

"It's true. Look at his colors."

"His clothes."

"Imagius, you've summoned him."

"We *are* free. The Sulfane's good as dead."

"I'm afraid the true picture is not so rosy as that," said the Imagius. "The Sulfane is far from dead. The Sulfane has a stone—also of Chloe's world."

At this, the crowd went cold. Even Guffaw could barely smile. Spenser thought it a great kindness that the Imagius hadn't revealed *who* had brought the stone into this world.

"What is to be done?" asked Gnarl, the hooded imagicator.

Rafalco turned to Spenser, waiting for *him* to answer the question.

"Well, I suppose we ought to get the stone back. And bring it to the Royal Wisps," he added, thinking of Elaine.

"That's easy, then," said Renard, the imagicator with the fox's face. "All we have to do is find the Sulfane, steal the stone from under his nose, evade the Clovens guarding the halls, get past the gargoyles, dodge the Dilemma, escape the army of Clovens waiting outside, leap the moat, avoid the scalemanders, and climb over the heavily-guarded 40-smoot wall of the city. What are we waiting for?"

It isn't easy to read a fox's expression, and Spenser had no idea if Renard was serious or mocking him. Spenser looked around at the others, who seemed to be waiting for a word of command.

Oso rose up on his hind legs and growled, "Young master, lead, and we will follow."

Spenser swallowed hard at the sight and sound of the immense talking bear.

Rafalco whispered in Spenser's ear, "One thing about imagication that may come in handy to know: if you *analyze* it too much, it hardly ever works."

"Right," Spenser nodded. He raised his voice, just a little. "Let's go. Quietly."

He turned and started down the stone spiral staircase, with his newfound supporters behind him.

After a few cautious steps, Guffaw started giggling.

"Shh!"

"I'm sorry. I can't help myself."

He tried to stifle his giggles, but that only made him sputter, which in turn made him laugh all the louder. Someone next to him laughed too, then someone else, then someone else.

"Ah, just like old times!"

"Shh!"

Spenser stood stock-still. Hopping sounds were coming up the stairs to meet them. He tried to turn, but his supporters had bunched up too tightly behind him for anyone to move.

A pair of Clovens charging up the stairs rounded the corner below. They saw Spenser, backed by his entourage of imagicators. They froze.

This time, Spenser didn't stop to think. He took advantage of the Clovens' surprise.

"Charge!" he yelled.

Spenser ran down the stairs two at a time with the Imagius and an oversized bear right behind him.

The Clovens didn't stop to think either. They turned and bolted.

Now all the imagicators yelled—except for the one who laughed out loud.

They reached another landing. Rafalco tossed the dead Cloven hand to Gnarl.

"See who else you can free. Don't leave the Rook until every door is unlocked! See you at Cloud Palace!"

"At Cloud Palace!"

The next landing down, corridors branched in all directions. The Clovens they had met on the stairs darted away down one. Spenser paused by another. The Imagius forged on, turning this way and that, with Spenser and the rest of the party hurrying to keep up.

Just as Spenser was about to ask the Imagius how he knew the way, the Imagius answered for him. "Left. Left. Left, right, left. It's the pattern of a march. No imagination."

"True," said Rockbane. "You'd never find your way so easily through Cloud Palace."

"Because it's never the same twice!" laughed Guffaw.

They turned the last corner into the triangular corridor that led to the Sulfane's audience chamber. The double doors with the ornate yellow S's clicked closed at the opposite end. Someone had just gone through.

Spenser wanted to hold back, a pit opening in his stomach, but the Imagius did not break his stride. What were they going to do? Just march in and ask for the stone back? Maybe say please? Shouldn't they stop and think first? He and the Imagius were side by side, reaching for the two knobs. At least this time there was no wind orchestra screeching in his ears.

Together, they opened the doors.

The room was empty.

The Imagius strode up to the throne. The bubbling sulfur bath in which the Sulfane had been half-submerged had turned to cold, yellow stone.

"Too late," said the Imagius. "He's figured out how to work it."

The pit in Spenser's stomach grew to a cavern.

"Imagius!" cackled Renard. "Look here!"

"Ow! Let me go!"

Renard the fox had caught a gnome in the corner where the orchestra had been, and held the little musician in the air by the side of one pointy ear.

"Ow! My ear! At least grab it by the tip! If you're not careful, you're gonna make it *round*!"

"What are you doing here?" growled Renard.

"I just came back for my crumpet—and my brother's bassinet!" He waved a pair of wind instruments in his hand. They screeched as wind flowed through them. "I don't know anything!"

"So you say," said Renard, "But just what is this *anything* you claim not to know?"

"Nothing!"

"Oh, so it's nothing, now, is it? One minute it's anything, the next it's nothing. Soon it'll be something, and *then* you'll tell us all about it!"

"I can't if I don't know!"

"Where's the Sulfane?"

"Gone."

"Where?"

"Don't know! Ow!"

"I said where!"

"Let him go," said the Imagius. "We need not stoop to the cruelty of our enemies."

"But—"

"I know where the Sulfane has gone," said the Imagius, "Let the gnome go."

Renard dropped the creature, a little roughly. The gnome scurried into the opposite corner with his crumpet, rubbing his ear.

"Spenser," said the Imagius, "Lead us out."

Spenser, who had been feeling increasingly wretched ever since he learned that he had brought the Sulfane the means to tip the balance of power in Windemere, hardly knew what to say. If the Sulfane won control of the land, it would be his fault.

"I don't—" he started to say, but when he looked into the old man's eyes, he swallowed and nodded. "This way."

He led the troop back out the double doors into the triangular hall. He paused, thinking about which way he had come in. Was that only yesterday?

Don't think, something inside him said. *Move.*

Two turns later, Spenser found himself at another branching junction, with corridors shooting out like spokes in all directions. He couldn't remember having been here before. Worse, a dozen Clovens, armed with crossbows, were coming down one hallway to meet them, led by the Clovens they had met on the stairs.

Spenser turned to his left. Another party of armed Clovens approached from that direction. Spenser looked to his right. A third party of Clovens raised their crossbows, aimed, and—

"Go!" shouted Spenser.

He dove across an intersection to an empty hall.

The Clovens fired.

Screams ripped the air. The Clovens had missed Spenser's troop and hit some of their fellow Clovens coming from the opposite hall.

Spenser led his group in a run, darting around corner after corner, following the same *left right left* pattern the Imagius had shown him, the footsteps of Clovens always just one turn behind. He took one more right turn and found himself at one end of the grand entrance hall, lined with gargling gargoyles, that led to the front doors.

Upon seeing Spenser and the imagicators, the gargoyles began spewing fountains of sulfuric acid back and forth across the hall, barring any escape. Hearing Cloven footsteps behind them, Spenser's group turned to face their pursuers. The Clovens didn't fire. They didn't need to. Spenser and the freed imagicators were trapped.

Spenser edged backward. A gargoyle spat sulfuric acid at him. A few drops landed on his sleeve, but that was enough. The steaming acid burned through the fabric and tore at his arm. Spenser let out a yell. He turned in rage to face the gargoyle. Without stopping to think, Spenser spat back.

His spit scored a direct hit on the gargoyle's cheek. The gargoyle shrieked in pain. Spenser could see where his spit had hit. The gargoyle's skin bubbled and blistered. Saliva from Chloe's world was just as toxic to the gargoyle as the gargoyle's acid was to Spenser. He snorted up some phlegm, preparing to spit again. The gargoyle hopped from his stone pedestal and scampered away. Spenser turned to face the next gargoyle, then the next. The entire hall stopped their fountains and cowered, putting their hands in front of their misshapen faces to protect themselves.

Spenser and the imagicators backed cautiously through the hall. The Clovens hesitated, having no commander, no orders.

Rockbane sidled up to Spenser and the Imagius.

"You two make a break for it. We'll hold off the half-wits."

The Imagius nodded.

"Cloud Palace, then."

"Cloud Palace."

The rest of the group, led by the immense bear Oso, blocked Spenser and the Imagius from the Clovens' view. Spenser and Rafalco turned and trotted for the front doors.

Locked.

Like the cell doors in the tower, there was not even a knob. There was the impression for the palm lock, but the Cloven hand Spenser had used before was now in some other part of the Rook. Hopefully, Gnarl was putting it to good use.

"Well?" said Rafalco.

"I don't have the hand," said Spenser.

"So imagicate another."

"I can't."

"The sooner you stop saying that, the better," said the Imagius.

A roar went up behind them. Spenser stole a glance back. It was difficult to see, for the gargoyles had resumed their fountains, cutting them off from their compatriots. Above the fountains, though, Spenser could make out Oso's great golden head and arms waving in the air, swatting down arrows mid-flight.

Spenser turned his attention back to the task at hand. Getting through the solid door was beyond him.

"How did you get the Cloven hand before?" asked the Imagius. "Do it again."

"I can't. Sorry. But I didn't exactly get it before. More like, it got me."

"Then just imagicate the door is unlocked!"

Spenser wanted to say, "I can't" yet again, but he held his tongue. He thought about the door being unlocked and pushed on it. It didn't budge. Meanwhile the roars and commotion behind him grew ever greater.

"Why can't you do it?" Spenser asked in frustration.

"I told you. The Sulfane's fumes prevent me. But your power should be stronger. It is stronger."

Spenser tried again. He imagined the door was unlocked. He pushed on it again—and met solid stone. He grunted, pushing harder.

"You're angry," said Rafalco.

"Of course I am!" yelled Spenser. "I can't do the simplest—"

"Focus your anger on the door. Get rid of the anger. Turn it. Channel it into energy. No thoughts. No will, even. Just *open the door*. There is a way. There is *always* a way, always some little chink into which you can drive a wedge."

At the word "wedge," the memory of fixing his skateboard with one popped into Spenser's head. He may not have understood a thing about channeling energy, but he understood wedges. The image of a steel wedge flashed in his mind, down to the finest details. He could see it. He could smell it. He could feel it.

Spenser had been focusing on the center of the door. Now he sent a sharp glance at the crack along the edge.

"There!" cried the Imagius, slamming his hand on the exact spot, as if driving Spenser's wedge with his palm.

Spenser felt it work. He knew it worked. The door cracked open. The wedge clattered to the ground, solid as could be.

"Hoo-hoo," laughed the Imagius. "The Sulfane may have the stone, but I have you!"

Spenser almost allowed himself a smile, but then—

An arrow thwacked into the wall just over Spenser's head. He and Rafalco darted through the door.

The door closed behind them the second they were through, nudged on its hinge by the great beast they now faced—the Dilemma, its breath spattering drool more rapidly than before. Razor-sharp horns on both ends of the brute glinted in the sun.

"Heads or tails?" asked Rafalco.

"Neither!" cried Spenser.

He dodged the bite from the beast's head and went straight for its hairy belly. Spenser scaled it as he would a steep grassy hillside back home, scrambling up, pulling his way by grabbing greasy tufts of hair. The Imagius followed.

The Dilemma spun around, nipping at its back like a dog after a flea. It thrashed its barbed tail, spiking itself in the side, adding to its own rage.

"Feed it a muckworm!" yelled the Imagius.

"I don't have one!"

"*Don't* say *don't*!"

Spenser dug in his pocket. No muckworm, but he discovered the last Fourré chocolate from Elaine's box. He had saved it for later, and later was now. The beast snarled as Spenser unwrapped the candy from the foil and tossed it in the Dilemma's gaping mouth. The Dilemma calmed for a moment, rolling the strange flavors around on its drooling tongue.

"You haven't given him anything *tasty*, have you?" asked the Imagius.

"Um, why?"

Suddenly, the Dilemma roared, foaming and spitting.

"Because it likes *muckworms*, for Wind's sake!" said the Imagius. "I'm afraid you've made it *mad*!"

"Like it wasn't before?!"

The beast whirled, more irate than ever, growling and thrashing, gnashing its teeth.

"Hold on!" cried the Imagius, as the Dilemma bucked and bellowed.

"No, *don't!*" yelled Spenser.

The Dilemma's tail smacked into its body once more, and the beast whipped around so fast that the courtyard blurred. The Dilemma bucked, snapping its body like a whip and launching Spenser and the Imagius up and off with such force that they flew over the entire courtyard.

Most of the drafters had already flown off with the Cloven army, but still several squadrons remained, adding the last supplies to their drafters. One Cloven happened to look up just as Spenser and the Imagius soared overhead. He rushed off to tell his superior.

Spenser imagined he and the Imagius had been thrown in slow motion, with his billowing, long, black coat catching the air in its rainbow lining. The Imagius clutched Spenser's arm, and they continued lazily over the wall, over the steaming, yellow moat, and landed bruised but mostly unharmed on the opposite bank.

"I thought that was going to hurt," said the Imagius.

"I didn't imagine it would," said Spenser, a smile breaking through his own amazement.

The Imagius shared the smile.

A half dozen hungry scalemanders reared their heads from the moat, and a Cloven voice rose from the courtyard, "To the drafters! After them!"

"Now, we've got to fly," said the Imagius. "As I'm now beyond the moat, allow me."

The Imagius went into a trance, trying to recover all his former powers. He held his hand aloft with an air of majesty, and produced—

A paper airplane.

He looked at it in dismay.

"But I'm beyond the moat..."

"It's a nice enough plane," said Spenser.

"Not for flying in! I was trying for something a little larger!" The Imagius was pacing now, more upset now than when facing all the obstacles of the Rook. "Curse you Sulfane!" he cried. "Curse you with a thousand nightmares!"

Spenser looked back at the Rook. The scalemanders in the moat were cackling, plotting in some infernal language, licking their lips, and considering crawling out. Drafter after drafter rose from behind the wall. Clovens on each drafter loaded the catapults with buckets of steaming, yellow liquid. Spenser had no idea what the weapons' range was, but he reckoned that at most, he and the Imagius had about thirty seconds to devise an escape.

CHAPTER 11

▼

CAPTURE

Thirty seconds. Maybe twenty-five by now. Come on, Spenser. Get busy.

Spenser's mind leapt into the air. They needed to fly. He needed an airplane. At first he thought of a passenger jet, but that was way too complicated. Too many controls, a long runway—He'd never get it off the ground. The idea faded almost before it formed.

Twenty seconds.

A small plane. A two-seater. Simple controls. But what about the engine? Spenser knew a lot about engines, how they worked. He could probably put one together if he had all the tools, but—What if he forgot some little screw? The whole thing would crash.

Fifteen seconds.

Okay, okay. Just imagine a plane that's already built. The engine's running. The door is open, ready to climb in. Now, how do the controls connect to the wing flaps?

Ten seconds. Scalemanders started emerging from the moat.

The plane began to materialize. Spenser turned his attention to the propeller, spinning in a blur—and the wing flaps dissolved. It was too complicated, too much to hold in his mind all at once.

I can't—

The whole plane disappeared.

Five seconds. Clovens on the lead drafters cocked their catapults.

"What about that flying carpet you were talking about?" asked the Imagius gently.

Spenser's mind clicked. A purple and red, woven carpet formed in front of them, two feet off the ground.

The Clovens fired. The first catapult hurled steaming yellow acid right toward them.

"Sustain it!" cried the Imagius, leaping onto the carpet.

Spenser could hardly believe the carpet supported Rafalco's weight, but seeing it happen made him accept it as reality. That acceptance made the carpet even more solid.

SPLAT! The sulfuric acid hit a nearby thornbush, dissolving it to a bubbling puddle.

Spenser leapt onto the carpet himself. He felt it with his hands. He inspected the weave—crude, but it held.

"Fly!" called the Imagius.

The carpet just hovered. Spenser didn't want to break his focus from the substance of the fabric to think about motion.

SPLAT! Another bucket of sulfuric acid landed even closer.

Spenser stood, finding his balance as if on a new, king-sized skateboard.

Another splat. Spenser imagined he was riding a giant aeroboard, dodging the assault. The carpet shot up twenty feet—shot up so fast that the Imagius lost his balance and fell over the edge. One hand grabbed the tassels. The Imagius dangled below. The carpet started to fray.

"It's holding," said the Imagius, with such authority that Spenser believed him.

And the fraying stopped.

The Imagius pulled himself back aboard, saying, "Weave it. Sustain it."

In Spenser's mind, the magic carpet wove itself back together, stronger than before, the pattern growing more intricate and richer in color.

Spenser stood in the center, Cloven drafters circling all around. One fired, then another. Spenser saw the steaming yellow liquid flying straight for him. He imagined he could control the flying carpet with the tilt of his feet. He banked right, skimming between the two flying blobs of acid.

A hole opened up beneath Spenser's toe. He could see the narrow streets of Dreck twisting below.

"Did we get hit?" Spenser asked.

The hole opened wider as Spenser feared the worst. The whole carpet was dissolving with them fifty smoots above the ground.

"No," said the Imagius sternly, "Everything is fine. Weave it back. Sustain it."

Spenser looked through the hole in the fabric to the ground far below. Drafters circled like vultures. They launched another attack. Spenser realized what was happening. Every time he took his attention from the carpet—even just to fly it—the weave unraveled. *This is too hard*, he thought. *No! Don't say don't!* He had to concentrate on every thread, tightly woven, or his whole invention would collapse. At the same time, he had to focus on flying, evading the attack, for the drafters now kept pace, launching a steady barrage from their catapults. *Keep it going.*

Out of the corner of his eye, Spenser saw a bucketful splash down on some cowering street-sweepers below. They screamed in pain as their skin boiled and blistered.

Spenser wove and re-wove. He dodged; he soared as he had in his dreams. He wouldn't let the Sulfane take his dreams away. All his years of anger at all the people who ever put a fence in his way came to a head; now was his chance at freedom. He imagined the carpet speeding faster. He banked left and right, escaping enemy fire.

"That's it! That's it!" called the Imagius, his great white beard billowing out in the breeze.

A blob of acid nearly clipped the front right corner. Spenser took the carpet into a barrel roll to the left, swooping, diving. He pulled out of the dive half a smoot from a building, and caught a warm updraft rising from the city wall.

The Imagius laughed aloud, like a grandpa on a roller coaster, reliving childhood joy.

"You've got it, boy! An ace flyer! An ace imagicator!"

Spenser allowed himself a laugh, too. He had outpaced the drafters. The catapults kept firing as they fled from Dreck, but the acid fell far short of its target. Spenser let out a whoop and took the carpet into a tall loop-the-loop, better than in any skate park. They were free.

"Just follow the river," said the Imagius. "Where the Samovar meets the sea, the steam rises into Cloud Palace."

Spenser nodded. He had gotten the hang of holding the carpet in one corner of his mind while thinking of other things. Still, he was reluctant to talk too much, so they flew for a good while in silence.

Spenser hardly needed the river as his guide. Below, alongside the river, lay a path of destruction. For five hundred smoots to either side, there were no colorful flowers, no rainbows, no daystars. All was flat, dull granite like a great cement freeway. The Sulfane, Spenser thought miserably, would probably call it progress. And Spenser had brought him the stone. Spenser's throat tightened with remorse; he had infected this beautiful world with a sickness from his own.

"Imagius?"

"Yes?"

"What would have happened if I'd never come—if I'd never brought the stone to Windemere?"

"What do you think?"

"I don't know…I guess…I guess I think none of this would have happened."

"Hmm…Maybe not…Maybe not…The Sulfane might still be without the stone. I might still be locked in the Rook…And Guffaw might have cried instead of laughing. What then? Guffaw's cry might have startled a hawk nesting outside his window. The hawk might have missed catching his morning rat. And the rat might have bitten a gnome, who might have spilled some soup, and a scullery maid bending down to wipe it up might have ripped her dress and tripped on the loose fabric and crashed into a rack of pots which might have wheeled into a pillar, which might have crumbled under the Sulfane's chamber and collapsed the whole Rook."

The Imagius' eyes twinkled brightly, letting Spenser in on the joke.

Spenser allowed himself a little nod. Still, he couldn't help feeling responsible. Part of him had known not to look behind the brick at Windy Hill—and he had ignored his instinct.

To the south, the horizon filled with dark storm clouds, churning and billowing like an ominous, fast-motion nature video.

"Imagius?"

"Yes?"

"Are you sure we're going the right way?"

"Look below."

"I know, but—That storm to the right—"

"Yes, that's some storm," said the Imagius, eyeing him.

Spenser fell silent again, trying to figure out why he had this urge to steer for the storm. It was ridiculous. Surely the Imagius knew what he was doing. And surely the Sulfane had come this way before them. Yet Spenser was bursting with the feeling they needed to change direction. He wouldn't ignore his gut impulse again.

"I should find Elaine," he blurted out. "She's the person I came here with. I— We're going the wrong way."

The Imagius studied him, seeming to understand. "Kayseri Caves...I was headed there myself before the half-wits caught me."

"And the storm?"

"All the more reason we should go."

Spenser banked the carpet for the south, his impatience growing.

"Ugh! Why can't we just imagicate we're there already?"

"Ah, transmigration...It's the stuff of fairy tales. Don't you know the story of The Girl Who Disappeared?"

Spenser shook his head.

The Imagius dismissed the lack of knowledge with a little wave. "It's a child's fable. Basically, when you try to imagicate you're there already, one of two things might happen. You might imagicate that somewhere else is suddenly surrounding you; you won't have moved anything, but will have created a duplicate somewhere else. Or you might end up disappeared. In order to appear somewhere else, you would have to disappear from here. But in that instant, you would cease to be—and be unable to reappear anywhere at all."

"Well then, what about imagicating we're going super fast—or imagicating we were falcons? Why did I need to make a flying carpet?"

The Imagius laughed, "Ah, Spenser, I underestimated you. At first I'd thought your mind was too scientific to be a great imagicator. Now I see my error. A scientific mind is really the same as an imagicating mind. Both rely on exploring, testing, even expanding the boundaries of the possible. Transform into a falcon? Try it at your own peril. Do you know the falcon's anatomy? Suppose you don't connect the muscles right. Or the heart."

"I see what you mean."

"As far as speed goes," the Imagius went on with a shrug, "Who knows? Everyone has some limit as to what they can imagine. Test it. Explore the boundary."

Spenser nodded. He put his attention back into the carpet, then he focused on speed. He imagined they were going faster, faster. The wind threatened to blow him off. He sat and found he could control their direction with his mind; he no longer needed to ride the rug like a skateboard. This enabled him to increase their speed until the wind threatened to fling them from their seats. Spenser imagicated an upward curve, like the front of a sled, to the carpet's leading edge. The curve shunted the wind above and below, and he drove the carpet faster still. He glanced back. The fabric behind started to fray. He rewove it in his mind, but as he did, the carpet slowed back down. He had reached his limit. At least for now. And for now, he was hurtling toward a more massive storm than he had ever seen.

Thunder and shouting echoed through the catacombs of Kayseri Caves, jolting Elaine out of bed.

"The Knights! The Knights!" came the voices.

"How'd they find us?"

"Who would have told?"

"Never mind! To arms!"

More thunder, crashing all around.

Elaine looked out the window carved into the wall of her cave. Her jaw dropped. She had expected to see a battle like the one she had seen before, where the Prince and Princess had simply danced rings around the attackers. But the forces that had tried to pluck Tyrrel and Tallia from their caravan had been only a tenth, maybe a hundredth, of what now assailed the caves. Everywhere, the sky and cliffs swarmed with Dark and Stormy Knights battling for control of the cave entrances.

A young imagicator Elaine recognized from the dining hall came into her room.

"Excuse me, please! No time to stop and gawk! Deeper in! Deeper in!"

He grabbed her by the arm, and only then did she notice he was bleeding from a gash on his forehead. She turned back for one last look out the window—just as the stone around it was blasted to rubble. Rock shards zinged across the room.

"Quick, quick!" said the young imagicator, touching his own forehead and healing it.

He pulled her into a connecting tunnel, packed with the chaos of troops under a surprise attack. The young Duke of Windham stood at one end, trying to organize his fledgling army.

"Go, go, go!" he urged, sending everyone on into the next cavern. Rocks showered down, threatening to crush all who passed through.

It hadn't been thunder Elaine had heard. It had been the sound of caves exploding and crumbling.

The young imagicator who had pulled Elaine from her room left her side and joined the Duke.

"All accounted for!" she could hear him say.

The Duke nodded, "Well done, Rivien. Take your troops to the Prince on the Sun Stage. I'll be with the Princess on the Terrace."

No one told Elaine which way to go, so she followed Rivien along the winding course she had taken with Tyrrel and Aster the day before. Dust rained from the ceiling as the whole mountain rumbled. Rivien's band hustled along with scarcely a word, but Elaine knew what everyone was thinking: Someone, some spy close to the Prince and Princess, had revealed the hideout's location.

"No warning…" whispered someone. "How is it possible?"

"Whose watch was it?" whispered another.

"The Duke's."

"The Duke's?"

"The Duke's."

"Hush now," Rivien commanded. "Look lively."

He quickened the pace and burst out onto the Sun Stage.

The sky above the platform was black with Knights, so thick that no sun made it through. Pterospies skirted the battle, disappearing now and then to report to their unseen master. Dark and Stormy Knights buffeted one another with wind lances and defended themselves with wind shields, each side vying for the chance to capture the Prince and Princess. Elaine might have thought it comical were it not so deadly. Whenever one Knight unseated another—which, with a thousand Knights filling the sky, happened every few seconds—the unlucky combatant would plunge to his death on the rocks below.

Rivien's band took up positions on the wall ringing the stage and imagicated their own weapons and defenses to hold off the Knights trying to get through to the Prince. Tyrrel, for his part, stood at the center, a whirlwind of imagication. Lightning flew from his fingertips. Flying leopards soared from his shoulders, clawing at the backs of any Knights who dared get too close.

Across a narrow canyon, Tallia stood on a wide ledge, flanked by the Duke and his troops. Above them, a dozen Knights had caught on fire and streaked down like shooting stars. The Duke, master of illusion, busied himself by imagicating cliff walls that weren't solid and passageways in the air that looked empty but weren't. Several flying horses reared angrily as they crashed into invisible walls.

Elaine stood by the passage back into the cave, amazed at the sights and sounds. At first glance, the imagicators looked invincible. True, they were outnumbered by a hundred to one, but they were so clever! They could imagine countless ways to thwart the attack. But on closer inspection, Elaine saw the problem the Prince and Princess's people were having; there was just too much happening all at once. She remembered how much trouble she'd had evading three fireballs at once. Now, every imagicator seemed to be under attack from three *hundred* sides at once. No one had time to sustain any object.

A Knight swept past the young Duke, penetrating the outer ring. The Knight swooped down at Elaine on his way to Tyrrel. The Knight swiped at her with his wind lance, blowing her hard to the ground.

"Tyrrel!" she cried.

Somehow, above the din of the storm around him, Tyrrel heard Elaine scream his name as she fell. He turned, warned just in time to face the Knight storming at his back. In an instant, Tyrrel imagicated a solid stone wall between them. The Knight crashed into it at top speed and crumpled in a heap. Tyrrel turned his attention outward again and the wall dissolved. There was simply too much happening even for Tyrrel to sustain it.

Elaine pulled herself to her feet and climbed onto the perimeter wall by Rivien.

"Defend the Prince!" he called to her.

For a moment, she watched Rivien at work. He seemed to be imagicating clouds of bees, swarming around intruding Knights' heads.

A Stormy Knight made it past a Dark Knight and headed right for Elaine's section of wall. She tried Tyrrel's trick of imagicating a stone wall in the air, but she was too slow. The Knight was through it before she had made it solid. Quickly, she tried one of Tallia's fireballs, but she missed. The Knight kept coming, his lance aimed straight at her. The Knight swatted himself on the helmet and veered off course. A bee had stung him in the ear.

Elaine turned to thank Rivien, but saw two more Knights had broken through the ranks. Rivien had his mind full. Out of the corner of her eye, Elaine saw Aster talking into Tyrrel's ear, advising on strategy. She tried another fireball to help Rivien. This time it hit the Knight's horse on the neck, but had no effect. She had imagined what it would look like, but not what it would feel like. Rivien's bees warded off the two Knights without her help.

But now a new threat, a wedge of five Dark Knights, plunged down for the center of the Sun Stage. No one could stop them.

Water, thought Elaine. *My element is water.*

She imagicated a sheet of pure water, as smooth as Looking-Glass Lake. Five Knights saw five Knights swooping right up at them. The first five continued their charge, and the other five did not yield. The leader saw the other leader was a Dark Knight identical to him. At the last second before a collision, both leaders pulled their mounts to the side, tricked by Elaine's illusion.

Across the narrow canyon, Stormy Knights blasted away not at Tallia's party itself, but at the cliffs and caves surrounding them. Wedges of Knights dove at the rock walls, battering them to rubble with hurricane-force winds. Tallia and the Duke found themselves cut off from the rest of their band, who had been forced to retreat into the relative safety of the crumbling cave. They backed farther away from the cliff wall, farther out onto the ledge.

"Look to your sister," Aster said to Tyrrel. "It's time."

Tyrrel looked. With no other imagicators nearby to support their defense, Stormy Knights threatened to drive Tallia and the Duke off the edge.

Tyrrel imagicated a white flag, billowing in the air above him.

"A truce! I call a truce!" he cried.

Knights on both sides wheeled and regrouped. The Duke took advantage of the pause and imagicated a stone arch across the canyon to the Sun Stage. He and Tallia scurried across it to join the Prince.

"You're surrendering?" questioned the Duke.

"Not a surrender," called Tyrrel. "A parlay."

Two Knights from each side rode down and landed on the stage.

"Tell your master the King, and your mistress the Queen, that we will parlay. But only with them both together."

Tallia had sidled up to Tyrrel.

"What mean you by this?" she asked in a hushed voice.

"We are outnumbered, outfought. At the very least, it bought us a rest, and the chance for you to—"

"Tyrrel!" cried Elaine.

It was too late. The two Dark Knights had flown off to convey the message to the King. A second later, the two Stormy Knights took to the air as well, but on their way, they plucked Tyrrel from the ground.

"Treachery!" cried the Duke.

The Prince struggled for only a moment. Then a Knight pressed a yellow cloth over his nose and mouth. He fell limp across the flying horse—and they were gone.

"We'll go after them!" cried Elaine.

But her command was too late. Armies of Dark and Stormy Knights closed the gap, pinning the imagicators to the ground. Elaine watched the Prince disappear, a warrior no longer, just a boy scarcely older than herself.

Spenser saw the Dark and Stormy clouds part, then come together again. He urged his carpet to its limit, following his feeling that he had to get there *fast*. Still, his questioning mind could not help itself.

"What are the Dark and Stormy Knights even fighting over?"

"The same as everyone," said the Imagius. "Power and control. No one has ever ruled Windemere without keeping Cloud Palace whole. And no one has ever kept Cloud Palace whole by himself. The King and Queen each need an ally. In former times, they had each other. Now, they each want at least one of their children on their side."

"What about the Sulfane?"

"Ah, yes, the Sulfane…The Sulfane has taken advantage of the moment. While the eyes of the world are on the battle between the King and Queen for their children, the Sulfane has been extending his reach. Yet as much control as the Sulfane has gained, he cannot quite subdue the land from his Rook in Dreck. True power emanates from Cloud Palace. Whoever sits in the thrones gains power over the Knights."

"But the Sulfane's heading for Cloud Palace. Can he make it whole by himself?"

"By himself, no. But with Chloe's stone, who knows?"

"What's so special about that stone anyway?"

"Nothing—and everything. Legend has it that, at first, Chloe was an ordinary girl who found an ordinary stone. Like many children, she imagined she had found a treasure that gave her special powers. Instead, by imagining this so clearly, *she* gave power to the *stone*. Power the Sulfane can now use."

Spenser felt the too-familiar weight sink in his stomach. The carpet slowed.

"Spenser," prodded the Imagius. "You are following a true feeling. What is it?"

Elaine, he thought, but said, "To find the Royal Wisps. And to go together to Cloud Palace."

"Yes. Together. That sounds like an excellent plan."

His resolve hardened, Spenser turned his attention back to full speed. The sky darkened as they approached the battle. Below, the cliffs and canyons surrounding Kayseri Caves plunged into shadow. Spenser drove his carpet like a falcon down into the heart of the storm.

He steered straight for the round platform below, which seemed to be the focus of all the combatants. He thought he could see Elaine standing on a wall at the edge. His heart leapt to his throat. But no, it couldn't be Elaine. The Elaine he knew couldn't be throwing lightning bolts—or could she?

"Your Highness!" called the Imagius in a shocked voice.

Rafalco had spotted Tallia, and now Spenser did too—though he knew her as Rosetta. The princess had been caught in a yellow net slung between a pair of Dark Knights soaring in the opposite direction from Spenser and the Imagius.

"Turn!" the Imagius commanded.

Spenser banked the carpet hard in a U-turn, swooping low over the Sun Stage, racing after Tallia's captors. Distantly, he could hear cheers of "The Imagius! The Imagius!" Then another pair of Dark Knights cut between him and the princess, obscuring Spenser's view with darkness. Spenser plunged through in pursuit. A crosswind blindsided him. A lance blew him and the Imagius from the carpet. They fell out of the darkness and crashed roughly to the stone platform.

Spenser's head cracked on the wall, and all was darkness once more.

When Spenser came to, the clouds had gone. He blinked away the bright sunlight to see Elaine and a young man sitting by him. Spenser sat up and his head rang like a gong.

"This is Rivien," said Elaine.

"Oh," said Spenser, still in a fog.

Rivien touched Spenser's head. The ringing stopped.

"I closed the gash on your head and set your arm," said Rivien. "But you'll have to do the inside work yourself."

Rivien could see Spenser didn't understand. Either that or he was too focused on Elaine to pay attention.

"You were lucky," said Rivien. "I have others to help. But Elaine thought I should see to you first."

"She did?"

"I did," said Elaine, her smile tinged with concern.

"Imagicate," Rivien instructed. "Feel strong, clear, whole."

Spenser nodded. He struggled to remember feeling strong and whole. He focused on his arm. The broken bones had been set roughly, but only Spenser knew how they should feel inside.

Rivien rose and set about treating others. Spenser looked around. Dozens of bodies lay crumpled on the stone slab. For many, Rivien would be too late.

"Elaine...," Spenser began.

She met his eyes. Then he looked away. He had so much to say, but no words. *I'm so sorry*, he thought. He shook his head. "I should have left with you. That dream box—I shouldn't have let myself get sucked in."

"It got you into the Rook, didn't it? And then you managed to get yourself back out—with the Imagius!"

"I'm not sure it was worth it."

"Not worth getting out? Oh, Spenser!" She wanted to reach out, but held back, not wanting to re-injure his healing bones.

"I meant, not worth it just to get the Imagius," he said.

"Well, he's got to be more use than I am."

"Are you kidding? Wasn't that you throwing thunderbolts? You were like—like a goddess!"

"Oh, you think?" she smiled.

"I mean," Spenser backpedaled, feeling a bit hot in the cheeks, "It was pretty cool."

"Well, thanks just the same…But a fat lot of good it did. Both Tyrrel and Talia are gone—the prince and princess, the Royal Wisps—the reason we came here."

"Can't we go after them?"

"If we couldn't protect them here, when half the Dark and Stormy Knights were busy fighting each other, we really don't have a chance. But I expect that's what the big argument's about."

She gestured with her eyes to where Aster, the Imagius, and the Duke of Windham were locked in a heated debate. Spenser got to his feet. He and Elaine walked over to the council.

"By my father's sword," said the Duke, "I will not let this treachery stand."

"I'm with you there," said Aster, eyeing him. "The traitor's connections are deeper than I'd feared. The yellow cloth—soaked in sulfur, I'd wager. And the yellow net."

"The Sulfane's own tools," said the Duke, "Used by the King's own Knights."

"What are you implying?" demanded Aster. "I've known the King all my life. He'd never ally himself with the Sulfane."

"Nor would my cousin the Queen," insisted the Duke.

"And yet," said the Imagius, "There was more to that yellow net than its color, or surely the prince and princess would have imagicated their escape. Whoever the traitor is, he has connections to both the Sulfane *and* to the King and Queen."

"By my father's sword, I'll find the traitor—"

"I'm sure you will," said the Imagius evenly, "But the matter at hand is even more pressing. By aiding the King and Queen with the Sulfane's tools, the traitor has distracted us—*and* the King and Queen—from the real prize."

"How so?" asked Aster.

"The Sulfane has left the Rook with a thousand drafters. He aims to take Cloud Palace."

Aster laughed. "Good luck to him! By now it's nothing more than fog."

"He aims to make it solid. And he now possesses the means to do it."

"Impossible!"

"How can he?"

"*Pebble, rock, flint boulder stone,*" intoned the Imagius. "*From Earth to Wind, make firm the throne…*"

"No…" breathed the Duke.

"He has a stone?" said Aster. "From Chloe's world?"

The Imagius nodded, "It would seem he does."

The Duke wheeled around, searching for Elaine, and saw her standing right by him with Spenser at her side.

"Traitors," he said. "You. From Chloe's own world."

He imagicated a gleaming sword in his right hand and raised it, ready to strike.

"Perhaps," said the Imagius, "you have never heard the rest of the verse. Few people have."

The Duke lowered his sword, if only by an inch.

"*Water's course and falcon's flight, sling shattering force, rend rock with light.*"

"Meaning what?" asked the Duke.

"Meaning these two may have added to the evil in this world, but they also have the power to heal it. If they so choose."

The Duke lowered his sword.

"I'd like to know how," he said.

Spenser and Elaine glanced at each other, then stared at the Imagius, each thinking, *And so would we.*

"The first order of business," said the Imagius, "would seem to be to rescue the Prince and Princess."

"Of course it is!" exclaimed the Duke. "By my father's sword, I'll do it! Rivien! Feral!"

With that, he strode off to rally what remained of his forces.

The Imagius eyed Spenser and Elaine with his penetrating gaze.

"I imagine you two had best be off, too. If you so choose."

CHAPTER 12

▼

THE CLOVEN
CONSEQUENCE

"You're the Imagius," said Elaine. "Can't you just imagicate them back here?"

"No, I'm afraid not."

"Then how about imagicating the King and Queen are letting them go."

"No again. Imagicating control over another thinking being has never been done. Not even the Imagius before me, the Imagius Accipteryx, could do it."

"Then what *good* is it all?!"

"That's frustration talking. Whenever frustration talks to me, I try not to answer. 'No, sorry,' I say. 'Not interested, thanks. I don't want any.' I should, however, try to provide you with some weapons…"

The once-great imagicator closed his eyes, concentrating, once again trying to regain his former powers. He held both hands aloft, and in them appeared—the Imagius opened his eyes—a pair of feather dusters.

The Imagius looked so sad, Spenser took his anyway.

"Thank you. They're very nice."

"Yeah, thanks," said Elaine.

The Imagius nodded, gritting his teeth, and turned away.

"Batty," said Elaine.

"No. Not batty. He's trying…Still, we're wasting time."

"Right. Where's your magic carpet?"

"I don't know. We need something stronger."

"Right. A flying horse like the Knights have."

"Yeah, and bigger."

"And tougher."

"Faster."

"Fiercer."

"Teeth."

"Fangs."

As they talked, they imagined, and a great beast started to take shape in front of them.

"Claws," said Elaine.

"Wings," said Spenser.

"Two heads."

"Sure, one for each of us."

"Chains to guide it."

"But a powerful will of its own."

"Yes, power."

"Armor."

"Fire."

"A dragon."

"A dragon."

"A two-headed dragon."

As they climbed on, the Imagius looked around.

"No...," he breathed.

They pulled back on the chains. The beast reared up.

"You're breaking Article Four!" The Imagius shouted. "Don't sustain it!"

"What's he saying?" Elaine asked over the dragon's beating wings.

"Sustain it," said Spenser.

Elaine nodded. They both sustained their creation. The beast lifted from the ground.

"No!" shouted the Imagius. "A beast with a will of its own—it can't be controlled! The consequence is a nightmare!"

"What?" said Elaine.

"Something about a nightmare," said Spenser.

"Oh. Good name for it. Our Night Mare."

They left the Sun Stage far below, and flew off in pursuit of the retreating Knights.

"I can't believe that Duke—calling us traitors!" Elaine called to Spenser. "Threatening us with that sword! He wouldn't have the *guts*. He was just *waiting* for the Imagius to stop him. I bet he's the traitor himself. All his talk of treachery—he was standing right next to Tallia when she was taken, and he didn't raise a finger. Of course, there'd be no telling Tallia that. She's in *love*."

"Well, we'll get to her before he does. Look below."

The Night Mare flew faster than his magic carpet, faster than any drafter or winged horse. Second by second, they gained on the Knights. They soared over a party of six imagicators, led by the Duke of Windham, flying along on what looked to Spenser and Elaine like skateboards with sails.

"Now *those* I'd call wind surfs!" said Elaine.

The Night Mare dove between canyon walls, its wingtips inches from rocky cliffs. They rounded a rocky corner and now had both the Dark and Stormy Knights in clear view. The Dark Knights veered off to the left, the Stormy Knights to the right. Spenser leaned to the left in pursuit of Tallia. Elaine leaned to the right, following Tyrrel. The Night Mare split like a Cloven.

Spenser fought for control. At best, he could only half control the flying beast, since they had given it a will of its own. And now he only flew on half of it. *Half of a half,* thought his mathematical mind, *that means I'm only a quarter in control.*

It also seemed the Night Mare had trouble controlling itself. With only one wing, it tumbled through the air. Spenser clutched its neck with his legs, and the chain with his hands. He and the beast rolled onto their backs, plummeting.

Any second now, I'll smash to the rocks.

Yet his mind was surprisingly calm. And perhaps that was why his one-quarter control was enough to help the Night Mare tuck its one wing into the shape of a hang-glider and right itself just in time to avoid a crash.

Elaine's half tucked its remaining wing too, and Elaine hugged its neck with both hands, forgoing the chain, settling the beast, guiding it with the force of her own will. They flew low to the ground, darting between cliffs, dodging tent rocks. Ahead, Elaine saw Tyrrel, tied with yellow cord to a white, flying horse. Next to him, on a regal mount draped with silver wisps of cloud, was the Queen.

In the chaos of wartime, the Queen had clearly come down in the world. Now she had to make do without either her beautician *or* her personal dresser. She fought to keep the clasp of her cape from coming undone, and to keep one rogue strand of hair tucked up where it belonged.

None of the Knights had spotted Elaine yet, and she glided close enough to hear.

"Oh, my Prince," said the Queen. "I'm so glad I've got you safe! I've been so worried! You're so thin! And just look at your *hair*!" she laughed. "You can't keep it out of your eyes!" She tucked her own rogue strand back in place before her son noticed.

"I could if my hands weren't tied," said Tyrrel.

"Soon, soon…We have to be sure—sure to get your father's wildness out of you. He was never a proper prince, you know. Not like *you*." The Queen paused to fiddle with her cape. "But I did think we'd taught you better than to run away. And your sister. The tutors we hired—no small expense either—I thought we'd at least taught you respect! No small expense getting you back, either!"

"Then why did you?"

"Because you're my son! Truly, I forgive you for running away. You were young, and young people make mistakes. I was young when I married your father."

"I ran because my home had fallen apart."

"Exactly. The palace doesn't hold with just one person on the throne. Now you and I can heal the kingdom—together!"

"But *you* let it fall apart."

"None of that, now."

"No! You talk about respect. What have you given me to respect? What about *your* responsibilities? You're the Queen, for Wind's sake!"

"Do not tell me what I should do. You are not King yet."

"And I won't be—not by your side!"

"No? Think of it, my Prince. Cloud Palace back together—isn't that what you want?"

"That's not fair! I was fine being a prince! We were all fine! Until *you*—you and Dad—this is *your* problem; *you* fix it!"

As they banked and turned, the Night Mare's huge half body suddenly threw a shadow on the Knights, catching their attention. One Knight spun around, then another, then the entire escort wheeled and charged Elaine. The Night Mare took a deep breath and inhaled the sudden storm. Seconds later, the beast exhaled and blew the Knights a hundred smoots away.

Elaine imagicated a sword. The Night Mare momentarily bent to her will, and swooped toward Tyrrel's mount. Elaine leaned down and sliced through the yellow cords that bound the Prince's hands.

"Jump!" she called.

"No," said the Prince, eyeing the Night Mare warily. "You jump here!"

Suddenly, against Elaine's will, the Night Mare dove for the ground.

"Elaine!"

Elaine imagicated a lasso and looped it over the neck of Tyrrel's steed. She held the rope tight as the half-dragon dropped from under her. Elaine swung like the troubadour acrobat who had trained her and landed perfectly on the winged horse in front of him. Tyrrel's arms steadied her, then wrapped around her.

"Tyrrel!" scolded his mother. "Come back here this instant!"

But Tyrrel had already set his mount into a dive so the Night Mare was between him and the Queen. He looked back, with only a hint of bitter regret.

"Well, young lady," said the King, "What do you have to say for yourself?"

Princess Tallia stewed. She sat on a plain wooden chair, the yellow net still around her, thwarting her ability to imagicate. Her father sat across the cave from her, a small banquet on the table before him, a crown of golden clouds slightly askew on his hairy head. Like the Queen, he had come down in the world. Unlike the Queen, he reveled in the chaos of war. He tore a piece of meat from a skewer with his teeth.

"Eh? Speak up," he said.

"'Tis not polite to speak with your mouth full."

"That's your mother talking. All prim an' proper princess. Humph. Shouldn'ta never fallen for her. You now, you got the fire in you. And not afraid to use it, I see."

The King laughed at this and nearly choked on a piece of meat.

"You're right," he coughed. "Shouldn't eat with my mouth full."

"Should not *talk*."

"Right, right. Your mother's right after all. But I still shouldn'ta fallen for her. Didn't really, if you must know. Was more of a challenge, like. Everybody wanted to marry the princess. So why not me? Was Aster who dared me to go for it, if you must know. Ah, we were hell-raisers. No wonder you've got the fire in you. That came from me. Aster really wanted to marry your mother more than I did. *Ambitious*. Oh, yes, he wanted to be king. But we were best friends, see, the sort of best friends who fight over everything. So of course I couldn't let him marry her. Had to do it myself."

He stabbed a strawberry with a golden knife, then pulled it into his mouth with his teeth.

"You're awfully quiet. Not like you at all. What's the matter, your fire gone out?"

"It must be the sulfur net. Why not let me out?"

The King shook his head. "We need to come to some sort of agreement first. The kingdom has fallen apart."

"Agreed. Now let me out."

"Nice try," the King smiled, "But no. Not yet. First, answer me this: will you come back to Cloud Palace with me?"

"Without Tyrrel? Without my mother, the Queen?"

The King waved his skewer with a shrug. "There are only two thrones."

"Never!" Tallia raged. "You're a fool to think I'd go with you!"

"*That's* my girl!" the King laughed proudly. "*There's* my little fireball! Rebellious like me. What a team we'll make! Now then. Windemere needs you to cooperate whether it *pleases* your royal highness or not. Captain—"

A Knight guarding the cave door saluted.

"Captain, secure a steed for my daughter. We fly at once."

Spenser had reached a wordless agreement with his half of the Night Mare. The Night Mare could fly as it wished, swooping in and out between rocky spires, snapping after pterodactyls, as long as Spenser could keep nudging it in what he thought was the right direction. He had long since lost sight of the Knights who had abducted Tallia, but he followed their route and soon could see a formation of Knights rallying to defend a cave against the Duke of Windham and his tiny band.

Spenser urged his beast toward the flying Knights, hoping to scare his way through. But the Night Mare would have none of it. The half-dragon wheeled in a cloud of its own smoke and soared around the back of the hill.

"Other way! Other way!" Spenser urged.

The Night Mare settled on a crag and tore into the rock with its great jaws. Its teeth and claws ripped a hole in the mountain, a cave in back of the one that had been so heavily protected. Spenser understood. The Night Mare was helping him after all. It spat out boulders like cherry pits and went for another bite. Spenser patted it on the neck. Before long, the Night Mare stopped digging.

"Go on," said Spenser. "Go on."

The half-dragon backed out of the tunnel and lowered its neck.

"What?" Spenser asked.

The beast gave its neck a sudden shake, and Spenser slid off.

"Hey!"

The Night Mare gave a breath of fire and flew up into the air. There, the cloven beast met its other half, and merged. The dragon circled low over Spenser. Spenser held up his hand, imagining the beast would land and join him in the back-door assault. The Night Mare dipped its wing to wave, but did not land. Spenser waved and hesitated as the Night Mare circled again. This time, it dove straight at him, not slowing for him to get on, but instead, snapping at him with its teeth.

"Hey!"

The beast made another quick circle. It opened its jaws. Spenser stood frozen as the dragon exhaled a fiery breath straight at him. Spenser dove into the newly-made cave entrance, the hairs on the back of his neck singed and smoking.

Spenser followed the tunnel the Night Mare had made. At the start, the cavern was large enough to accommodate a standing dragon, but quickly it narrowed to the diameter of the beast's neck and head. Spenser crawled on all fours until he came to a window the size of his own face. He peered through, onto the back of a man's hairy head, a head encircled by a crown of golden clouds.

"So your young Duke's come to rescue you," the King was saying to Tallia. "I must say I admire that kind of reckless passion."

The King picked up a skewer of meat and tore off a bite.

"Of course," he went on, "I could be persuaded to let him accompany us…"

"You'll have to catch him first," retorted the Princess.

Spenser worked at the boulder blocking his way. If he could just roll it back quietly, he could sneak into the chamber without the King noticing. He tried to imagicate that the boulder wasn't there, but it didn't work. He remembered the Imagius saying something about the Sulfane being the only one who could destroy. Silently, quickly, he went to work with his hands, digging at the dirt supporting the boulder.

"Turn and look, my daughter" said the King, sounding genuinely concerned.

Spenser glanced up from his work, but the hairy head blocked his view.

"My Knights pick off your Duke's men one by one. Come with me without a struggle. Call them off, and you could save them all."

Spenser pried a small stone from under the boulder. The larger rock shifted, then stopped.

"There goes another," the King said. "Tallia, don't let your own fiery pride burn you."

One more small wedge to pull out…

"You'll come with me one way or another," the King went on. "This fight is for nothing. I feel for your young Duke; I really do."

"Then you stop fighting *us*!" said Tallia, fearing for the Duke. "Stop fighting us and fight the Sulfane!"

"Don't you see that's what I'm doing? Don't you see the best way to stop the Sulfane is by taking back Cloud Palace?"

"Not without my mother! Not without my brother!"

Spenser pulled the wedge. The boulder crashed back and cracked into the cave wall. The King turned.

"What the—" he began as Spenser leapt into the cave.

The King grabbed for him. Spenser feinted one way, then the other. Then—in a move perfected by years of getting out the front door past his parents—Spenser dodged under the King's grasp.

"Guards!" cried the King.

Spenser grabbed the golden knife from the King's table and darted over to Tallia's net. With three quick strokes, he sliced through the cords that bound her.

"Thanks," she said.

Two Knights appeared at the cave entrance. They drew swords and charged at Spenser. Tallia, freed from the sulfur net, imagicated a pair of fireballs zinging straight at their visors. The Knights ducked and held back.

"Thanks, yourself," said Spenser.

Outside the cave, the Duke and three others were putting up a desperate fight against the King's whole army. These four had imagicated a misty, impenetrable bubble around themselves. It protected them but made it difficult for them to see their own targets.

Dozens of Knights swarmed at the cave opening. Tallia imagicated a wall of fire to keep them at bay. The King, meanwhile, held a skewer in each hand. He and Spenser circled one another like gladiators in a pit.

"Come on, boy, let's see the blade. Plain combat. No magic."

"What's the point of that?" Spenser bluffed, "Afraid of my powers?"

The King laughed, "No, boy, be afraid of mine."

With that, the King squinted, and a hundred skewers shot out from the two in his hands. Spenser saw them all fly. His mind shifted them into slow motion. His knife flashed in real time—and he cut them all down.

Spenser considered the situation. The King was certainly a danger, but not his true enemy. Keeping one eye on the King, Spenser recalled his flying carpet. He remembered the pattern, the feel, the speed. As he remembered, he imagicated, and another magic carpet came into being, hovering two feet above the cave floor, just to his left.

"Hop on," he said to Tallia.

"Tallia," said the King sternly, "The future of the country is at stake."

"True," Tallia retorted. "Which is why I cannot leave it all to you."

She hopped onto the carpet beside Spenser.

"No!" roared her father.

The King imagicated a sprinkler above Tallia's wall of fire, dousing it, and the Knights stormed in, grabbing the sulfur net from the floor. The King blocked the back door Spenser had come through. The Knights threw the net, but Spenser was too quick.

The carpet shot to the side. Tallia almost fell off.

"No seatbelts," said Spenser. "Hold on."

Spenser imagicated the carpet to fly one way, then the other. Again, he faked out Tallia's father, darted under his grasp, saying "'Later," and bolted out the back door.

"Parents," said Spenser. "For some reason, they always fall for that move."

They soared out into the open sky.

"I'm Spenser, by the way."

"Tallia," said Tallia. She almost added "Firstborn child of Queen Quoirez by King Orrozco, Heiress to the Airs, Princess of Whales, Dauphina of—" but then thought it better to be modest.

They soared over the cliffs, back over the main cave entrance on their way to their base. The Duke of Windham's party still held off an army of Dark Knights from their misty bubble. As Spenser flew overhead, the Duke managed to get a glimpse inside the cave and saw that Tallia was gone. The Duke reluctantly gave up his battle and retreated.

An uncertain mood hung over the dining cavern that evening. One of every five seats around the great table stood empty, a reminder to all that while the prince and princess were safe, many of their companions were not.

"Your highnesses," said the Imagius, "I think we would do well to counsel a while in private. Raise your glasses to your devoted followers, then let us go."

Tallia stood at the head of the table and raised her goblet.

"My dear, brave friends. Today, we discovered we are not invincible. And yet today has made us stronger and more committed to success than ever before. We have had our first taste of one possible future, the future where war and chaos reign supreme. We cannot let this future come to pass. We *will not* let this future come to pass. With you by our sides, we will restore Windemere to balance and peace."

"To Windemere!"

"To the Princess!"

"To the Prince!"

"By my father's sword," said the Duke on the tail of the cheers, "We will not let you down."

The assembled crowd drank as one.

Aster, standing by Tyrrel's side, said, "Now then. Let us counsel."

The Imagius studied Aster thoughtfully.

"No, it would be better that you stayed here in this chamber. You and the young Duke."

"But Imagius—" the Duke protested.

The Imagius raised his hand. "Some must stay with your followers. We cannot have them think they are without leaders."

The Duke raised himself up proudly, "Yes. Yes, of course."

"And I, Imagius?" asked Aster.

The Imagius answered in a voice too low for others to hear, "You may keep an eye on our young Duke."

Aster nodded, already eyeing him. Then Tallia, Tyrrel, Spenser, and Elaine followed the Imagius into the next chamber.

"You do not suspect the Duke, too!" exclaimed Tallia.

The Imagius waved her comment away with a shrug. "There is a traitor here somewhere. And as I said, I do not intend to leave your people here without leaders."

This chamber opened out to the outside world. The Imagius studied the Night Mare circling overhead, harassing a squadron of Knights, its fiery breath glowing deep red in the fading twilight.

"Are we leaving, then?" Tyrrel asked.

"With the Knights surely regrouping for another try?" asked Tallia.

The Imagius's eyes twinkled. "All the more reason to leave Aster and the Duke behind."

"Surely we can not abandon our followers," she replied.

"Ah, my princess," said the Imagius, "I appreciate your passionate dedication. But sometimes, the way to serve your people best is to strike out on your own. The way to win this battle is not by fighting; it's by going around the fighting to the solution. You yourself have always held that the battle between the Dark and Stormy Knights is a distraction from the true danger." He paused, making sure she was with him. She considered, nodded for him to continue. "That the Sulfane's troops have not arrived here can mean only one thing: he hopes to take Cloud Palace while everyone's attention is elsewhere."

Elaine smiled, "And you hope to catch him off-guard. We sneak out the back door, and the Sulfane's spies don't know we're coming."

"Precisely. All agreed?"

"Agreed," said everyone except Tallia.

A moment later, she nodded, "All right."

"Excellent," said the Imagius. "Then let us just imagicate some speedy transportation…"

The Imagius focused his attention on the ledge by the cave opening. The others could see the effort of his concentration. Beads of sweat formed on his forehead. And there, on the hard rock floor, appeared—a leaky rowboat, filled with water.

"It's okay," said Spenser gently, "I've got it covered."

He imagicated his carpet flying in from where he had left it. The carpet hovered two feet above the floor, waiting.

"Nice work, Spenser," said Elaine.

"Thanks," he beamed.

Tyrrel nodded and said, "To Cloud Palace."

The prince climbed on, taking Elaine's outstretched hand.

Seeing their gazes meet, Spenser's previously proud expression sank into a jealous funk. He sighed and took his place at the front.

Tallia and the Imagius followed, echoing "To Cloud Palace."

CHAPTER 13

▼

THE NIGHT OF THE
DANCING STARS

From his watch on the wall above the Sun Stage, the Duke of Windham could have sworn he saw five people soar past on a scrap of carpet—with no sail, no bottled jet stream, nothing to harness the power of the wind—just flying all on its own. Stranger still, he was sure Princess Tallia was among them. Couldn't be. She wouldn't leave without saying goodbye.

Unless, he thought, *those traitors from Chloe's world—*

A blast of fire shot across the sky. Giant, leathery wings beat the air as the Night Mare dragon flew after the carpet. Taking a cue from the dragon, the circling Knights broke off their skirmishes and followed.

The young Duke listened to the wind. He stared and thought.

They've all gone and left me.

"Rivien!" he called.

"Ho there!" came the response from a nearby cliff.

"Report, please!"

"Nothing. I mean, it seems everyone's gone, my Duke. Even the pterospies. Flown east. All clear."

"Prepare our people to travel! Break camp and fly to Cloud Palace. By my father's sword, we will not be left out!"

Spenser felt the Night Mare's presence before he heard or saw it. Elaine, too, felt the hairs on the back of her neck prickle, that uneasy feeling that comes with a bad dream, even before anything bad starts happening.

Perhaps because they had created it together, Spenser and Elaine turned as one, and saw the beast bearing down on them. Its leathery wings shone silver in the moonlight, and seemed to flap in slow motion. The Night Mare screamed. For kilosmoots around, children cried out in their sleep. Grown men awoke in cold sweats.

"Turn it away!" cried Tyrrel.

"They can't," said the Imagius, "They have broken Article Four. They have created a beast with a will of its own—a nightmare."

The Night Mare reached out its talons.

Spenser swerved. The dragon missed but turned its head and breathed out a blazing fireball that put Tallia's to shame. The carpet's back fringe caught on fire. Elaine imagicated a bucketful of water and put it out.

"Why is it after us?" she asked.

"It has no 'why,'" said the Imagius. "A nightmare is not a rational being, never fully awake."

The dragon circled back. Spenser sent his carpet into a dive, just on the edge of Kayseri Valley. The dragon tucked its wings and followed. The Imagius' beard streamed back in the wind, cracking like a flag in a gale. Again the Night Mare screamed. In the forest below, a tigeroceros hid in his den, whimpering.

The dragon let out another fiery breath. Spenser raced ahead of this fireball down through the air, plunging faster than a falcon. He dove fast, but the fireball dove faster, gaining on them every second.

Spenser reached the cover of the trees and steered the carpet into the thick forest. He slowed, not wanting to crash in the dark. But it didn't stay dark for long. Behind them, the fireball hit the canopy. The treetops erupted in flame. Elaine conjured a thunderstorm to keep the fire in check.

Spenser slalomed between the trees. Overhead, the dragon shrieked again, farther away this time, and flew on.

When Spenser took the carpet above the treetops for a look, they could see the glow of the dragon's breath fading into the distance, flying ahead of them into the east.

"Will it fly to Cloud Palace as well?" Tyrrel asked.

"Why not?" said Elaine. "Everyone else is."

"I suppose we shall find out when we get there," said Tallia.

"Should be quite a party," said Spenser.

"It has a scavenger's hunger," the Imagius mused. "And there will be blood."

On the horizon, Spenser could see the steam rising from the Samovar River, shining silver in the moonlight. He would keep this on his left, and follow its course east to the sea, and to whatever awaited them at Cloud Palace.

The night grew darker and colder. Elaine scooted against Tyrrel to keep warm. She caught Spenser's jealous look and felt a pang of guilt. Spenser looked away.

"Ah, I did it!" cried the Imagius suddenly. "Hot chocolate for everyone!"

The others looked around. The Imagius was beaming, proud of his returning powers. He handed everyone a steaming mug.

Spenser sniffed his. Tyrrel took a sip and sputtered it out. The others looked askance. The Imagius took a sip.

"Oh," he said sadly. "Sorry. Mud."

He poured his out over the side. The others followed suit.

"Here," said Elaine, gathering the mugs, "Let me try." She caught Spenser looking at her doubtfully and added, "I *do* know chocolate."

She stared deep into the cups, imagicated some water to rinse them, then stared some more. As she conjured the smell, the heat, the rich, soothing flavors in her mind, steaming cocoa filled the mugs. Confident she had it right, she sustained the imagication, making it complete.

She handed out the mugs proudly.

"Don't you want to test it first?" Spenser asked.

"I will," said Tyrrel.

He took a sip. He froze. He gagged. He keeled over with all four limbs sticking up in the air.

"Tyrrel!" cried Tallia. "Tyrrel!"

The Prince sat up laughing.

"Delicious, Elaine. Really. It's delicious."

Elaine punched him playfully on the shoulder.

"You watch out or next time it won't be!"

The others laughed and drank their cocoa. The Imagius settled in the back corner of the carpet, stewing sullenly over his cup.

Spenser wanted to say, "Thanks, Elaine," but, seeing her with her back now leaning into Tyrrel's chest, the words didn't come. He turned his back and studied the stars.

"I wonder how come I can't imagicate at home," said Elaine.

"Maybe you can," said Tyrrel. "Maybe it's just that no one ever taught you how."

"Or maybe the rules are different in your world," said Tallia. "Maybe there, 'tis just not possible."

"Mmm," said Elaine. "If that's the case, I don't think I want to go back."

"Then don't," said Tyrrel.

"Well, it's tempting," she said, with a bittersweet smile.

Tyrrel studied her sad face, then said, "Come, let me teach you Mirage."

He imagicated a Mirage board and several figurines. The board looked something like a map of Windemere, with a grid overlaid.

"At the beginning, everyone starts out as a peasant, a wind serf, or a student. So you choose a figure to match—one with a shovel, a wind bottle, or a book."

"I'll be a peasant."

She reached for the peasant figure holding a shovel.

"No, you don't have to touch it. Remember, this is a game of imagication. I shall be a student."

He glanced at the board, and the little silver figure holding the book sprang to life and trotted to his side of the board. It flipped open the book and began studying intently. Elaine looked at her figure. It scooted to her side of the board and stiffly dug a little hole. Instantly, a miniature peach tree sprang up.

"Excellent first move," said Tyrrel. "Now, the object in Mirage is to create your own castle before the Angst can break it down."

"The what?"

"The Angst. It's a shapeless blob that eats away at all you try to create. It lurks everywhere, and the only defense is to create more and more imaginatively. The game is a race between the players, but the real opponent is the Angst."

Without looking back, Spenser knew all about the Angst. It was that pit that opened up in his stomach whenever he thought about his stone in the Sulfane's hands, whenever he thought about Elaine with Tyrrel, whenever he thought about his parents poisoning his home with their fighting.

"To build your castle," Tyrrel went on, "you need to gather materials, power, wealth, and allies. But how you go about it is up to you. For example, you could use your shovel to threaten people into helping you—'Build my castle, or I'll beat you over the head'—but that probably wouldn't work as well as trading favors and the food you grow, and thereby gaining friends and accomplices."

He moved his student one square, to a small stream. The student bent down and filled a leather canteen with water.

"Your turn."

Though curious about the game, Spenser forced himself not to look at Elaine having so much fun with the prince. *I just need to concentrate on flying.*

"Oh, excellent move!" he heard the prince say after a bit. "I have never seen someone get the aeros so fast. Now you can play in three dimensions. You're amazing!"

I just need to concentrate on flying.

Spenser familiarized himself with the night sky. The constellations were brighter here than in his world—and the stars comprising them were closer together, too, like an easy connect-the-dots where you hardly have to draw the lines to see the shape.

Over to the left, a poodle constellation stood by the trunk of a tree. Straight overhead, a pig seemed to be nibbling on a pineapple. And right in front of Spenser in the East, a silver bear was surely kissing a starry toad on the cheek. The constellations were so whimsical that Spenser let out a laugh. He looked back up at the poodle and stared. The stars had moved. They *were* moving.

"What the—?"

The poodle circled the tree once, sniffed it, then squatted down.

"It didn't just pee—!"

Tallia sat next to him at the front of the carpet, laughing with him.

"Yes, 'tis Priscilla the Poodle. No telling what she is going to do."

"But how—? The stars moved!"

"Yes, 'tis a lucky night, the Night of the Dancing Stars. It only happens once every seventeen moonths."

"Moonths?"

Tallia nodded, "Moonths. You do not have moonths? One moonth is about thirty days—the time between fool moons—those being the nights when the moon looks most foolish. 'Tis not a fool moon now or you would see it making rude faces at you. But the Night of the Dancing Stars is far more of a treat. I had forgotten it was tonight."

"I had forgotten as well," said Tyrrel. "A good omen for our task, I'd warrant."

"Aye," Tallia agreed, "And 'tis a relief to see the Sulfane's destruction has yet to reach the stars."

"But are they dancing?" Elaine asked.

"They are just warming up to it," said Tyrrel. "Watch."

The toad hopped over to Priscilla the Poodle and made a low bow. The poodle nipped at its heels until the toad hopped away. In another corner of the sky, a rooster, its sparkling crest formed by shooting stars, picked up a violin and started to play.

"Oh, I wish we could hear it!" said Elaine.

"I wish you could, too," said Tyrrel. "We used to have grand concerts on the turrets of Cloud Palace. Oh, it seems like ages ago...Have you heard our music?"

"No," said Elaine.

"I have," Spenser shuddered. "At the Sulfane's Rook. If you can call it music."

Tallia scoffed, "No, that you cannot. Not at the Rook. That is just horrid noise. Nothing of the Sulfane's shows any imagination or creativity. How could it?"

Spenser shrugged.

"Our music," the princess went on, "is woven of air itself. It sounds like crystal...Music befitting the stars."

They gazed up as the dance began. The forgotten Mirage game dissolved and disappeared.

Even without music, the starry dance was almost beyond belief. Constellations whirled and waltzed through the sky like elegant fireworks, while the feisty poodle nipped at the other creatures' heels, spilling their cocktails and upsetting trays of hors d'oeuvres.

After what seemed like hours, the stars settled back into their normal, static positions, except for Priscilla, who kept sniffing about the sky, looking for spilled crumbs.

"Is it over?" Elaine asked.

Tyrrel shook his head. "They are merely resting. It will go on all night."

"Speaking of rest," said Spenser, with a nod at the Imagius, snoring in the corner, "You all should probably get some sleep. I have a feeling tomorrow—" He felt the Angst again opening a pit in his stomach—"Well, we'll have our work cut out for us."

"What about you?" Tallia asked. "Why do we not take turns flying so you can sleep, too?"

"I don't think that would work. The way I imagicated it, it's steered by my thoughts. If I fall asleep—Well, I'd better not."

"Then I shall stay awake with you. To make sure you stay awake, too."

"I'm all right. You get some sleep."

"No, really. I am not yet tired. And—I would like to. You can tell me about your world...What is your family like?"

"Oh, there's a question to keep me up all night...Why don't you tell me what it was like growing up as a princess?"

Tallia laughed, "How do I answer that? For me, it was normal."

"Yeah, I guess it would be."

He glanced back at Elaine, curled up on the carpet in Tyrrel's arms. Then he looked at Tallia, sitting inches away. She spoke gently, so the others could sleep.

"'Tis a fair question, though. I knew not what normal was. I mean, I knew that not everyone was a princess—after all, I am the only one in Windemere—so I knew *that* was not normal. But I mean, is it not normal not to feel normal?"

Spenser smiled, "Yeah, I guess so."

"Oh, what is normal, anyway?"

"Did you *want* to be normal?"

"Does not everybody?"

Spenser shook his head. "I think everybody wants to be a prince—or a princess."

"And every princess just wants to play prickleball in the dirt with the other kids."

"But couldn't you—if you really wanted?"

"It would not have been the same. The other kids would still have known I was *Princess Tallia, heiress to the airs.* And they certainly could not have understood that a princess's life was not all that great either."

"Wasn't it?"

"No. With my parents, well, it always seemed as if Tyrrel and I were in the middle. 'Tis difficult to explain."

"You don't have to."

"No?"

"No. My parents fight, too."

"Really?"

"Really. Ever since I was born. Oh, there were some good times in between, but they couldn't even agree on my name—so they gave me a few extras just in case. Of course, they don't have armies of Knights on flying horses. I guess you've got me beat there."

"You mean they fight directly with each other?"

"Sure."

"Well, that is even worse, then. When you're king and queen you can make other people do your fighting for you."

They flew in silence for a bit, each thinking private thoughts.

"Tallia?"

"Mm?"

"Why can't you just imagicate your parents are back together? Imagicate that they're happy."

Tallia let out a sigh. "I wish it were that easy. I cannot tell you how many times I tried. All the great imagicators—even the Imagius over there—they told me it could not be done. But they also taught me that ours is a young world, with much still to be discovered. So I kept hoping—and trying. Every night. Every night for years, while other kids were watching troubadours, I would go up to bed early. I would lie in my bed and try to remember. I would try to remember my parents being happy together. And when I could not remember it, I would imagine it. But I guess the Imagius was right. The one thing imagication cannot do is change what other people think or feel. No matter how hard you wish it."

Spenser swallowed hard, remembering his own years of going up to bed early just to escape his own parents squabbling. He would put a pillow over his head because that was the only way he could make the fighting stop.

"At least you didn't just run away from it," he said.

"Didn't I?"

"No, I mean, we're going to *do* something about it. Aren't we?"

"I do not know...Maybe growing up and living our own lives is all we *can* do." She yawned and looked up. "Oh...They're dancing again..."

Spenser looked up, too. The great waltz of the constellations had renewed, a more formal dance this time. For a while, Spenser let himself be mesmerized by the stately, swirling movements.

Spenser felt Tallia's head bob, then settle against his shoulder as she dozed off. He started to pull away, not used to having someone so close. In her sleep, she snuggled closer.

"Um, I think it's getting lighter in the east," said Spenser. "It'll be morning soon."

"Mmm," she said, not stirring.

Spenser took a deep breath and let it out. Her head on his shoulder, it was a new feeling for him, but a nice one—the first nice, warm feeling he could remember in years. He breathed it in...and closed his eyes.

▼

CLOUD PALACE

Elaine awoke with a shriek. She had been having a pleasant dream, something about floating on a marshmallow raft on a hot cocoa sea, then suddenly she was falling, screaming. She opened her eyes. She *was* falling. The wind blew back her hair as the ocean rushed up to meet her, seconds away.

"SPENSER!"

Spenser awoke, along with the others. He had fallen asleep, and now the carpet was little more than a few colored threads tangled around him and his friends. They plunged down together, too fast to do anything about it, and splashed into the Sweetwater Sea.

"Ah, how thoughtful of you, Spenser," said the Imagius, "A morning bath. Though I must say it would have been nice to hang up my robes first. Still, one can't always imagicate perfectly. Better luck next time."

"Sorry," said Spenser.

"'Tis fine," laughed Tallia. "A bit of a shock, but the Imagius is right. 'Tis a nice way to start a day."

Tyrrel agreed, splashing on his back like a carefree boy, "My sister's not just saying that to be kind. When we were young—before all the troubles began, I mean—first thing in the morning, we would jump right out a wind-door into the sea."

"Besides," said Tallia, "You got us as close as we could wish. Look there."

Spenser and Elaine turned to the coast, five hundred smoots away.

"That is the city of Veil to the left," said Tallia. "And the Samovar steaming into the sea. And above it, well, what is left of Cloud Palace."

Spenser and Elaine raised their eyes to the wondrous apparition suspended above the bluffs. Rows of braided columns flowed into gilded archways, which supported ornate facades, which in turn help up a dizzying assortment of parapets and spires. The palace swept to the sides like wings, and climbed to the heavens in towering thunderheads and delicate brushstrokes. The sun rising in the east cast a rosy hue over the walls while the corners shone with silver linings, and the tallest towers became fringed with gold.

The structure gradually shifted shape, as one would expect with a cloud, but always to an equally stunning new design. Ramparts stretched and spiraled into new spires. Pillars bent and met to form new arcades. Balconies reached out to create bridges and aerial passageways.

The whole fabrication gave the appearance of a grand confection—more solid than an ordinary cloud—a castle woven of cotton candy, with every crystal of spun sugar sparkling like a jewel. Spenser wondered at the connection between the crystalline structure of the building and the sugar in the ocean around him. Elaine merely tasted the Sweetwater Sea on her lips and smiled.

"It's fan*tas*tic…"

Tyrell shook his head. "Nothing like what it was."

"But the swirls, the patterns…Those turrets up top!"

"They *were* turrets," said Tyrrel. "It's nearly all dissolved. Now, it would barely support a fly."

"Oh, 'tis so much worse than when we left!" cried Tallia.

"Well, that's what we're here to fix, isn't it?" said Spenser.

Tallia nodded, "Yes."

"Shall we swim for it, then?" Spenser asked.

"No need," said the Imagius. "Allow me to provide our transport."

"Oh, no," said Elaine, "You really don't have to."

"No trouble, no trouble."

With that, he sank beneath the waves. A few bubbles rose up from where he disappeared. Spenser thought he heard some high-pitched squeals. A moment later, the Imagius resurfaced. His head broke through to the air first, then his shoulders and body, moving forward like the conning tower of a submarine. He rode on the back of the old Sailphin Leeee and was followed by four others.

"Climb on," he said.

Elaine followed Tyrrel and Tallia's example and stood on a Sailphin's back the way one would ride a windsurfer.

"Hello again!" squealed the young Sailphin Eee to Spenser. "Don't just flop about! Climb on!"

Spenser hesitated, remembering his earlier experience, and asked, "Um, have you had breakfast yet?"

The Sailphin let out a high laugh and said, "Oh, don't worry. We'll get some on the way."

"That's just why I'm worried," Spenser muttered to himself.

No sooner had Spenser climbed on than Eee plunged beneath the waves in search of fish. Seconds later, he caught one in his teeth, surfaced, and flipped it back over his head to Spenser.

"Um, thanks."

"Don't mention it. Oh, too late," the Sailphin laughed. "You just did."

The early morning breeze seemed to blow directly from the rising sun in the east, and the companions reached shore almost before they knew it.

The Imagius squealed a thank you in the Sailphins' own language. They squealed back and disappeared into the foam. Spenser gave a little wave with the fish Eee had caught for him. Then, after he was sure the Sailphins had gone, he set the fish back into the sea.

The company had landed on a rocky beach. Perched on a bluff to the south, the city of Veil glowed orange in the morning sun. To the north, the Samovar River branched and stretched into the ocean. It had cooled substantially since flowing from its volcanic source in the mountains above Dreck. Yet it still steamed upon hitting the waters of the Sweetwater Sea. The mist billowed, rose and swirled into Cloud Palace, which filled the sky directly overhead.

"Oh, it's even worse up close," said Tyrrel.

"We've been away too long," said Tallia.

"Our *parents* have been away too long," said Tyrrel.

"Enough of that!" said Tallia. "'Tis up to us now."

"Up to us to bring them together. Listen. They're on their way."

A low roll of thunder echoed in the distance, the Dark and Stormy Knights on the move.

"Yes," mused the Imagius. "All the forces of Windemere gather in this one place. It is fitting."

"Well, let's not just stand around," said Spenser, anxious for his part to be over. "How do we get up?"

"Good question," said Tyrrel. "The Palace has always been protected from access by any kind of flight. I guess that was to guard against the Sulfane's drafters. In the old days, the only way was to ride a thermal updraft. But it looks as if the serfs have all scattered to the wind. Skittish folks."

"Wait!" cried Elaine.

She scrambled over the rocks and pulled a wind bottle from between two boulders.

"I don't suppose it's a thermal updraft," said Spenser.

"No," said Elaine. "No, it isn't..."

"Well, what *is* it?"

"My milkshake..."

The thunder rolled again, almost on top of them.

"We need speed," said Tallia. "At least to the bluff. Another carpet?"

Spenser tried to imagicate one. Nothing happened. He shook his head.

Tallia held out her palm, testing her own powers. No ball of fire appeared.

"What's happening?" she asked, her voice quavering for the first time in her life.

The Imagius let out a low whistle. "The Sulfane. His powers have grown."

Tallia choked down her fear. "By foot, then," she said boldly.

The others nodded and started the climb.

The thunder rolled once more—only this time, it cut out mid-roar, like someone switching off a radio.

"Come on," Tallia urged. "Silently now."

As quietly as they could, they scrambled the rest of the way up the cliff. Two smoots before the top, a figure came crashing over the edge, bowling Tallia into Tyrrel. Tyrrel grabbed the short stranger by a billowing cheek and spun him around.

"Begging your pardon! Begging your pardon!"

The wind serf bowed low and scraped his nose on the ground.

"Ooch!"

"Zephyr!" Elaine cried. "What are *you* doing here?"

"The Cloven hurricane was blowing me here. Two days ago, when I was meeting you."

Spenser grabbed the serf. "Meeting us! *Stealing* from us! You're the cause of *all* of this!"

"Begging your pardon! Begging your pardon! I'm knowing it. It's being my fault. I shouldn't have been meddling. I shouldn't have been even talking to you! Oh! Being *so sorry!*"

He crumpled into a puddle of tears.

"Oh, I was smelling the Clovens coming. I was feeling the wind. Seeing the stone and the Clovens coming! I was trying to be saving it! Saving it from the coming Clovens! Clovens can never be catching wind serfs. No one can."

"I don't believe you for a second," said Spenser. "How did the Sulfane get the stone?"

"That, I'm not knowing. I was thinking—that was being my problem; I should never have been thinking—but what luck! When the hurricane was blowing me here to Cloud Palace, I was meeting a great imagicator, a gentleman of the royal court. What luck, I'm saying. I'll be getting the stone into royal hands where it's belonging!"

"But you gave it to the Sulfane!"

"No! I was giving it to a gentleman of the royal court! He was wearing a silver wisp on his shoulder!"

Tyrrel and Tallia exchanged looks.

"I don't believe it," said Spenser.

"Believe it," said the Imagius. "Wind serfs may be flighty, but they are not given to lying. And he's right. No one can catch a wind serf. They're too airy. It was actually a pretty smart thing this young serf did."

"Oh, your imajesty!" said Zephyr, bowing low again.

"This gentleman," said Tyrrel, "What did he look like?"

"Oh, I couldn't be saying. I couldn't be seeing—too much bowing, snuffling my nose in the dust, then—oh—too much sneezing."

"But you saw his silver wisp. What else?!"

"Just seeing his wisp—and spectacles. Star-shaped spectacles."

"No," said Tyrrel, refusing to believe it. "It could not be!"

"But it *was* being."

"Aster was father's best friend! And one of my own…"

"He was father's rival, too," said Tallia, putting it together. "If he were father's friend, why did he not stand with the King? Why did he come to us?"

Tyrrel had no answer.

"Who? What?" asked Spenser.

The Imagius cleared his throat.

"Tell me—Zephyr, is it?"

"Being Zephyr the Lesser, your imajesty."

"Tell me, Zephyr, do you have any wind about you?"

"Of course, your imajesty. I'm having been harvesting here for two days, but—"

"Good. We may need all you have."

"But, your imajesty, it's being up there—up on the plain."

"Wonderful. Just where we're heading. Come along."

"Oh, but the Sulfane," Zephyr moaned. "Worsening and worsening. And the Knights! The Knights are freezing!"

Tallia scoffed, "On a sunny morning like this? You heard the Imagius. Up you go."

With a whimper, the wind serf found his feet and led the company the few remaining steps up onto the bluff.

"Keeping hidden! Keeping hidden!" urged Zephyr as they poked their heads over the edge.

The others hardly needed to be told. They scrambled for the cover of some low, wind-swept shrubs. Surrounding them on the plain, all the powers of Windemere had gathered.

To the north, King Orrozco stood at the head of his Dark Knights. To the south, Queen Quoirez stood proudly in front of her Stormy Knights. To the west, an army of Clovens spilled out from their drafters. Alone at the center, with his scaly arms upraised, stood the Sulfane. Just seeing him again—even from a distance—filled Spenser with a sick, gut wrenching feeling that threatened to devour him from within.

"What has happened to the Knights?" asked Tyrrel. "Why are they not fighting?"

"I was telling you!" whimpered Zephyr. "The Knights were attacking. Finally! Dark and Stormy Knights—both being back on the same side, siding against the Sulfane! And then, he is holding up the stone. And the Knights are freezing."

On second look, Tyrrel, Tallia, Spenser and Elaine could all see the Knights weren't just hovering in mid-air above their king and queen. They were frozen there.

"But how?" Tyrrel asked.

"Before he had the stone," said the Imagius, "the Sulfane merely had the power to dissolve. Now he has the power to make things solid."

"The Knights—?" Elaine asked.

"—appear to have turned to stone," the Imagius answered.

"And Mother?" Tyrrel wondered aloud.

"No," said the Imagius. "He does yet not seem to have power over people. The Knights and their winged mounts were always something more fanciful, never thinking beings with wills of their own. Look. She turns her head."

Indeed, the Queen drew herself to her full height.

"Sulfane!" she cried in that punishing voice her children couldn't help but dread, "You have no right!"

"Silence!" screeched the Sulfane. "I have every right! The right given to me by Chloe's stone!"

"Given!" Spenser started to protest, but Elaine held him back.

"Not yet," she cautioned. "We need a plan."

"By the power of this stone," the Sulfane went on, "I declare myself Lord Protector of the Realm. As you can see, I alone possess the power to stop the warring between the Knights. I alone can bring peace to Windemere. And once I attain the throne of Cloud Palace, I promise you, I will bring a new order to this land."

Just then, a daystar, flickering silver and gold, had the misfortune to flutter past the Sulfane's ear. As if to remind all those present what sort of order he would impose, the Sulfane turned and breathed on the daystar. Its sparkle vanished. It withered and fell to the ground like a dead leaf.

King Orrozco could not contain his anger. He strode boldly toward the Sulfane.

"I will not allow it!" he cried, even as armed Clovens blocked his way with black knives and spears. "Windemere was created to be a land free from absolute control, a land free to imagicate beauty and fancy."

"Aye," said the Queen, as more Clovens moved to cut her off as well.

"Bah!" the Sulfane sneered, "Such fancy only leads to chaos. Look upon what you yourselves have wrought upon the land—upon your own children! Shame on you! Look about you as King and Queen for the last time! But look in silence, for I have work to do."

He held aloft the stone once more. A bead of yellow sweat appeared on his forehead. For the first time in his life, the Sulfane imagicated something into being. A slab of cold, gray stone appeared at his feet.

The King and Queen struggled against their Cloven captors, without success.

"This is all your fault!" spat the Queen to her husband.

"Humph!" grumbled the King.

The Sulfane imagicated again. Another granite slab appeared, perched mostly on top of the first. Then another. Then another.

"A staircase!" Spenser exclaimed.

"Stone stairs to Cloud Palace?" Tallia cried. "How dare he!"

"Tallia," said Tyrrel. "We must restore our parents to the thrones—before the Sulfane gets there."

Tallia nodded as the Sulfane imagicated another stair and began to climb.

"Serf!" Tallia called "Serf! Ach! Where has he gotten to?!"

Zephyr appeared from a nearby bush, his rope of canisters around his neck. "Being at your service!"

"What do you have?"

"Two cans Jet Stream, two cans Thermal Updraft, two cans Toucans—they're being gorgeous. Look."

He opened a canister and let out a small flock of tropical birds.

"What else?" Tyrrel asked impatiently. The Sulfane had quickened his pace. Already his staircase cast a long shadow over the plain.

"Oh, a bit of Hurricane, Breath of Fresh Air, Misty Breeze, Drizzly Sneeze, and Assorted Gusts stashed in a bush."

"All right," said Tallia, taking the bottles of Jet Stream and tossing one to her brother. "The prince and I will take care of the Clovens. You provide the Thermals for the King and Queen."

She pointed the nozzle of her Jet Stream at the Clovens holding her father. She opened the valve. A high-powered wind shot out of the nozzle, sending her crashing back into the next bush.

"Ah," cried Spenser, running to her, "Don't you know your physics?! For every action, there's an equal and opposite reaction. Plant your back against something. Plant your back against your brother's! Here!"

He stood Tallia and Tyrrel back to back, aiming out at the two sets of Clovens.

"On the count of three, now. One—"

A Cloven general had spotted them.

"Two—"

A wedge of drafters bore down on them from across the plain. Elaine saw the danger and grabbed the hurricane bottle.

"Three!" she cried in unison with Spenser.

Backed against a rock, she aimed her hurricane at the wedge of drafters, broadsiding them and sending them crashing into the sea. At the same time, Tyrrel and Tallia blasted the Cloven guards away from the King and Queen.

"Ha!" said the King proudly, "That's *my* brains they're using."

"What," chided the Queen, "that cold, splattering wind?"

"No, you rotten custard," said the King, "Their strategy."

Elaine next turned her bottle on the Sulfane himself. The Cloven guards, now onto her game, cut between with a drafter, wind shields raised, protecting their master.

The moment it was clear, Zephyr boldly dashed out to the King and Queen.

"Your flynesses!" he called. "Updrafts for your flynesses. To the thrones!"

"Thrones?" said the Queen haughtily. "I'll not share my thrones with this insect, this gnat who calls himself King. Flyness, indeed! He's not a fly; he's a flea—no, a flea on a flea!"

"Nor will I share with you, you stale crust of last month's moldy pie! So putrid even this fly will not go near!"

"But your flynesses," Zephyr whimpered, "Begging your pardons for calling you so, but begging you more to be looking at the Sulfane!"

By now, the Sulfane had built a hundred stone slabs, slanting nearly halfway up to the swirling palace. The King and Queen, their eyes locked on each other in pride and anger, did not even glance up as the Sulfane took yet another step higher.

"I'll not be so insulted!" said the Queen to the King. "You were a tiny fleck of nothingness before you met me. And now see what you have become—a great, infinite *mountain* of nothingness."

Spenser, whose attention had been shifting between the royal insults and the Sulfane's staircase, could take it no longer. He strode from his hiding place right up to the bickering royals.

"Cut it out! You're wasting too much time!"

"Excuse me?" said Queen Quoirez. "Who do you think you are?"

King Orrozco looked him over, "Why, you're that ruffian who blasted into my cave!"

"Begging your pardon," Zephyr bowed again, "This is being no ruffian. This is being Just Spenser, Count of Cauliflower!"

"I don't care who he is. This is none of his business," said the King.

"Guards!" said the Queen, forgetting her Knights were frozen stiff. "Take him away!"

King Orrozco laughed, as no Knights appeared, "Ah, what have we for a Queen! You're about as bright as the bottom of a pit on a moonless night!"

"Ha! You're as fit to be King as a festering sore."

"You're only Queen because your parents got you the job."

Spenser choked up. The arguing was all too familiar. And it was so beside the point!

"Please," Spenser practically cried. "Just *stop*! This isn't about you. Look around. Look at the Sulfane. Look at the whole country! *This isn't about you!*"

For one moment, King Orrozco and Queen Quoirez took their glaring eyes from each other and looked at Spenser.

"Look," said Spenser more quietly. "The Sulfane builds another stair. You're the King and Queen. You're like—You're like the parents of this whole beautiful, amazing place. If you don't *do* something—I don't know…I don't know…Everything that's good and fun, I guess it'll all turn to stone."

He paused. He looked down at his feet.

"You don't have to like each other. But—" He looked up again. "You do have to work together."

The King and Queen looked from Spenser to each other.

The Sulfane built another stair and took another step higher.

"Serf," said the Queen. "A thermal."

"Two," said the King.

Solemnly, Zephyr opened his bottles, giving the King and Queen a smooth ride up to what remained of the throne room. Cloven drafters wheeled, trying to find an angle in, but the moment the King and Queen took their thrones, the room around them became more solid. The drafters could not penetrate the cloud.

"Now what?" Elaine asked.

Tyrrel answered, "Now they'll make the palace solid, and balance will be restored."

"But the Sulfane—" said Spenser.

"Once the palace is solid, the Sulfane will not be able to pass through the gates."

Spenser studied the situation, not convinced. While Cloud Palace slowly became more palace than cloud, the Sulfane continued his meticulous labor, protected by circling drafters. Another forty stone slabs and the Sulfane would reach the gates.

From her throne, the Queen surveyed the damage to her former home.

"Just look at this place," she said, casting a disdainful eye toward the remnants of carpets stained by rain, the film of algae covering almost every surface. "How could we have let it come to this?"

"Oh, are you speaking to me now?" said the King.

"I do not see anyone *else* here."

The Queen felt the floor beneath her throne creak.

"Watch your mouth, woman, or you'll make this place dissolve once more."

"I? I?"

"Yes. Now calm down. Didn't you notice that when we speak civilly to one another, the palace grows stronger? When you rankle and curse, you bring it down again—and us with it."

The Queen took a breath, calming herself.

"Yes, I did notice that."

Her throne stopped wobbling.

"There now," said the King. "You see how easy it is to bring it back together?"

He smiled. She forced a smile herself. He held out his hand. She hesitated, then took it. At their touch, the haze above them condensed into silver chandeliers. The walls solidified, with silver drapes about the windows.

"Oh, Orrozco, how beautiful it is. I had almost forgotten."

"Well, that doesn't surprise me, you witless—"

The whole east wall dissolved again.

"—I mean, I'd almost forgotten, too."

He smiled tentatively at her, throwing nervous glances at the east wall taking shape once more.

"Dare we get up and look around?" Quoirez asked.

"Let's just sit awhile. Give the palace time to come back together. Look—the entrance hall."

"And out the wind-door—the fog garden."

"I can't believe you let it dissolve."

"Do not start with me."

"It *did* start with you. I was perfectly happy being king, but you could never let me forget that I started life as something less than you!"

"You *were* less than I. 'Tis a simple fact."

"A true princess would have had the grace to see beyond it."

"How could I when I had to face it every day? How could a farmer ever stop seeing his pig is a pig?"

"And how could I ever stop seeing that you were a—Oh, help!"

The pair had been so focused on their renewed quarrel that they hadn't noticed the whole floor giving way. What a moment ago had been hard as crystal quickly thinned to the consistency of mushy mashed potatoes. The Queen fell through her throne, through the floor, and plunged into the chamber below. The King clung to a footstool, which had so far managed to escape dissolution.

"This is all your fault, you beastly wench!" he called down to her. "Oomph!"

The footstool dissolved in his hands, and he plummeted next to her.

"Yes! My fault for marrying you! Oh!"

From below, Spenser could see the palace falling apart.

"Oh," he groaned, "They're not working together!"

The walls and floors had become transparent enough to reveal the King and Queen grasping at any wisps they could reach.

"And Spenser," said Elaine, "our Night Mare."

Spenser turned to see the Night Mare flying in low from over the ocean. It wheeled below the palace like a scavenger, waiting for one or both of the royal couple to fall.

"We've got to stop the Sulfane," he said. "No one else can."

She nodded, aimed her hurricane bottle at the Sulfane once more, and opened the valve. Only a faint breeze and a last few raindrops sputtered out.

"Your bottles, Zephyr," she cried. "All of them!"

"Coming with me!" he said, leading Elaine to his stash.

Spenser looked up at the Sulfane, now towering two hundred steps above him. Thirty more and he'd reach the Cloud. Spenser glanced back at Elaine going through Zephyr's bottles. He couldn't wait. He swallowed his fear and took off at a run for the stone staircase.

When he reached the bottom stair, the Clovens spotted him. Tyrrel and Tallia did their best with their jet streams to keep the drafters away from Spenser. But by the time he hit the sixtieth step, the bottles had been emptied.

Spenser looked up. The Sulfane stood a hundred and fifty stairs ahead of him, with just twenty more to build before he reached the thrones. Nineteen.

Spenser climbed at top speed, closing the gap. As he drew closer, all the sadness and despair he'd felt in their previous encounter began to ooze back into his soul. He fought against it. He couldn't give up yet. He couldn't let the same sadness flood the whole country. Out of the corner of his eye, he saw Clovens on the lead drafter loading a catapult.

From the ground, Elaine saw it too. She grabbed the best bottle left—Strong Gusts. She aimed it at the Sulfane. She then turned it on the drafters. She could feel the gusts bursting out, but could see no effect.

"Wind shields," said Zephyr, shaking his head. "They're all having wind shields."

The lead drafter fired. A steaming ball of yellow liquid splashed on the stair behind Spenser.

Spenser looked around. The acid sizzled on the granite, and started to eat into the hard stone.

"Not *that*, you fools!" the Sulfane hissed. "Just knock him off!"

The drafters regrouped into a line and dove at Spenser. He sprinted another ten stairs toward the Sulfane, then dove flat as a drafter swooped. The drafter's runners nearly hooked Spenser's collar with their leading edge.

Another drafter buzzed low, missing Spenser by inches. The wind from the passing machine almost blew him off, but he hung tight. He looked up. Yet another drafter bore down on him.

A Cloven pair hung from the running board, black knife outstretched. If Spenser didn't get out of the way fast, he'd be sliced in two. If he rose to move, he'd be knocked off the staircase entirely, falling to his death on the rocks—if the Night Mare's flaming jaws didn't snatch him first.

The blade closed in—seconds away.

No time to think, the knife upon him, Spenser rolled. The dagger ripped into his jacket, grazing his back. Spenser fell sideways from the staircase—and hung on by his fingertips. The Cloven blade shattered on the stone—and the drafter passed above. The next drafter in line changed course, trying to get at Spenser hanging below the steps, but the drafter's momentum carried it straight into the staircase. The drafter splintered. The staircase shuddered. The Sulfane looked around, nervous for the first time. But the staircase held. The Cloven pair tumbled into the scavenging Night Mare's two mouths, which snarled and snapped, fighting with each other for every bloody scrap. Eighteen stairs left for the Sulfane to build. Seventeen.

"It's pathetic," said Tyrrel, pacing. "What a sorry excuse for parents."

"I know, I know," said Tallia, studying the shifting palace, "But Tyrrel, I said something to Spenser last night…"

"This is not the time, Tallia. We've got to *do* something."

"Exactly what I said to Spenser! Hear me, please. If we cannot imagicate our parents to work together—"

"Why not? Why *not*?!"

"You know the answer to that."

Tyrrel exhaled through gritted teeth. "I know. I just—Go on."

"But what I was saying—what we *can* do—is grow up, maybe faster than we want to, and live our own lives."

"Take the thrones ourselves?"

Tallia nodded. Tyrrel looked up at his parents grasping at wisps, then back at his sister, an ocean of doubts suddenly welling up inside him.

"No, but—No. The thrones aren't ours to take. We're not the King and Queen."

"No," said Tallia bitterly, "But our parents aren't acting like King and Queen either. Tyrrel, someone has to take control. Someone's *going* to take control. If we don't, the Sulfane will."

While Tyrrel considered, the Sulfane built another stair. Tyrrel set his teeth and sighed, "You're right…You're right."

"Zephyr," said Tallia, "The thermals."

Spenser didn't know how much longer he could hold on. His fingers ached. His hands ached. His arms practically tore from his shoulders.

Out the corner of one eye, Spenser saw Tyrrel and Tallia rising slowly toward the throne room. A pair of Clovens saw them too, and quit harassing Spenser to intercept the Prince and Princess.

The stone stairs slanted up, out over the ocean. Two hundred feet below, breakers crashed on the rocks. Spenser tried to pull himself back up onto the stairs. He swung his legs, but—So close to Cloud Palace, fog condensed on the stone slabs. Spenser's right hand slipped. He held on with only his left now, and his own Night Mare circled below, waiting for him to fall. Spenser tried willing the beast back under his command, but the dragon had found its freedom and would not yield.

Elaine saw Spenser's hand slip. She saw him dangling by four fingers. She, too, tried to will the Night Mare to rescue her friend, to no avail. The beast was a lone scavenger, intent only on its next meal.

She stomped her foot. "I can't imagicate the simplest things!"

"Yes," mused the Imagius, "The Sulfane kills all creativity. Under his rule, there will not be a single new act of imagication."

"But what about *old* acts?"

The Imagius shrugged. "They might still work, for a time. Anything previously imagicated still exists. I don't suppose you have any old magic about you?"

"No, I—" She felt in her pockets. Her fingers touched the aeros, the Mirage game piece the gift horse had given her. "Wait."

She looked at the silver triangle in her hand, then up at Spenser.

A drafter headed straight for him, the Cloven drivers grinning fiendishly as they aimed to run him down.

"No!" cried Elaine.

Spenser saw them coming. He had no choice. He let go.

Elaine threw the aeros like a paper airplane. Its silver wings caught sun and the breeze. The aeros shot under Spenser's feet, growing big enough for him to ride like a skateboard. His feet connected to the metal triangle. The aeros responded to the slightest shift in weight, better than any skateboard he'd ever ridden, better than the Aeroboard of his dreams. He did a loop as he would in a pipe, but did not have time to play. Above him, the Sulfane was six steps from the thrones.

"What ho!" cried Tyrrel from below. "It's Aster!"

"And the Duke!" cried Tallia.

From the west, riding on the sailboards Spenser had seen them use before, Aster and the Duke of Windham led the rest of Tyrrel and Tallia's followers into the fray. Now the battle began in earnest. Spenser slalomed between drafters, trying to get to the Sulfane. The Duke's army fought their way through countless Clovens. With no imagication to help them, they bravely grappled hand to hand, many going unarmed against the black daggers.

An angry growl tore through the air, followed by echoing giggles. Oso the bear, Guffaw, and the other imagicators Spenser had freed from the Rook appeared over the horizon to join the fight.

Elaine couldn't just stand on the sidelines. She still held the only bottle with any wind left in it—Strong Gusts. She opened it, this time to use as jet propulsion. The gusts blew her about in spurts, almost impossible to control. On the other hand, it made it almost impossible for the Clovens to chase her. She sputtered and zigzagged her way up toward Spenser, hoping to interfere with the Clovens blocking his way to the Sulfane—the Sulfane, with just three more steps to build.

Tyrrel and Tallia were nearly to the thrones themselves when a drafter moved to cut them off. Rivien shot his sailboard at the enemy drafter. Aster followed, a sword in hand. Just as Rivien was about to intercept the Clovens, Aster raised his sword and slashed at Rivien's sail. The mast shattered. The sail crumpled, and Rivien fell screaming past the Night Mare's tail into the ocean below. The Night Mare wheeled and dove like an overgrown, two-headed pelican. Just as its dragon's jaws were about to snatch Rivien from the surf, a Sailphin shot up from below, caught Rivien on the leading edge of its fin and plowed him through the waves to safety.

"Aster!" shouted Tyrrel, full of confused anger.

The drafter Rivien had tried to intercept held back, watching, waiting.

"Rivien was a traitor," Aster explained, circling the Prince and Princess, his star-shaped spectacles glinting in the morning sun. "He would not serve his true master. I'm sorry, Tyrrel. I like you—and Tallia—but your family is not fit to rule this land. Look what Windemere has become."

"And what have you become?" Tyrrel spat, bitter at the betrayal.

"Nothing more than I have always been. A man with the best interests of Windemere at heart."

"A jealous, greedy heart," put in Tallia. "I know you wanted to marry our mother. I know you always wanted to be king."

"And so I shall be," said Aster. "But it takes two to sit on the thrones of Cloud Palace. Two people, working together."

"You and the Sulfane?" spat Tyrrel.

"Why not? After all, it was I who conjured the stone from Chloe's world so he could make it solid."

"You?" Tyrrel's heart sank with every word.

"Of course. The Sulfane has tremendous power, but he could never imagicate an incantation into another world. And you poor, trusting fools—trusting me to counsel you on strategy. Yes, I counseled you to waste a year skirmishing with your parents while the Sulfane's power grew. Then you yourselves sent me on the mission to Cloud Palace—where the stone practically fell into my hands. But I'm afraid that's all I have time to explain. It has been an honor and a pleasure to serve as your tutor, but now the lessons are over."

He raised his sword and moved closer.

Meanwhile, Spenser and Elaine had both managed to dodge and weave through the drafters protecting the Sulfane.

"Race ya!" called Elaine, aiming her Strong Gusts like a jet pack.

Spenser gritted his teeth and aimed his aeros up toward the top step, but Elaine got there first. Another gust shot from her bottle, propelling her right into the Sulfane's shoulder, knocking him from his perch. With only two more steps to go, the Sulfane fell. Before Elaine had a chance to cheer, the Sulfane shot a scaly hand through the air and caught the bottom of Spenser's aeros, sending Spenser into a spin. In his other hand, the Sulfane still held tight to Chloe's stone.

Spenser leaned, struggling to regain control of the aeros before he and the Sulfane both dropped into the Night Mare's waiting jaws. He reached down, stretching desperately for the stone in the Sulfane's left hand. The Sulfane laughed, holding it out of reach. Spenser adjusted his stance, and stepped on the Sulfane's right hand. Instinctively, the Sulfane brought his left hand back to the aeros. Spenser grabbed Chloe's stone, but the Sulfane would not let go. Spenser put the entire force of his will into the stone. The Sulfane clutched it tighter. Spenser could feel the Sulfane pouring his soul into the stone. Spenser did the same. The stone glowed orange, then red, as opposing wills battled within it.

"You shall not have it," croaked the Sulfane.

Spenser answered through gritted teeth, "Just what I was going to say to you."

"Ha!" said the Sulfane, and he blew a foul, yellow breath out at Spenser.

Spenser winced and held his breath just before the acid fog reached his face. But the Sulfane's cloud engulfed him and reached around his heart like a hot metal claw. Spenser scrunched his eyes closed and felt his life begin to boil away. His skin bubbled and blistered, but that was nothing compared to the pain he felt inside, where all the joy—those few, small, happy memories he had kept carefully sheltered—curdled and corroded in a searing acid burn. Small thrills like soaring off his garage roof evaporated, leaving only the pain of landing and the awful feeling of facing his parents. Even the newfound pleasure of being with Elaine fizzled away until all he could remember were the times she had chided him, the times they had disagreed.

All the meager happiness Spenser had ever felt dissolved in a fog he could not grasp. All that remained was sadness, despair, pain, and then—finally—vacant horror. Spenser whimpered a last, pitiful cry, without a single good feeling left. How could he have done this to himself, to this beautiful world, hardening into cold gray stone? It was too awful to live anymore. Out of the corner of his eye, he saw Elaine, struggling with her bottle of Strong Gusts. It sputtered, running out of air. She would fall. She *was* falling. He remembered her admonishing him to *do something*. She had tried to be his friend, but he had already been too stone cold to let her in.

A last feeling welled up inside him, a feeling of anger—anger at the Sulfane, at the awful world, and at himself. Spenser clung to this last feeling, this last bit of human life left in him. He couldn't let go of it. And he couldn't let go of Chloe's stone.

The stone glowed white as the aeros spun more wildly out of control. Spenser's anger built. He imagined his fingers sinking deep into the stone's core. The heat from his fury railed against the Sulfane's own. And then—with a flash of light—Chloe's stone exploded into a million, sparkling grains of sand.

The Sulfane screamed, "No!" clutching at the fragments in the air—and fell.

The Night Mare swooped underneath, catching the Sulfane in its open jaws. The Sulfane propped his hands against the roof of the dragon's mouth. The dragon let out a breath of fire, but the Sulfane, who had been born of the volcanic coals of Cauldron Mountain, was not scathed. Together, he and the Night Mare crashed into the sea with a steaming sizzle—and disappeared from sight.

Spenser righted his aeros and gasped for breath, trying to suck his own life back in. With sadness in his eyes, he saw the battle raging all around. The instant the stone had shattered, the staircase crumbled, and the Dark and Stormy Knights resumed their fight. The King and Queen still dangled from wisps below the thrones. The country was in chaos once more.

"*Spenser*!!"

Elaine called, falling. Her bottle had sputtered out its last gasps of wind, and she plummeted toward the sea.

"*Spenser*!!"

Spenser spotted her. He tucked in his elbows and dove down on the aeros to catch her around the waist.

"Oh, Spenser! I saw the Sulfane's breath! I thought you were going to—" She threw her arms around him. "Oh Spenser!"

The acid pain the Sulfane had left in him began to ease, neutralized by her touch. He yearned to put his arms around her as well. He tried to summon the will, to remember what it felt like to be kind and loving. He started to raise his hands, to reach out, but then—

"Look at Aster!" she cried.

Spenser banked the aeros, turning toward Tyrrel, Tallia, and Aster.

Now that the Sulfane was gone, Aster had been free to imagicate a second sword. He threw them both at the Prince and Princess, aiming for their hearts. Tyrrel and Tallia quickly imagicated shields, and the swords clattered off.

"Relent, Aster!" Tyrrel shouted, "The Sulfane is dead! It's over!"

"Never!"

Aster produced a length of yellow rope from among his robes and twirled it into a lasso.

From above Aster, the Duke of Windham put his sailboard into a dive. As Aster threw out his lariat, the Duke caught the loop and flung it back over Aster's head. The Duke then grabbed the middle of the rope and pulled the loop tight, pinning Aster's arms to his sides, catching him in his own snare.

Tyrrel and Tallia, Prince and Princess of Windemere, eased themselves off the thermal updrafts and onto the thrones. Immediately, Cloud Palace took shape around them. Tyrrel put his hand in Tallia's. The Dark and Stormy Knights stopped fighting and looked at each other as if they had all just woken from a strange and terrible dream. The Knights then turned as a united force on what remained of the Cloven army, and pursued them into the northwest.

CHAPTER 15

▼

RESTORATION

The Great Hall shone almost too brightly for Spenser and Elaine. They sat at one of the head tables, squinting out at the nobility of Windemere, awaiting the celebratory feast. Remembering how his body should feel, Spenser had managed to heal his own skin, even getting rid of a few old blemishes on his face. The late afternoon sun sparkled through all the walls and wind-doors of Cloud Palace, a silver lining shimmering on every edge of every table and chair. The silver thrones, now empty, glittered as if radiating their own light.

"I wish I'd brought my sunglasses," whispered Spenser.

Elaine laughed. "Are you an imagicator or what?"

She imagicated a pair of gold-rimmed sunglasses wrapped around each of their faces.

"Oh, right. Thanks," said Spenser, sharing her smile.

The room fell silent as the Imagius rose to his feet and clinked a spoon on his crystal goblet.

"My dear, dear friends. I welcome you back to Cloud Palace on this most solemn—"

Guffaw couldn't help interrupting with a peal of high laughter.

"Sorry," he said, and snorted, trying to stifle himself.

The Imagius smiled, "That's all right, my friend. While this is a solemn occasion, it is also one of great joy, for we need stifle our laughter no longer."

"Hear, hear!" the crowd cheered.

"Today, we have wrought a great change, a change that is not yet quite complete. May I present Orrozco and Quoirez, King and Queen of Windemere."

The King and Queen appeared through doors to either side of the thrones. They looked out at the assembly, a strange mix of emotions in their eyes. No one cheered. No one said a word. Even Guffaw was silent.

"The time has come—" began Quoirez.

"I think—" said Orrozco simultaneously.

They both broke off and stared at each other. The Queen raised her head regally and began anew.

"On consultation with the Imagius—"

"And with our children—" put in the King.

The Queen, hating to be interrupted, shot him a barbed look.

"Sorry. Go on," he said.

"I—I mean *we*—for the good of all Windemere, hereby abdicate in favor of our children, Tallia and Tyrrel, Princess and Prince of Windemere."

With a final look and nod at each other, Quoirez and Orrozco removed their crowns. They held them in front of their bodies, then let go. Instead of falling, the silver circlets dissolved into swirls of cloud, hanging in the air.

"We sustain these no more," said the former Queen.

"Tallia and Tyrrel," the Imagius called.

From the same two doorways appeared the Princess and Prince of Windemere. Quoirez and Orrozco stepped aside as their children took their places and knelt beneath the wispy circlets that once were crowns.

"By the powers invested in me by the Imagius Accipteryx before me, invested in the See of the Imagius in Mezmir by Chloe herself, it is my solemn duty—and great pleasure—to crown you, Tallia and Tyrrel, Queen and King of Windemere."

With a supreme effort, the Imagius took the crowns in his hands and made them solid. Red and green jewels appeared, embedded in the silver. As the Imagius placed the crowns on Tallia and Tyrrel's heads, the jewels wobbled out. One fell into the Imagius' hand. He put it to his tongue.

"I was afraid of that," he muttered. "Jell-O."

Elaine gave Spenser a nudge. In silent agreement, they imagicated the jewels solid, gleaming perfect, and back in place. The Imagius looked around, knowing he had been helped. He nodded his thanks, then went on with the ceremony.

"Please rise, and take your thrones. Ladies and Gentlemen—my friends—I present to you Tallia and Tyrrel, Queen and King of Windemere."

The crowd cheered. As Tallia and Tyrrel sat in the thrones, the palace around them became even brighter and more beautiful than before. Every surface shone with all the colors of a brilliant sunset.

Tallia smiled, "In our first act, we proudly announce the return of our royal chef. Let the feast begin!"

A small woman at the table opposite Spenser and Elaine rose. With a nod of her head, a fantastic banquet appeared on all the tables.

"Oh, man!" said Spenser. "I wonder if she can wash the dishes that fast, too!"

"No, she's a terrible washer," said the Imagius, taking the seat next to him. "We all have our special talents."

"Something for drinking?" asked Zephyr, blowing in behind Elaine. "You must be trying this. It's being my latest invention—being my best ever. More being an accident really. I never would have been thinking of keeping milkshake in a wind bottle, but trying it! Trying it! It's being so frothy, it's making you float like a cow!"

The wind serf began pouring milkshakes into goblets, and soon, nearly all the guests were floating about the Great Hall, laughing as they ate mid-air. Spenser watched as the young Duke of Windham floated over to Tallia and took her hands. Elaine saw the forlorn expression cross Spenser's face. She followed his gaze and saw the young Duke waltzing through the air with Tallia.

"Spenser," she started gently, "Oh, Spenser…They *belong* together." When Spenser didn't respond, she reached out and touched his arm. He met her gaze.

Out of the corner of her eye, Elaine caught sight of Tyrrel, the Tyrrel who had held her close only last night, now holding court among a throng of admirers. Now her own expression fell. Spenser saw the reason and gave a sympathetic smile.

"You know, Elaine—I think, after dinner, maybe we should go home."

"I thought you hated home."

Spenser shrugged, "Yeah, but it's still home. Besides, somehow, I just don't think the problems there will seem quite so big."

"I know what you mean…"

They ate for a moment in silence.

"Do you think," Elaine asked, "If something from our world has so much power here, that something from here will have special power at home?"

"I don't know. But, oh—This is yours."

He handed her back the silver aeros, now lifeless and back to its normal size.

"Right. Thanks," she said.

"And Elaine—"

"Yeah?"

He struggled with all the words he'd meant to say to her—"thanks" and "sorry" and "that's okay"—all the words he'd never been much good with.

"Just—Thanks and—" he faltered, "I don't know, you know?"

Elaine smiled. She had been through too much with him not to know just what he was feeling—and to feel a good bit of it herself. Maybe he didn't have that warm, entrancing look the prince had once given her, but he was Spenser— Just Spenser, the thinker, as passionate about doing the right thing as she was— Spenser, with his crazy rainbow lining always struggling to be seen beneath the black surface. And now he was trying harder than anyone she had ever known to show that he cared for *her*. This was better than a dream box. This was better than any magic. She broke into a broad grin. "Yes. I know. I think I know *exactly.*"

The Imagius walked down to the beach to see Spenser and Elaine off. They waded out into the warm Sweetwater Sea, far enough for the Imagius to duck under and call the Sailphins. Soon, Leeee appeared, leading his pod in a circular dance, swirling the waters into the whirlpool funnel that once began the world.

As they churned the water, something else started bubbling up outside the whirlpool. To the north of the Sailphins' circle, the water began to roil and steam. Suddenly, the Night Mare rose up from under the waves and took to the air. Spenser and Elaine gasped. The Sulfane rode astride the dragon's back, clutching a handful of sand. The Sulfane cackled as the Night Mare wheeled and flew off to the northwest.

"Well," mused the old Imagius, "It's always a struggle to find balance in the world, isn't it?"

"But—Shouldn't we do something?"

"Oh, it'll take some time before the Sulfane regains any power to speak of. My imagicators turned his Rook into a flower garden. His army has been routed. See, even now he flies to the northwest, to the Blank Spot on the map. He knows he must start from nothing."

"But the Night Mare!" said Elaine.

"And the sand!" said Spenser.

"Yes, the sand...I'm afraid the sand might be a problem. But if Windemere needs you, I'm sure, somehow, Windemere will find you."

"But Imagius—I—It's my fault *again*. The sand was from the stone I brought!"

"Ah, Spenser. Do you remember about the rat and the gnome and the scullery maid? If the Rook had indeed collapsed because you hadn't ever come here, would you have been responsible for that? You see, the Sulfane will always be the Sulfanest Sulfane possible. That's his nature. All *you* can do is be the best Spenser you can imagine. Understand?"

Spenser gave a little nod.

"Good. The funnel is nearly complete. The Sailphins have swum the perfect dance. And now, we must all go our separate ways."

"And you?" asked Spenser. "Where will you go?"

"Oh, there's a quiet little town south of Aleili Bay. There's a fine hospital for imagicators there—the Doldrum Hill Sanatorium. I hope, with time, I shall regain my full powers."

"Imagius—" Spenser began.

"Rafalco," the Imagius smiled.

"Rafalco, I imagine you will."

"Ah, perhaps that's all it takes. Imagicate well. The funnel grows."

The ride back home was gentle, nothing like the wild spin cycle that had brought them to Windemere. Spenser felt the water tugging at his body. Elaine saw the turrets of Cloud Palace swirl into nothingness. In the darkness, Spenser reached out. His fingertips found Elaine's. Her hand gave his hand a squeeze.

Elaine wanted the comfortable floating to last forever, but she soon found herself back on Windy Hill, back with Spenser in the ruins of Chloe's corner room. The sun was setting and they were dry. Except for the aeros in Elaine's other hand, they would have had no proof they had ever been away.

After what felt like an endless, quiet moment, Spenser shyly pulled his hand from Elaine's.

"Well."

"Well, yourself," said Elaine.

"I guess you'd better get back to your library."

"My what?"

"Your library. You were talking on your phone about a library."

"Oh, *that*." She shifted awkwardly. "Spenser—I told you the truth. My parents *do* own Fourré Chocolates. They're off in Luxembourg half the time, and who-knows-where the rest. But Spenser—" She took a breath. "Spenser, I may lie to some people. But that's only because, well—because before, I didn't—I didn't have someone who would believe me."

Spenser wished he hadn't let go of Elaine's hand, but since he had, there seemed no way to hold it again. He remembered the touch, the warmth, but remembered too that imagication had no power over another thinking being. Besides, he wasn't even sure he *could* imagicate anymore, now that he was home.

So he just nodded. They walked silently back through the ruined corridors, back down the path.

"What will you tell your parents?" Elaine asked after a time. "We've been away for days."

"I know. I don't think I'll tell 'em anything. It's not like they ever believed me when I told them something believable. Maybe—Maybe I'll just ask them if they want to have some hot chocolate together."

"Sounds nice."

"Yeah. We'll see."

They reached the bush where Spenser had stashed his skateboard. He reached in and pulled it out.

"No way…"

He pulled from the thicket the board he'd dreamed, the fat wheels, the repaired front truck. He looked around. No one else could have fixed it.

"It changed…" he said to himself. "I—I changed something *here*…"

He looked around, wondering what else might have changed.

Elaine shifted impatiently. "Well," she said. "You were right. I really should get back to my library."

"Elaine—Will I see you again?"

"What do you think?"

"I don't know. I guess—I guess I think anything might happen."

"Yes," Elaine smiled. "I imagine it will."

The End

"Chloe?" said Elaine.

By now Elaine and Spenser had inched far enough around the old woman's bed to see her face. A clear plastic tube ran from an oxygen tank on the floor to a clip between her nostrils. More disturbing still was her vacant stare. Her right eye gleamed the clearest blue, while her left eye swirled with clouds, as if it contained an entire, dissolving world...

From ***The Imagicators and the Wind Between the Worlds***

Coming soon.

Visit <u>www.imagicators.bradmarshland.com</u> to learn more.

978-0-595-40471-1
0-595-40471-5

Printed in the United States
67156LVS00002B/208-339

9 780595 404711